T0063106

ESCAPE TO THE
FIFTH DIMENSION

ESCAPE TO THE FIFTH DIMENSION

DEAN YANG

PARTRIDGE
A Penguin Random House Company

To order additional copies of this book, contact
Toll Free 800 101 2657 (Singapore)
Toll Free 1 800 81 7340 (Malaysia)
orders.singapore@partridgepublishing.com

www.partridgepublishing.com/singapore

CHAPTER 1

He was again late for work. No, Danny Ong didn't work for someone else, he had enough of that, but he was late to open his small stall. It was supposed to be open every day by 11am but today he only woke up at 10.25am and to wash, eat breakfast and travel in the slow Penang traffic, he will surely be late. For readers unacquainted with Penang Island, it is a a state in Malaysia a little smaller in size than Hong Kong, with about three quarters of a million people and a fairly high population density. Penang came back to the world's attention several years ago when Inner Penang became a UNESCO World Heritage site and thus protected from the construction boom elsewhere on the island.

Danny's stall is at the 4th Level of Gurney Plaza, one of the happening Malls on the island. Stall owners can open their stalls for business anytime, unlike the shoplot owners who are bound by a strict contract which even stipulates opening and closing times, and he surely hates to lose the morning crowd of coffee drinkers, for he also sells cakes, pastries, and snacks of all sorts at his stall.

He was late because last night he had met up with an old friend, Johnny Santiago, a man of nearly fifty years of age while Danny is only in his late thirties and recently divorced. They had gone for some tea and snacks at the Muslim restaurant near the suburb of Farlim, the hideout locality of Johnny. He had not caught up with the drifter Johnny for a very long time and both had lots to talk about, and they were not finished even when the clock showed 2.15

a.m. By the time Danny got to bed it was already 3.50 a.m., way beyond his usual bedtime. As for Johnny, the half-Portuguese and half-Chinese Malaccan, it makes no difference what time he gets to bed. Nobody knows what he does for a living and nobody likes to ask him. And Johnny is never short of cash. In fact, Johnny is a big spender.

When Danny got to his stall, his two workers were waiting for him to unlock the padlocks on the chains that took the place of protective shutters. The workers, Hartono and Muljadi, are Indonesians as he could not get any locals to work for him. Oftentimes Danny had wondered where all the locals had gone. He suspects that many had gone over to Shanghai to work, as he personally knew of many locals who had gone to China to find a job. These were young local men and women with qualifications not recognised by the government and so they had to seek job opportunities abroad. But even though Danny needed only unskilled workers, no locals were available to fill up the posts. Really where have the young ones gone, he thought. Since getting these two foreign workers, it has eaten a huge chunk of his earnings as hiring them was not cheap, with government levies rising all the time. In addition to that it was not easy to get foreign workers these days. Many Indonesians prefer to work in countries like Hong Kong, Singapore and Middle East because of better pay. Danny is not the only employer facing such difficulties but is a problem across the board for small businesses in Penang. And business, sad to say, had been going from bad to worse.

Although Danny has his two Indonesians, actually they were illegals and he lives in constant fear of the local authorities coming anytime to arrest him and the workers. And this is not the only headache he has: his present girlfriend, Linda, has also increased his burden many times. And Danny does not want to talk about his previous marriage that ended in a divorce. No one could pry anything out of Danny about this sensitive issue.

Linda Chua is an attractive thirty - something woman, very independent and outgoing, far too outspoken for Danny's character. She works as a clerk in an architecture firm, a nine-to-five job and that's it. Don't ask her to stay back in the office for you will not only get a stern 'No!' as an answer but also an earful of words from her. Although she is quite hard to handle, she has a very kind heart and Danny seems to be able to put up with her and thus they had been going steady for the last two years.

It was while waiting for customers on that slow day that Danny's attention was caught by some commotion near Wing Onn, the goldsmith's shop not too far away on the same level of the building. Three men, still wearing their crash helmets, were seen running away from the goldsmith's and in Danny's direction, each carrying a brown sack and at least one of them was waving his gun as he ran past shell-shocked customers along the corridor. Danny had to step back as the men ran past him and disappeared around the corner.

It happened so fast, Danny appeared dazed and confused by the episode. However, he was very troubled at what he thought he saw and recognised. Throughout the day he was very reserved and this was not his usual self. Both Hartono and Muljadi also noticed that their boss looked worried and troubled. Surely, they thought, the boss was not too worried about getting a robbery at his stall. Business had been very poor and surely the stall is not worth robbing. Hartono and Muljadi looked at each other and they shrugged their shoulders. Soon it was closing time and it had been a terrible day as far as business went.

Two days have passed since the robbery at the goldsmith's and Danny is back as his usual self. He was planning to go fishing in his favourite spot at the Batu Ferringhi beach, a tourist haunt, not far from the famous Miami beach. His fishing spot is a bit more north than the popular beach in a more secluded part covered with rocky outcrops. The rocks can make fishing more difficult but he seemed to enjoy better luck here than anywhere else. However it could be dangerous as the tide comes in and he could be marooned on a rock. He was caught once in this situation and his sheer good luck saved him as he tried to swim against the strong tide back to the beach which now seemed so far away. Like most Penangites his age, he loved fishing along Penang's beautiful beach. However fishing enthusiasts are fewer these days than back in the 1980's. Today more youngsters prefer to ride their sports bikes along the winding road of Ferringhi in full bicycling gear or they prefer to stick to their iPads or iPhones at the shopping Malls which are fully air- conditioned.

However his fishing plans were spoilt when he got an unexpected visitor to his place. It was Ah Keat, his childhood pal from the area they grew up, Tanjung Bungah. Danny really had hoped Ah Keat would not show up because if he did, it would only mean big trouble. You see, Ah Keat is no ordinary man but quite a high ranking member of the triad that controls Tanjung Bungah area. Ah Keat is slimly built and only slightly taller than Danny who is rather more stocky. It was Lim Ah Keat that Danny had recognised running out of the goldsmith's shop that day, although Keat had his full face helmet on. But it was unmistakable; Danny can recognise Ah Keat anywhere, anytime, any day. Worse still, Ah Keat knew he had been recognised by Danny.

With a big grin on his face, Ah Keat greeted Danny in the local patois and invited himself into Danny's apartment and sat down on the sofa. Almost instantaneously, he whipped out a cigarette and lighted it. Before Danny could even speak, Keat spoke about the goldsmith shop. But he kept vague about it, only making it clear to Danny that for old time's sake he should keep real quiet about what he had seen.. Keat left just as quickly as he came.

It was only a brief visit by Keat but it troubled Danny to the core. Back in the old days when they were growing up in the back lanes and countryside roads of Tanjong Bungah, Ah Keat was already committing petty crimes in the village. Danny was at first amused by the episodes of chickens missing from the neighbours or the ripe mangoes disappearing before the owner could harvest them from their trees. He knew it was Keat's work because he was with him, as his look-out! It was fun to see how angry fat Uncle Ho was when he discovered his sweet and juicy mangoes would go missing every time when he was about to harvest them.

Keat would play truant from school and finally dropped out of school altogether while Danny continued his studies. That was how they drifted apart but somehow managed to keep in contact with each other. While Danny went on to college to take up Accounting, Keat got in with some big time crooks and would disappear from the village for years, coming back only to celebrate Chinese New Year in the village with his aging parents. Sometimes Keat would be very generous with his money on such occasions but of late Danny noticed Keat's long absenteeism from the village and even in the last two Chinese New Years, he had not been back. Unfortunately their latest meeting was when Keat was running out with the loot from the goldsmith's shop. The irony of life. But Danny need not be told, he would keep his mouth shut anyway. He was this sort of person.

CHAPTER 2

Just when Teoh Kim Heng was about to eat his late lunch of curry noodles in the sweltering heat, his walkie talkie crackled to life and called for action. The boys, known as runners, were out roaming the island on patrol duty to look out for road accidents and had just spotted their third business prospect. It was the team composed of Mokhtar, Ramu and Ah Boey. This team seemed to be either very lucky or just plain hard working. They topped the list of getting car accidents customers to the car repair workshop that hired them.

"Ah Heng, you better get here fast. This is a bad one!" shouted Ramu into his walkie talkie.

"It is just near Tesco along Tanjong Tokong road."

As Ramu was talking to Kim Heng, Ah Boey had already called for the ambulance while Mokhtar tried to help the dazed driver to open the jammed car door, but to no avail. The driver had smashed into the traffic lights and the pole was completely knocked down, which caused a bad traffic jam on both sides of the road.

By now, another two runners from their rival workshop had joined in the confusion to help direct traffic and talk to the trapped driver. Ah Boey was then seen arguing with the rival runners about this being their 'prize' as they got here first. Now curious onlookers were gathering to witness all the drama being unfolded – the wrecked MPV, a trapped driver, runners gesticulating and arguing loudly, and busybodies taking note of the car number plate of the

MPV, hoping to strike it rich by using it as a lucky betting number in the four-digit lottery.

Kim Heng, who is in his late forties and deeply tanned, jumped into his tow truck and sped towards the accident site; there was no time to lose as other tow truckers might be there to claim their prize. Traffic was bad, as usual, and especially so at this lunch hour break. There is one thing about Penang drivers, they are among the worst types in Malaysia. Many are too slow but occupy the fast lane, and they turn without using any signal and all of a sudden too. Nor will they allow you to change lanes so they will try to obstruct you. Some drivers of the smaller cars will weave in and out of traffic and tight spaces, thinking their cars are like motorbikes. However Kim Heng's driving skills are excellent – safe, quite fast and not taking unnecessary risks. Perhaps being in the tow truck business, he understands what a stupid thing accidents are.

He arrived at the accident scene to see the chaotic situation. Traffic was badly snarled and some of the boys were already directing traffic as no police had arrived yet. Due to Ah Boey's aggressiveness, it was easy for him to prevent the other runners from another workshop from laying their claim to the damaged vehicle. The dazed and slightly injured driver had already been rescued from the damaged vehicle and was sitting by the roadside awaiting the ambulance.

The driver was a young lady whose injury was unclear as there were no cuts or bleeding but she was in pain, unable to stand and still in a daze. There must be some internal injuries, perhaps a fracture, thought Kim Heng, who from his years as an accident tow- truck driver by now is almost as good as a doctor in guessing the kind of injuries an accident victim has sustained.. He had also obtained her permission to get her damaged vehicle to his workshop as she was whisked away by the ambulance with siren blaring to a private hospital. It is getting quite common to hear ambulance sirens screaming away in the distance daily these days.

After getting the car to his boss's workshop, Kim Heng felt dizzy
and nauseous. He thought it was because of missing his lunch, but
he had missed lunch or dinner several times before and had not felt
like this. Anyway he got something to eat and hoped this would
solve the matter.

It was nearly 7 p.m. and Kim Heng was still feeling unwell and
so he had to visit his old and familiar GP, Dr Looi Tat Meng, who
is in his late fifties and looked every bit like a scholar, and had been
in practice for over 25 years. Dr Looi's clinic is small but very neat
and clean and situated in a housing area where most of the residents
are the lower middle class group.

"Hey, Ah Heng, what brings you here today?"

"I must be getting old, Doc. Just feeling not so good and also a
bit of giddiness." They were speaking in the local dialect, Hokkien.
Dr Looi then went on to examine his old friend and patient. He
took his blood pressure, pulse and temperature and then went on to
check his blood circulation..

'Found anything wrong with me, Doc?"

"Unfortunately, yes! You have a blood pressure of 170/110, no
wonder you felt dizzy. It is really high."

"Really? But I don't feel dizzy always, and besides I slept late these
few nights," protested Heng but to no avail and he was convinced by
Dr Looi to be treated for hypertension and also to get a full blood
check to look into the possibility of diabetes and high cholesterol.
However this needs to be done in the morning before breakfast as a
fasting blood sample is required.

It was easy for Dr Looi to convince Heng to be treated but it
was not so for many of his other patients. Many could not believe
they needed treatment for their hypertension or diabetes. Some of
these patients would rather try some unproven alternative medicine.
However their disease will relentlessly march on and after many
years, a good number will come back with complications like renal

failure, heart attack or stroke. It is a scene that is frequently repeated and Dr Looi had seen enough of such.

Kim Heng was Dr Looi's last patient for the day. It was a slow day at work for Dr Looi. Today he had seen just a handful of patients. He should have retired a few years ago but he wondered what he would do with so much free time. Besides, a General Practitioner never really retires, they can work until it is no longer possible. Although he is nearing 60 years old, Dr Looi looks very much younger – he is medium built and has not put on much weight. His mind is still as sharp as when he was a medical student and his medical knowledge is very much up to date, thanks to his wide reading of medical journals and the attending of many medical conferences and seminars.

'Good night, Alice," he said to his nurse as he left the clinic.

"Good night Doctor," replied Alice Lim as she prepared to close the clinic up. She is Dr Looi's most loyal nurse and is still working for him ever since he opened the practice almost 20 years ago. How time flies!

Before heading home, Dr Looi decided to drop in at his close friend, Albert Yap's condominium. It has been quite a while he had met up with the retired engineer, who is still a powerfully-built man. Albert's wife had died a few years ago of lung cancer although she was no smoker and neither was Albert. They have a daughter who is now working in Singapore.

"So what have you been up to, Albert?"

"Same as before, spending lots of time on the internet surfing. How are you, Doc?"

"Fine, life goes on. So what new stuff are you reading from the internet?" asked Dr Looi. Albert is interesting because he would discover new things on the internet and they would sit and discuss for hours, usually till the wee hours of the morning.

"Energy healing! It is very interesting. This one is called Universal Healing."

Dr Looi himself believes in energy healing as he himself uses Reiki healing when it is appropriate and indicated. There have been some remarkable experiences with Reiki healing – some people had their chronic pains completely cured even after just one 45 minute session with Dr Looi. Some other cases needed more therapy sessions and yet others were never cured of their complaints. It is almost impossible to know who will respond but Dr Looi understands that everyone will benefit one way or other. He sometimes uses Reiki as a mode of diagnosis and this is the unique ability of Dr Looi and his usage of this therapy.

"Well, I have not heard of this before," replied Dr Looi.

"Me too. That is why I intend to find out more about this. What drink would you like to have, Doc?"

"Please, make your special coffee!"

They discussed numerous topics, from local politics, fengshui, religion to meditation. They both possess an in depth knowledge of these subjects and by the time Dr Looi said good night, it was already 2.40 a.m!

As Dr Looi drove back to his condominium, the road was very quiet and only occasional cars were zooming past. This is such a contrast to during the morning rush hour when there would be so many vehicles on the same road that it is indeed a chore to drive. In fact driving in Penang is a real headache as well as a hazard. As we have said, the drivers on this island have a peculiar way of driving found nowhere else in the country. It just makes your blood boil especially if you are in a hurry.

As he drove on the deserted street and was enjoying a smooth drive, something caught Dr Looi's eye. There was a flash of bright coloured lights in the sky. They moved right across the night sky, slowly at first and followed by a 90 degree turn before vanishing from view, at an unbelievable speed. The doctor stopped his car by the kerb of the road and got out to make a quick survey of the sky, but it was blank, now he can only see the twinkling of the stars.

He was sure of what he had seen, as on this occasion, he had had no alcoholic drinks at his friend's place. At once he thought about a UFO, as of late there had been many such sightings reported in many countries. Definitely it was a UFO, reasoned the doctor, now his brain was working extra fast and his heart pounding fast.

It was too early in the morning to call anyone and besides the vision had already disappeared from the skies. He proceeded home, all the while thinking what he had seen. It was his first encounter with something so puzzling. At the back of his mind, Dr Looi had a hunch it must be a UFO sighting, the question is from which planet it had come.

In his research, Dr Looi had discovered that there had been numerous types of alien visitation to the Earth since pre-historic times. There is indeed archaeological evidence but this is rejected by mainstream scientists. Even the so- called modern day evidence like the Roswell, New Mexico crash in 1947 has been covered up by the US Government till today. Many believe that badly injured aliens were recovered when a UFO crashed at the place and that a total cover up has since been in place.

Could the UFO be anyone of the friendlier visitors from Andromeda Constellation, Pleidians, Sirians or Arcturians? Or the more hostile and dreaded Grays? Yes, Dr Looi realised not all aliens that visited Earth were of the friendly type. The hostile ones had wanted to colonise Earth several times but were driven away by many of the Galactic Federation forces, a coalition of the benevolent aliens that watch over the welfare of Earth, according to Dr Looi's understanding.

This doctor is really one of a kind because he is so open minded about life and all its possibilities and at times he just seemed to "know" the situation, truth, fact, whatever, during his periods of meditation.

CHAPTER 3

There were no newspaper reports whatsoever about a possible UFO sighting the next day, as Dr Looi expected. However he did not need to depend on newspaper reports to convince him of what he had seen. He had rung up his friend Albert to tell him about it but Albert had gone to bed immediately after he left and thus saw or heard nothing.

For years Dr Looi had been researching on the topics of aliens, UFOs, the Mayan prophecies and implications for the year 2012. The year of 2012 is the most significant of all the years because not only had the ancient Mayans ended their calendar on 21st December 2012, but many mediums, psychics and shamans of various indigenous people all pointed to the Earth's uncertain future after this date. Even his own feng shui calculations showed that the year 2012 would be a year of great upheaval and uncertainties. All these independent experts in their field had come almost to the same conclusions, so it must be really significant, thought Dr Looi.

The hottest topic among the esoteric circle is that of Disclosure and Ascension of Earth into the Fifth Dimension along with her inhabitants. In Disclosure, governments can no longer deny the existence of intelligent alien life forms that had visited Earth. Once people all over the world accept this as the truth, the next step is the transference of knowledge and technologies for the quantum leap of people's lifestyle. The entire world will never be the same again.

Originally the aliens had wanted a mass effect by their appearance in great numbers all over the world within a short span of time. However they had to change this strategy as it would have caused pandemonium all over the world resulting in complete mayhem. They decided that the best way was to appear in small numbers and let it be reported in obscure channels so that small groups of people would be exposed to this.

In Ascension, it is a much more complicated process as it involves the entire human population changing their vibrational frequencies to a higher one with the appearance of 12 stranded DNA again. This is also known as The Shift, for humans are shifting to their Fifth dimensional bodies which is Light and no longer physical in form. Again the aliens are to guide humans in this Shift along with the Lightworkers, people who have the knowledge of how to handle such a Shift.

Ever since he had knowledge of the Shift, Dr Looi had been keeping a very close watch for UFOs and other phenomenon. He also has an extensive network of friends in several countries and kept in contact with them. His network of friends spans across Asia, Europe and the Americas and these are mainly from his Facebook and Twitter accounts. Today he will write to his friends about his experience last night and asked if any one of them saw, read or heard about any UFO activity in their locality.

Meanwhile, the Police had formed a team to track down the goldsmith shop robbery and one of the detectives assigned to the case was Hassan bin Rashid, a stockily built man in his early 30's with a light complexion. As a schoolboy, Hassan was the product of a great rugby playing school, King Edward VII School of Taiping, Perak and he used to play as a forward in his school rugby team. He is thus quite athletic and occasionally was called to represent the Police Rugby Team, which has some of the finest rugby players in the country. Although rugby is not that popular when compared to badminton or football in the country, rugby players had a special respect, for they are the ones tough enough to take up the game.

Hassan is being assigned to pay a visit to Danny Ong to ask Danny some questions as routine police work since Danny's shop was so near the goldsmith's that was robbed. It was just past lunch hour and Hassan rode his brand new Honda motorcycle bought from Boon Siew, the wholesaler for Honda in Penang. He is very proud of this machine and polishes it whenever he can but today it rained while he was on the way to Gurney Plaza and what a mess this beauty will be, thought Hassan. He did not mind getting wet in the rain, it just reminded him of some very satisfying games of rugby he had while playing on a rain soaked field in one of the most memorable matches he had in Alor Setar, against Kedah All-Blues in which he made a fabulous try to help Police win the match 12- 9.

Danny was at his stall and although it was at lunch hour, there were only a handful of customers these days. Where had all the customers gone? Business was really bad in the last few months and looked likely to continue to be so this month. And almost everything had gone up in cost: electricity, water, rental, petrol, highway tolls, cooking oil, and the list goes on and on. Alcoholic drinks and cigarettes are now not affordable to many people but people are still smoking. However most likely these were counterfeit goods and according to Danny, they were as good as the real ones. Danny has proof for this opinion; he saw a documentary on the Mafia and the Boss asked for the counterfeit cigarettes from China, since they taste like the real ones and are far cheaper.

Hassan introduced himself to Danny and started to ask questions. At first it was very general and then it began to be more direct and intense.

"So you said although the robbers ran by your stall, you didn't have a good look at them?"

"Yes, I have said so many times, all of them had their helmets on and they ran so fast it was impossible to have a good look."

"OK, how about these photos of some of the suspects we think carried out the robbery? Recognise any one of them?" Hassan laid all the photos, eight of them, on the table.

Danny took a brief look and one caught his eye- a mug shot of Ah Keat! There was no mistake, it was his old buddy.

"No". However the sharp detective eyes of Hassan has caught the surprised look on Danny's face when Danny saw Ah Keat's photo among the three he held in his hand. But Hassan was not too sure which of the three photos took Danny by surprise.

"I don't think you are telling me the truth! One of these 3 men's photos caught your attention, Danny!" Hassan said.

"No! I don't know any of them, all these eight photos! If I can be excused, I need to attend to someone now."

Whether it was good or bad timing, it was Danny's girlfriend, Linda who dropped in. Actually she had witnessed the whole scene of Hassan asking questions to Danny before Danny noticed her. Hassan picked up the photos, preparing to leave but walked towards Danny and said, "I'll be back with better photos to jolt your memory, Danny." He gave a cold hard look at Danny, frightening Linda even more.

After Hassan left the stall, Danny faced another round of severe interrogation by Linda. It was far worse than what he had gone through with Hassan. She wanted to know why he had not even mentioned to her about the robbery at the goldsmith's, what the Police suspected about him and the robbery, whether he was really involved in it, whether he recognised anyone from the photos Hassan showed, and on and on. The questions went rapid fire, not giving Danny time to focus his thoughts and answer her.

"I trusted you so much and this is what I get from you!"

"Linda, let me explain….."

"Enough! In my heart I never liked any of your so called friends, especially that Johnny Santiago!"

"Johnny? Now keep him out of this, he has nothing…."

"There you go! Defending your so-called friends again. What about me, me, me! Looks like they are more important than me!" Linda then rushed out with tears in her eyes and her heart pounding. Danny just stood there frozen, not knowing what to do. This was the most severe fight they had for a long time. He just sank on to a nearby chair and started to stare into empty space. After a while, Danny tried to phone Linda on her mobile but she did not answer the call. Let her cool off, thought Danny.

It was more than a day after the quarrel and still Linda had not answered all his calls to her mobile. This is unlike her, as Linda will always be the first to try to patch things up after every misunderstanding they had in the past. When he phoned some of her friends, they told Danny that she wanted to be left alone for a while and yes, she is fine.

Meanwhile, Hassan the detective kept his word. He visited Danny again and now he had only three photographs of the suspects but this time with a helmet superimposed on their heads. This should jolt Danny's memories, thought Hassan. However this time Danny knew what to do and to do it professionally- he kept on saying even with this help, he really could not identify the robbers in the three photographs. On the previous occasion he thought he saw a resemblance with one of the robbers but not now Danny explained. The wily detective still thought Danny knew more than what he is willing to say. Watch out Danny, I'll keep a close watch on you, thought Hassan to himself.

Danny is really troubled on two accounts. First is what you call girl problem with Linda. She refused to answer all his attempts to talk to her or meet her. Second was the question of Lim Ah Keat, should he be warned that the Police are suspecting him of being involved in the goldsmith heist? The trouble is, Danny did not have Ah Keat's contact number. He will have to go looking for Ah Keat and this is next to impossible for Keat has no fixed address and is also dangerous, for Danny is sure the detective will be shadowing him from now on. The third problem (actually there are three issues) is financial, how is he to pay the wages of his two workers if business continues to be so bad? He is in need of a second income.

Danny knew he would be in serious trouble soon if nothing is done to solve these problems, one a heartache and the others a headache. He needed to think and so he went to the local Bar, Kheng Hoe Bar in Air Itam, to find some peace of mind. This Bar is special because it has stood at the same location since the early 1970s. Even his father and uncles had frequented the same Bar. The other fact is that this is the only Bar in the area which is really a locals' Bar which had never served any tourists, unlike most Bars in Penang which are located around George Town area and where many visitors gather. So the crowd here thus only speak in the local dialect, Hokkien, and Danny hoped to be able to bump into some of Ah Keat's friends as well. This is killing two birds with one stone

Danny chose a corner seat all by himself and took orders for two bottles of "Or Kow" – what the locals called the Guiness Stout brand whose reputation is that only macho men knew how to appreciate the drink, which is bitter sweet in taste and gives a good punch or "oomph". He noticed only a few customers but many idle and bored "China Dolls" working as waitresses. Many of these young China girls would come to accompany Danny but he asked them to leave him alone. Some of these sweet young things were quite persistent though, but Danny got rid of them anyway.

Some old men were singing their favourite Hokkien songs at the karaoke set while others would cheer them on and Danny noticed they were quite good singers. The atmosphere was one of merrymaking after a hard day's work. The place was filled with cigarette smoke that lingers in the Bar, drifting away slowly. Danny then began to think about his life and how he met Linda.

His own marriage had broken down five years ago and his divorce was finally completed. Danny never believed that this would happen, he had thought that marriage was for life. However events began to take over and soon he knew that it had to be over. It was heart breaking to see it end and his little boy followed his mother. Since they had parted, he never got into contact either with his son or his ex- wife. It had to be a complete break to ease the pain of the divorce.

To recover from the trauma, Danny decided to look forward to a better future by concentrating on his business. He thought that he might end up being all alone in the remainder of his life and so was thinking of checking into an Old Folks' Home when the time comes. He had even driven around the island to take note of which Old Folks' Home he thought would be to his liking. The one near Jalan Utama was on his list.

One rainy evening about 2 years ago, he was at a local secondhand bookshop at One Stop Complex along Burma Road in Pulau Tikus. He was about to leave the bookshop when a lady reminded him about his umbrella which he had forgotten. She was Linda Chua and she was just being helpful.

"Oh, what makes you think the umbrella is mine?" replied Danny, with a mischievous smile.

Linda was shocked, and her face went red with embarrassment.

"I am sorry! I thought it was yours since it was so near you," replied Linda sheepishly.

"Well, the umbrella looks very old and weather-beaten, surely you don't think I can own such an umbrella?" Danny was getting a kick being cheeky now. He was certainly more like his usual self today.

Linda then thought to herself : "Oh, this one is trying to be funny."

"I knew it looks old and sort of discarded but I thought it must belong to a man," said Linda, now ready to do battle with this smart alec.

The China Doll waitress came to ask Danny if he wanted another bottle of stout and this broke Danny's daydreaming of how he met

Linda, who he really misses very much now. As politely as he could, Danny said he was about to leave and so he would have no more orders for the evening. The waitress walked off in disappointment as she will have no more commission earned from this man.

As Danny was about to leave, he bumped into Rajkumar, his old friend from school days. Raj works as a car wash attendant full-time but is also doing a part-time job in Keng Hoe Bar as a bouncer. Raj always wore short sleeves to show off his muscular biceps. With gold ear- piercings, Raj actually looks more like a DJ than a bouncer. Some say he looked like the late Michael Jackson if only he had been less muscular.

"Raj! What are you doing here?" exclaimed Danny.

"Hoi! Danny! Never seen you here before! What's up?" replied Raj, just as surprised.

The old friends then gave a bit of news to each other to catch up with the latest. Danny took the opportunity to ask Raj if he had met with Ah Keat as Raj too had known Ah Keat for years before the latter went to mix with people of shady backgrounds. Raj mentioned he had been busy and not kept in contact with Keat but said he would get in touch with Danny once contact was made as Raj has a large circle of friends. With that they parted and promised to stay in contact.

CHAPTER 4

It was past 11 p.m. and Dr Looi was at home and he was on the internet surfing for world news and when there was nothing interesting but just stupid political news, he signed into his Twitter account. He prefers this to Facebook because he has no time to waste on long winded write ups.

He wrote: "Saw some thing like UFO few nights ago". Almost immediately he had a direct message from one of his friends.

"Really? No joking?" wrote "Hawk" from Los Angeles, California, one of his contacts.

"Honest but no media report."

"Describe it," Hawk wrote back.

"Colored bright lights, very fast."

"Could be meteorite?"

"Unlikely, it made 90 degree turn."

"Now u r talking."

"Why u say this?" queried Dr Looi.

"UFO need 90 degree turn to get into the next dimension."

'Then I saw a real one?"

"Very much so" replied Hawk

Then Doc heard his doorbell ring. "Gotta sign off, visitor here," and he went to the door. It was his old friend Albert.

"Come in Albert! Say what's up?" said Doc

"Nothing much, Doc. But anything new you discovered about UFOs and the like?" asked Albert while making himself comfortable and at home on the rattan chair. When he visits Dr Looi, he always sits on this rattan chair. The TV was on but low volume and thus was not a distraction from the conversation.

"Just wrote about it on Twitter and someone thought it could be a genuine UFO from my description." said Dr Looi while shutting off his Notebook.

"Wow!" was all Albert could utter. Then they talked about the rising cost of living, inflation, some scandals involving the government and how irresponsible politicians are in general. Even taxi drivers were picked on because of a recent report of how one cab driver in Kuala Lumpur charged a tourist RM450 for a trip from Museum Negara to KLCC, a trip for which even RM 40 was excessive. This came to be known only when the tourist wrote a letter to a local newspaper, The Star, in the "Letters to the Editor" section. It is well known that cab drivers in the country are a recalcitrant lot.

"So Doc, assuming it was really a UFO, do you think it is friend or foe?" asked Albert, who is always amazed at the facts that Dr. Looi has at his fingertips.

"Well, it is hard to say. As a matter of fact, UFOs have been visiting our planet since ancient times. There are several evidences as seen in stone carvings on temple walls but archaeologists refuse to document these as genuine. In modern times many government agencies will try to cover up such sightings by explaining these are weather balloons, freak weather phenomena and so on. Governments are afraid that the truth will terrify the populace and panic will spread. However I think finally the UFOs will reveal themselves more and more as it is about time people know the reality."

The doctor continued: "I think we are in very exciting times in view of the coming 'Disclosure" – a term used by UFO specialists about the mass appearance of UFOs when finally humanity will come face to face with these Extraterrestrials or ETs. The visitations have increased since we exploded the atomic bombs in WW2.

Most of these ETs are benevolent types and they are keen to uplift humanity's life with their superior knowledge. They see us as their very own brothers and sisters and in fact that may be the case. Many of us are Starseeds, we have on purpose been reincarnated on earth to experience and learn life on the 3 Dimensional Plane. I know of many people who somehow felt that their real home is somewhere in the stars up in the sky, thus the reports of alien abductions. These people were abducted in their sleep to be brought to the spaceships to be studied by the ET scientists. As a matter of fact, these are not real abductions. The abductee had a prior understanding with their ET families to be brought up to their ships for information to be extracted and then returned to their earth lives and families as if nothing happened. It was only under hypnosis that such abductions were discovered by the medical community.

The hostile ETs like the Reptilians and Greys are totally different in their intentions. Those abducted by these groups sometimes are never seen again and these abductions are more like kidnapping but with no ransom. In the history of Earth, there have been several attempts by hostile ETs to conquer Earth and capture humans as slaves while they plunder for the raw materials their planets require. But these attempts were derailed by the Galactic Federation of friendly ETs. Mind you, a group of ETs known as the Annunaki had successfully colonized Earth thousands of years ago and their descendants, known as the Illuminati are the ones controlling Earth right now! Both behind the scene and also at the scene!"

"Doc, can you name a few planets where these ETs may come from?"

"OK, before they come to our planet, their starships must enter a stargate or portal and in order to do so the vibration of the Starships must change to that in sync with our sun. Not only that, they must calibrate it to our sun's special signature code. There have been over 100 extraterrestrial races over time that have visited us and will continue to do so. Some come from planets with names like Namo,

Heina, Topaki, Nunk, Ummo, Acart and many others. Some of these races are very closely related to us- like Pleiadians, Sirians, Arcturians, Antareans, Andromedans and those from Procyon, Aldebaran and Deneb. And since 11.11.11, it has been made far easier with the opening of more portals of entry. The 11th Star Gate Portal began formation since 1992 and is just completed. Altogether, 33 new portals are being opened and radiating the light of the 12 rays. And our cells are changing over to resonate at 528Hz, which is the source Code of Creation. The signal of the coming change had been the Asian tsunami of December 2004. It was in fact Mother Earth's first push into the 4th Dimension. Then, nothing of low vibration of Darkness has been allowed to enter."

"Doc, you mention about the Greys- who are they?" asked Albert.

"These Greys are artificial humanoids that continue to reproduce their kind and they have no spiritual spark. They are short, less than 5 feet and have a very pungent smell."

"But who created the Greys?"

"Beings of E'lohim"

"These ETs- do they look like humans?"

"The human form generally exists throughout the Universe, the basic blueprint type being called Adam Kadmon and variations arise due to planetary differences. Sirians, Pleiadians and Venusians are similar to us due to genetic linkage, especially the Venusians who can pass off as Earth people.' explained Dr Looi.

"And what about the others?"

"Well, the Antarians are very tall with large eyes, small mouths and no ears since they communicate without speech. They also have no nose but small narrow nostrils and bony skulls. They have no body hair. Andromedians, Pleiadians and Lyrans are generally of same height as us while Sirians, Arians and those from Perseus are very much taller, with males over 7 feet tall(2.13m) and females above 6 foot 4 inches(1.93m). Many of them have a very long lifespan and their bodies do not age."

"Doc, you mention about the baddies like Reptilians, tell me something more, if you don't mind." Now Albert is so excited that he can't help asking. Dr Looi went to get themselves some cold drinks from the kitchen and some titbits as well, knowing that Albert is going to stay a while longer.

"OK, these Reptilians are very tall, about 7 feet and have skins that are scaly with quite long tongues, so they talk with a hissing sound that sounds like whispers as their tongues flick out. However apart from these differences, they look like humans. Sometimes their tails may be seen. The more troublesome ones are actually known as the Archons."

"The what? Ah Chongs?" interjected Albert.

"No, Archons. But they have several other names and are among the worst because they played a big role in hijacking and derailing the evolution of Earth and Mankind and have been a big nuisance and problem in the entire Universe. These are low 4th Density beings, mostly unseen, which the Elites invoke in their rituals for power to control others."

"Your knowledge on this subject is most amazing, Doc!" exclaimed Albert, now helping himself to some snacks.

"But you can get this from many sources. However sometimes I myself am confused which source I got it from."

"Meaning…?" asked Albert, munching a mouthful of titbits.

"I mean it could also be from my meditations, apart from books and the web."

"What I don't understand Doc is how come these Reptilians, these snakes and lizards, can be more advanced than us?"

"Well, the whole story is as follows. These beings chose to be evolved as the dinosaurs but with climatic change, many were dying. Due to their large size, not many were saved by their original stock who came in spaceships to take them back to Orion Constellation where they originated. Some smaller ones went on to live in underground caves and survived while others that were even smaller went on to evolve into modern day snakes, lizards and birds.

In their own planet they formed two groups according to whether they were meat-eaters or vegetarians while on Earth. These two groups kept on fighting each other but the vegetarian group retreated into underground caves. They developed spiritually and their bodies glowed allowing them to illuminate the dark caves. Later their skin became lighter coloured and their scales thinner and softer. They developed longer tails and gills to swim in the underground rivers and later wings developed to allow them even to fly.

But they never had Love emotion until they met the Arcturians, who were attracted by their spirituality. With Love, they developed even faster and higher in the spiritual realms, along with their intelligence."

"Do you have any information of their flying saucers, Doc?"

"In fact I do! They have a Mother ship which is of immense size, like a small city. It is indeed larger than the whole of our Penang Island! From the Mother ship, smaller crafts are sent out for their various missions. Many are specialized in certain jobs, like surveillance, laboratories for conducting experiments and sample collecting. Then ships that are tasked with environmental clean ups, yes these mop up radioactive debris from nuclear tests that we conduct or like that from the Chernobyl and Fukushima disasters. Of course they brought along too their combat ships mainly for their own protection."

There was a change in tone of Dr Looi's voice here and Albert sensed it.

"To be honest, Albert, I am very uncomfortable with the last one about the combat ships they have. Though many psychics and channelers convey messages that those from the Galactic Force and Andromeda Council are benevolent, coming to help Earthlings to progress especially with their superior technologies, I still have some reservations about their roles in overcoming the Cabal and Illuminati that try to control the world. I mean do you think they come all the way, light years in distance, just to help us?"

"It is more likely to plunder Earth's natural resources for their own consumption!' interjected Albert, proud to offer some of his own theories.

"And Albert, my friend, I have information that three gigantic motherships had left Gootan planet for Earth, and two of them have a diameter of 200 miles across! And no one knows of their intention! This seems like an Armada of Battle Ships."

"If these Aliens are hostile, what can we do?" asked Albert.

"Nothing.....I mean I don't know.' replied Doc. There was an eerie silence between the two good friends, each thinking deeply. Then Albert rose up to say it was time for him to go and he left. They promised to talk about this when they meet again, hopefully soon. And in Albert's heart, he hoped he would not run into an Alien UFO on his way home.

CHAPTER 5

Mokhtar is accompanying Ah Boey today in their rounds of the accident prone areas, looking for cars involved in accidents that would need towing away or repairs that their workshop can do. They are paid to roam and this suits both of them very much. Ram was ill and on medical certificate leave today. They had roamed Jalan Mesjid Negeri, Air Itam, Farlim and now they are in Paya Terubong area. No luck, no accidents. Seems like all drivers were behaving well today.

They decided to try their luck around Pulau Tukus area and so they headed there on their modified bikes that make a very loud noise but do not necessarily go any faster. When they reached Peel Avenue, which is close to the Pulau Tikus area, both of them stopped under the shade of the palm trees to observe the traffic and rest for a while. It was Ah Boey who noticed the snatch thief snatching the handbag from the basket in front of the Honda motorbike ridden by a middle aged woman. It happened so fast; the woman did not react until the snatch thief and his accomplice were far ahead. Ah Boey shouted to Mokhtar and pointed to the situation and both of them gave a nod to each other and gave chase, with Ah Boey being first to go after the thief.

The snatch thief was a pillion rider and his accomplice was driving the bike, weaving through the heavy traffic and being pursued by Ah Boey with Mokhtar close behind. While chasing the snatch thieves, Mokhtar was talking on his walkie talkie to other groups of tow truck bikers alerting them of the situation. These boys then swung into action and tried to cut the escape route of the snatch thieves. Since Ah Boey was closing in, and what seemed like a bunch of other such bikers in front, the snatch thieves threw away their loot and disappeared into the traffic at McAlistair Road.

The thieves escaped but lost their loot. Ah Boey retrieved the hand bag and went to the Police Station to hand it over to the Police to trace the owner. Crime rate has been rising throughout the country, both petty crimes and serious ones. The number of snatch thieves cases is really troubling the tourism industry because many tourists have also been targeted and several suffered injuries when they fell and hurt themselves while struggling with the snatcher. A few had even died from the serious head injuries they sustained when they fell. As most tourists will not stay on to appear in court to give evidence when the thieves are caught, they are the favourite targets now.

In the capital city of Kuala Lumpur the crime situation is far worse. In Lebuh Ampang area, snatch thieves are most active. In the Jalan Ampang- Menara Great Eastern locality, cases of assault and kidnapping are well known. Strangers may come up close to ask for directions and then strike suddenly. Another area for snatch thieves is Changkat Thambi Dollah, off Jalan Pudu where plenty of bikers hang around looking for potential victims. In fact in the area from Swiss Garden Hotel to Hentian Pudu Raya and Menara Maybank, even if you are using your mobile phones, it will be snatched at lightning speed, leaving you talking halfway. The worst areas seem to be at Wangsa Maju Putra LRT and TAR College areas- they are now worse than Jinjang, Balakong or Puchong.

Those who go shopping at Wisma Shaw should park their cars at official parking places. This is because roadside parking bays have been "booked' by certain gangs who do not allow anyone else to park there. If one happens to argue, then they are in for serious trouble.

After the excitement of chasing the snatch thieves, they were back to patrolling the streets for accidents but things were very quiet and these boys thus could not earn their commissions. With the cost of living going up frighteningly, it is rather tough for these boys to survive only on their basic wages. That is why they sometimes end up fighting over a "claim" with other groups of riders from rival car repair workshops. In such explosive situations they need seniors like Kim Heng to settle these disputes.

Riders like Ah Boey, Mokhtar and Ramu work very hard. They will have to patrol the roads the whole day long, in the hot tropical sun or under the rainforest type of thunderstorms and rain. It is a job for the young boys, for it is only them that can take the strain of riding round the whole day regardless of the weather. Also at night they each have their own small side incomes to attend to. For Ah Boey, it is peddling pirated DVDs for sale in Batu Ferringhi, the hot tourist beach area, just like Kuta Beach area of Bali. Although he was caught several times in police raids, each time he was released uncharged after intervention by his Boss.

Mokhtar will be helping his brother sell *satay* at their stall in Hillside, Tanjung Bungah Food Court while Ramu gives home tuition to some lower primary school kids in his area. Actually Ramu is the brightest among the three friends as he was supposed to study in Lower Sixth Form but because his parents were very poor, they could not afford to let him continue with his education. That is why Ramu has to come out to work.

The next day Ramu was back to join them at work and the three started their patrolling along Tanjong Tokong heading to Kelawei Road. Then a sudden heavy downpour started and the boys sought shelter at a Shell petrol station along the road. Then their walkie talkie crackled with the voice of Kim Heng, "Hello! Ah Boey, you people go to Chulia Street now. There is a flood there and many cars are stuck. I am already on my way."

Without wasting any time, the three of them rode their bikes out into the downpour, heading to Chulia Street. This is the street where backpackers go to as there are plenty of budget hotels there and it is in the heart of George Town. The rain this time is accompanied by unusually strong winds and many branches had fallen on to the road making it a hazard.

The three of them reached Chulia Street and saw the floods. They were shocked. The whole of the street was flooded with above ankle depth water which seemed to be rising fast. Many cars were stalled with their drivers sitting inside helplessly. Some were seen to be making frantic phone calls on their mobile. Those with 4WD vehicles were able to drive on fearlessly and the drivers seem to enjoy the situation, some even had the cheek to laugh at cars that were stalled.

Mokhtar talked to Kim Heng to give feedback on the chaotic situation and Kim Heng replied that he was just round the corner. The boys got to work. Ramu directed traffic away from the unseen drain while Mokhtar and Ah Boey were pushing a stalled Kenari car with a lady driver and her two kids inside to the side, but avoiding the deep drain they knew was there. Kim Heng appeared with his tow truck and was directed by Ramu to the owner of a Wira who had got the wheels stuck in a pothole or drain. Ramu had already got the driver to agree to be towed out of trouble and Kim Heng expertly hooked his truck to the Wira and pulled it to safety. This helped to solve the traffic jam to a certain extent as those cars that were still running could continue their way.

The boys and Kim Heng did an excellent job in rescuing stalled cars and keeping traffic flowing as best as they could. No policemen were in sight. The police, when you need them, are nowhere to be seen, as always, thought Ah Boey, who must have known about half the police personnel in the Air Itam Police Station, the place where he is usually locked up after getting arrested for peddling fake DVDs.

Communicating via their mobiles and walkie talkie sets, they learned that several parts of Penang were flooded. The worst affected area was in Jalan P. Ramlee, which was impassable to any traffic. In fact the Emergency Response Team of Penang had deployed boats to the area to rescue stranded residents. It was chaotic. The weather these days seems to be very different – either it is too hot or it is getting too much rain. In fact one part of Penang can be raining while another part is very sunny. However, today it seemed that the whole of Penang and parts of the mainland were having very heavy rain. The sky had turned dark and grey and dark clouds could be seen to change shape and size very fast.

Other groups of riders for many other car repair workshops were also busy helping stranded motorists just like Ah Boey and his friends in other parts of Penang. Now they were relaying news among themselves. Although they were all rivals to each other in this business, when it came to times of emergency and disasters, they were all very united and helpful. That was how the news of a very bad landslide that occurred Batu Ferringhi came to their knowledge. Landslides had also occurred in the Paya Terubong area and at the winding road near Hotel Equatorial.

These boys knew that their help was needed and so they organised among themselves which group should go where to lend a helping hand. All their differences and old grudges were left aside. The Hup Aik group will go to the Paya Terubong area while Seng Lip Seng group will head to Hotel Equatorial area to help. Ah Boey and his friends, belonging to Tong Aik group, were to go to Batu Ferringhi. The respective groups then went on their way.

Meanwhile Linda Chuah had just come out of Boutique at Prima Tanjong, Fettes Park, when she discovered the underground car park was completely flooded up to waist level and her car was thus stuck there, along with so many other cars. She thought for a second and decided to call some friends but none could come to help her as they too were stuck somewhere. Now what? She knew now she needed to call Danny but she had not been answering all of Danny's calls and messages for the last few days. She took all her courage and decided to call Danny, thinking any way this is a good chance to break the ice between them.

As her mobile number flashed in the display of Danny's phone, he couldn't believe his eyes.

"Hi Linda?" said Danny.

"Danny, yes it's me. Look, I am stuck at Prima Tanj……" even before she could finish her sentence, Danny knew she was in trouble as he heard from several people that there were floods in several parts of the City.

"Just stay there! I will come now to pick you up. Stay put!" yelled Danny, as he prepared to get two helmets. Danny knew that cars will be quite useless in this situation and he is prepared to go there by bike. Linda felt so much better now. Danny was so glad that Linda called him for help as this will bring them back together. The storm meanwhile is still going on, lashing the island with strong winds, huge waves and driving rain.

Elsewhere, when the three friends got to the road to Batu Ferringhi, it was already jammed with traffic but as they were on their trusted bikes, they managed to make their way towards the area of landslide. It was a few kilometres from Rasa Sayang Hotel that the landslide had occurred. It completely blocked the hilly road. Huge boulders were now blocking the road together with earth and fallen trees.

'We better turn back and fetch the MPPP men here. They have equipment which will make the job far easier than just digging with our own hands," said Ah Boey to Ramu and Mokhtar, referring to the MPPP lorry with workers stuck along with other cars in the gridlock. The MPPP are the efficient and people-friendly City Council workers deployed in times of urgency to make the roads safe for the public by the current State Government. They turned their bikes around and sped to the MPPP lorry which made no progress at all in the bad jam. The boys explained the idea to the MPPP workers in the lorry and managed to get three men with equipment like shovels and chainsaws to the place. Leaving the three men there to start clearing the landslide, they went back to the MPPP lorry to fetch another three more men and equipment.

As for Danny, he had reached Prima Tanjung and located Linda. Both were so relieved to see each other again! But there was no time for small talk, as Danny surveyed the flooded car park and thought he could try to drive the car out before even more flood waters came. Some other drivers were also trying to start their cars. Danny went into action and managed to start and drive the car out of the basement car park, followed by several others. He then picked Linda up and started to drive her back to her Apartment. He can't allow her to go alone now.

"I called you several times, Linda" said Danny as he drove through the rain.

"I..I know...I am sorry I didn't return the call."

"Never mind, now that we are back together, let's not be stay out of touch again, OK?"

Linda just nodded her head. Danny then switched on the radio to listen to the news and it was reported that a bad storm had caused severe flooding in Penang, Ipoh and Kuala Lumpur. It seemed that KL was the hardest hit, especially at Raja Chulan area, which is under 1m. of water. Several houses in Pandan Jaya had their roofs blown off, trees had been uprooted and there was just plain chaos. Both of them were shocked at the news, learning that Penang was not the only place to suffer this storm.

Mokhtar and the boys had been in the thick of the action along with uniformed personnel like Fire Brigade, RELA and Non-Government Organizations in helping to do relief and rescue work. The speed at which some of the NGOs sent their members to help was simply amazing.

Soon traffic was back to some normalcy when blocked roads were again functioning and the heavy rain eased off as well. However, Kuala Lumpur was not so lucky. Flood waters were not receding and the amount of destruction and chaos was unbelievable. The whole City was thrown into disarray. And there were reports that a major landslide had occurred somewhere near Fraser's Hill and it was believed to have caused some casualties. The Meteorological Department had not expected such a severe lashing from the weather although from their weather data they knew of an impending tropical rainstorm, not much different from any typical tropical rainstorm. But one man deep in the northern forest named Jatek knew more than any of these weather scientists.

CHAPTER 6

Jatek lives in the forest fringes of Pahang state, not too far from Rompin, the nearest town. He belongs to the tribe called Temian of the Senoi people. They are the indigenous *orang asli* people of the forest of Malaysia. These aboriginals only compose less than 1% of the total population of the country, around 141,000 in the census taken in 2006. During the Second World War, these hardy and silent people of the forest gave the Japanese invaders great problems, so much so that the Japanese soldiers had to avoid the jungle routes in the march to invade what was then colonial Malaya. And they only had poison darts from their blowpipes to kill the soldiers. Then in the Emergency Days from 1948 to 1960, the British and later the Malaysian Government used these expert jungle survival guides to track the Communists down and raid their hideouts deep in the jungles. They were so successful that 2 platoons of Rangers were formed entirely by the Orang Asli to help drive off the Communists. Though having contributed so much in both wars, they are largely the forgotten people of the jungle. Many still live in remote small settlements near the forests and come into contact with ordinary people only when they go to small towns to sell their jungle produce of honey, rattan canes, carvings and local fruits.

In 2005, researchers from Glasgow and Leeds Universities discovered and published their findings about the mitochondrial DNA of these people. It was discovered that it resembled a sample of DNA from a 65,000 year old sample from Africa. This could mean that right out of Africa, early humans had come to the Malay Archipelago.

One week ago, Jatek noticed strange behaviours in the jungle animals and birds. Along with his keen sense of observation, he also possesses a kind of sixth sense, for he is the community medicine man, or shaman. Jatek, a man in his early 40's, is quite tall for his tribe. He also looks different because his mother is Chinese, hence his features. He is thus well known among the local Chinese villagers in the area. He sensed some kind of disaster would be inflicted upon his small band of villagers. Their small shelters and bamboo huts were quite close by a river and lately the currents had been stronger and levels rising almost imperceptibly. He then went into his meditation or trance and was given the advice to lead his people out of danger from the impending floods.

His band of Temian comprises about 9 families of 35 individuals and they never argue with his leadership and decision making. He told them to move to higher grounds and to make temporary shelters there and within 3 days of moving, the heavy rains came and the small river near their tiny settlement overflowed its banks and inundated their settlement. Thus they were safe and suffered minimal damage to their properties. When the flooding subsided, they returned to their settlement to make the necessary repairs. Life goes on. It was once again peaceful and cool in the jungle. Again Jatek had saved his tribe people from disaster and danger with his special gift of understanding Nature and Energy.

Back in George Town, Penang, things are getting back to normal with people going about their daily routines after doing the big clean up after the floods. The famous Penang hawkers were back in action, the heavy traffic jams due to office, factory workers and school children's parents or servants' unique way of driving were also back. The island people's driving habits do not make for a smooth flow of traffic at the best of times.

In all the renewed daily routines, one life was discovered tragically cut short. It was the gruesome murder of an old lady who lived alone in Lorong Selamat. There were several knife wounds and blows to her head. The neighbours had not seen anything unusual. They only noticed a stench from the old house after the floods. Police came to investigate and had to break down the front door to find her body sprawled on the floor in the kitchen. Although there were frequent petty crimes throughout that area, nothing in the way of a murder had ever taken place. Detective Hassan was also roped in to investigate the crime. He has yet to get any useful leads in the goldsmith shop robbery and now this murder investigation on top of that. Hassan will be busy along with the forensic team as now the Police will depend on them to get clues to the murderer. So far there have been no witnesses and no leads.

After the floods, many car owners went to car wash centres to get their cars cleaned up and Rajkumar was over- worked. However he took the opportunity to ask those he knew he could trust about the whereabouts of Ah Keat. It wasn't long when a stranger came to ask Raj why he was looking for Ah Keat. Rajkumar then knew that this must be the go between man and told him that Keat's old friend has some important news for him. The stranger asked for Danny's mobile phone number and said there is a good chance that Keat will contact Danny. Raj took the risk and gave Danny's number. When the stranger left, Raj phoned Danny immediately.

"Danny, Hey! Someone will contact you about Ah Keat" said Raj.

"Really? When?"

"I was asking around for you, then just a few minutes ago, someone I don't know wanted to know why I needed to get in touch with Ah Keat. So I explained to him and then he wanted your mobile number to get Keat to call you."

"OK, thanks." replied Danny. Danny was wondering if it was a good idea for Raj to give his mobile number to the stranger.

It was exactly three days later when Danny got a call from Ah Keat.

"Danny, what is it? This is Keat."

"Oh, Ah Keat! I need to tell you that one police detective came to me asking me questions about you."

"When?"

"Sometime about last week," replied Danny. "So I said I don't know the person in the photo. It was your photo!"

"OK. You said the right thing, old friend!"

"You better not be around in Penang. Things will get hotter."

"I know. And thanks for the news."

"Is this the number where I can get you if I have any further news?" asked Danny.

'No, I am calling from a phone booth. You can leave a message with Yu Toh of Kheng Hoe Bar. I gotta go now."

Danny was relieved that he had conveyed his encounter with Hassan to Ah Keat. He was surprised that Ah Keat also knew he had been to Kheng Hoe Bar recently. This man has a lot of tentacles spreading all over, thought Danny.

Although Hassan was busy with the murder case, at the moment he is waiting for some evidence to turn up from the Forensics Team. Meanwhile he had better use the time to pursue the gold robbers, he thought. Word got back that some of the loot from the goldsmith shop had been disposed of in a pawnshop in Air Itam road, very close to Shell petrol station.

A visit to the pawnshop yielded some very useful information indeed. Part of the loot to be found in the pawnshop was positively identified and the shop owner was brought in for questioning. He produced the photostat copy of the identity card of the person pawning the items. Although it was a stolen ID card, the owner managed to identify the photo of Ah Keat when he was showed by Hassan. Now the effort put into the search for Ah Keat is doubled.

Ah Keat is now in hiding in Bukit Mertajam on the mainland and a hotbed for illegal activities. His network of friends is extensive in that town and he felt safe. However he made an error. He could not wait for his friends to melt the gold jewellery later to be got rid of. He collected some of his share and went to pawn it to get some urgent cash. He hoped by using a stolen ID card, the police will not be able to connect the loot to him. Although the photo in the stolen ID card has no resemblance to Keat, he was able to get the transaction done because the owner of the pawnshop was well known in the underworld for doing all sorts of business. When questioned by the Police about this, the owner said it must be the work of one of his workers although he had reminded them countless times to check for such a trick. In normal circumstances, the owner of the pawn shop will have his licence revoked and he will be charged with buying stolen goods, but this time he was released. It seemed that almost everything can be settled with a bribe. Besides, the Police got a very good lead and co-operation from the owner to call them if Ah Keat comes in again.

Hassan then organized a search team for the elusive Ah Keat and if he is caught, the police may be able to round up the rest of the gang members whose identities are still a mystery. Hassan decided to put a watching team on Danny Ong to follow his every move. This team will be composed of of Mustafa and Sobri mainly, with others moving in if they need help.

This is not a difficult job to Mustafa or Sobri as they are very experienced in this type of covert work. It was just routine work for the two of them. However Danny is no easy target. He was already very careful and suspected that Hassan or some other detective might follow him. He was thus very observant of his surroundings wherever he went. When Danny drives, he will be looking at the rear view mirror every few seconds to see if anyone was tailing him. However, due to their experience, the two seasoned detectives knew at once that their target is no easy meat so they had to be extra careful on this case. It was a real cat and mouse game.

However it didn't take long for Danny to confirm that he was being followed because Sobri made a small error one day by following too close behind Danny when Danny was walking along Burma Road. Actually with any other suspect, Sobri did not make a mistake, it is only because Danny is too observant and on high alert. Since Danny now knows that they are really tailing him, from now onwards he will have to be smarter and more careful. As for now his strategy is to pretend he is unaware of their stalking him and never to do anything to link himself with Ah Keat. But he needed to tell Yu Toh of Kheng Hoe Bar to get the message to Keat that he is being closely monitored, so that Keat himself will be careful.

Late one night, Danny had a phone call from an unknown number.

"Hi Danny, it is me Keat. Be careful, you are being followed by two detectives. Good night, old friend." Before Danny could speak, the line went dead – Keat hung up the public phone. It is unbelievable because he didn't notice that both he and the two cops were being followed by Keat's man. Now that man is a real expert, to remain unseen both by Danny and his two sleuths.

The Forensics Team had meanwhile made important discoveries at the crime scene of the murder and Hassan was being briefed. They had lifted some good fingerprints and these were being checked at the national database. Moreover the murder weapon, a small knife, was recovered in a drain not far from the crime scene. The Police are confident they will wrap up this case quite early.

CHAPTER 7

It was quite late in the night and Ah Keat was sitting alone in his rented room thinking. This can't go on, he thought. He is now quite short of cash again. He needs to do some serious thinking. He lit another contraband cigarette. The duty on a pack of cigarettes is so high now that it is really unaffordable to smoke. That is why many smokers resort to buying these contraband smuggled foreign cigarettes as they are much cheaper.

He had a small stall selling mobile phones and accessories in Kompleks Bukit Jambul, Bayan Baru, but it soon became a non-viable business. Rentals kept going up and customers were getting fewer from severe competition. He knew of the folly of resorting to loan sharks to keep his business going and thus he had to close down his stall.

He tried looking for suitable jobs such as being a helper in the local coffee shop, but it could not even pay for his monthly expenses so he had to give up the job. Besides it was very hard work and long hours- being up by 5am and work done only by 11 p.m.. Sometimes it would be even later.

Then his whole life changed when he met an old friend, Ah Seng, with a missing front tooth and who works as an air-conditioning serviceman. Although he was paid little, Ah Seng always had cash to splash around. Keat had to ask his friend how he managed to be so loose with his money and Ah Seng said point blank that it was from ill-gotten gains. It was not long before Ah Seng roped his old friend into his small band of burglars. Being an air-conditioner repair- and service man, Ah Seng had access to many houses and he took mental notes of how rich the owners were and would break into those houses and apartments very much later to loot their valuables.

When their appetites grew for more money, they graduated to be robbers. Keat proved to be an asset to the gang and he quickly became Ah Seng's right hand man. He needed to meet Ah Seng to make a proposal for he had forged a plan in his mind. He found Ah Seng at the usual place, a small coffee shop at the edge of town, drinking beers. He was in shorts and white T- shirt and of average height but rather slim and sinewy, his muscles could be seen under his tanned skin.

"Hey, old friend! Come join me," exclaimed Seng when he saw Keat coming. With folks like Seng and Keat, they always sit facing the crowd and with easy and quick access to the exits. The China Doll waitress who was accompanying Seng left to bring more beers.

"Can't sleep tonight?" asked Seng.

"Yes, also because I have an important suggestion for us." replied Keat.

When the waitress came back with the beers, Seng asked her to leave them alone. She did not protest. Seng turned serious, no longer was there the smiling face with a missing tooth showing that he had a few minutes earlier.

"Well?' asked Seng.

"I think we should do another job and I have a place in mind." said Keat softly. There were very few customers at this time and thus it was rather quiet. Keat knows that sound can travel clearly and he was being careful. Seng was even more attentive and curious, since he was the one that had done all the planning in the previous heist at the goldsmith's as it involved a lot of planning since there were CCTVs and security guards that were heavily armed.

"Don't worry, this is a far simpler job and far safer as it will be on the mainland!" said Keat proudly.

They all knew how dangerous it would be if a robbery were done on the island as their getaway would depend only on the bridge to the mainland as the ferry service is too slow. Once a Police roadblock on the bridge is set up, they would be virtually done for.

"So what is your bright idea?" asked Seng.

"We hit a petrol station in Sungai Petani, nearest to the Highway. It is all in cash, no goods to dispose of." said Keat proudly. There was a moment of silence.

"Have you any station in mind?' asked Seng after some quick thinking as to the feasibility.

"No, but once you OK the idea, we will have to make detailed planning and some groundwork."

"I like the idea!" hissed Seng.

A broad smile flashed on both their faces and they continued to drink. This is indeed their 'Happy Hour". They agreed to fix a date to do the groundwork.

Although the forensic team had lifted several fingerprints at the crime scene of the murder of the old lady, no matches were found in the database. It was frustrating. This could mean they were criminals with no police records or they were foreigners, which means a very slim chance their prints could be found in the Immigration database so this request was sent to the Immigration Department. However, if the killers had come into the country as illegal immigrants, then it is back to square one. And to everyone's disappointment, there were no matches. The lead has gone cold. Now two high profile cases are at a dead end and this makes Hassan very uptight for you see his chances of a much needed promotion is greater if these two cases are solved.

For Muljadi and Hartono, it was their day off and they were enjoying themselves roaming around KOMTAR, a favourite place in George Town for foreign workers to meet and socialize especially at weekends. This building is situated along the famous Penang Road. One can see Filipinos, Burmese, Thai, Vietnamese, Bangladeshi and Indonesian workers hanging around the place. Sometimes it is rather intimidating for the locals who could easily be outnumbered. Clashes among the foreign workers are also rather common and could be among their own kind or against another nationality, in which case, they are more serious ones.

Muljadi had separated from Hartono to be with his own friends who were construction workers while Hartono went to chat up some Indonesian girls who worked in the factories of Bayan Lepas. They would be going back separately as usual.

It was while mingling with the construction workers that Muljadi heard the talk about the murdered old lady of Lorong Selamat. One of them whom he hardly knew was boasting of how he managed to 'get hold of' some valuables from an old lady. He said he thought the house was empty as the area was under one foot of water and many owners had been evacuated to safer places but apparently the old lady was still in the house and she started to shout and he reacted swiftly and managed to silence her.

Muljadi had heard about the robbery and murder from his boss Danny as it was the talk of the town. He edged closer to hear more and tried to have a good look at the man. He asked a friend who this chap was and was told it was Ambon of East Java. Ambon was very talkative that day because he had some alcoholic drinks.

Muljadi could not stand it any longer hearing the evil Ambon boasting and so he decided to leave quietly so that no one would notice. He slipped out and went to look for his friend Hartono but Hartono could not be found. He decided to enjoy a movie before going back to their rented apartment in Farlim.

It was a difficult night for Muljadi. What is he supposed to do now? He had stumbled upon the man who is responsible for a most heinous crime. Should he tell the police or just let the police find the man themselves. He decided not to be a busybody and so he told no one about it, not even his close friend Hartono.

For the next few days Muljadi tried to keep the murderer's face out of his mind but he could not. Danny noticed that Muljadi was quieter and kept more to himself, not even talking to Hartono, who is only thinking about girls. Something is not right with Muljadi and Danny decided to ask.

"Muljadi, I noticed you are very quiet these days. Is there anything?"

"Uh, nothing Boss."

"You can't hide, Muljadi. I know you. Something big must be troubling you." replied Danny.

There was silence from Muljadi, he was thinking deeply.

"If you don't want to talk now, we can talk later, OK?" suggested Danny. Muljadi just nodded his head. The very next day, Muljadi signalled to Danny that he wanted to tell him something when Hartono was out on an errand to buy some items that Danny needed.

"Boss, I need to tell you something important!"

"Yes, Muljadi. I am listening."

"I know who killed the old lady."

"What old lady? What are you talking about?" said Danny in a surprised tone

Muljadi then gave the whole story of how he came to know who was responsible for the crime. Danny listened without interrupting at all. He was trying to understand Muljadi who was speaking in a half whisper while looking right and left. When he finished, Danny was shocked. Both men were quiet. The case had hit newspaper headlines because of the brutality of the senseless murder.

"What to do now Boss?" asked Muljadi. "Please don't let anyone know and get me in big trouble!" pleaded Muljadi.

"We need to let the police know, but the question is how. I mean, you need to be protected." They both thought for a while and then "Let me think of something first," said Danny.

Back in the Police HQ in Dato Kramat Road, Hassan was looking at the case files, flipping over the pages. In the murder case, investigations had stalled while in the robbery case he felt he might get something out of Danny. It is time to pay Danny a visit again.

Hassan arrived at Danny's place in Gurney Plaza and that jolted both Danny and Muljadi, who thought Danny had informed the police for he knew Hassan was a detective. The look on Muljadi's face didn't go unnoticed by Hassan who instantly knew that something is going on, perhaps Danny knew about the robbers more than Danny would admit. Danny himself was very nervous, thinking now what?

"Hello, Danny" greeted Hassan.

"Oh, What can I do for you today?" Again there were no customers and Danny really wished there were some so that he can pretend to be busy with the customers instead of talking to Hassan. Muljadi was getting really nervous.

"About the robbery case, I am sure you knew one of them, Danny" said Hassan right to the point, without wasting time.

"I told you before, I don't know anyone of them. You are wasting your time here. You can get the culprits faster if you interview others in your list."

"Danny, come on, I know you knew something about the suspect, you were old friends, right?" said Hassan. This really got Danny off balance. But as quickly as he was off balance, Danny suddenly turned it around by saying "OK detective, I do have something to tell you, if you are interested." Danny took Hassan to a more secluded spot and they sat down.

"Actually I don't know how to start but I have some information about something else.."

"Stop it Danny! I am not here to play games with you…."

"OK, if you want information about the robbery, then I have nothing to say but if you want to know about the murder, then I have!"

"What? Murder? What are you talking about?"

"Yes, the murder of the old lady of Lorong Selamat."

"Are you sure? Or are you diverting me from the purpose of this visit?"

"I am serious, *Enche* Hassan!" replied Danny.

"OK, how do you know I am also investigating this murder?" asked Hassan, who was curious to know everything now.

"Oh? This I didn't know for sure about you being in the investigations but I would think you are police and surely you want to know," replied Danny, who is equally surprised. "Anyway I heard it from my Indonesian worker, but please don't get him into trouble. He is very scared."

"Go on." said Hassan impatiently.

"He was with some friends on his day off......" went on Danny and explained the whole story. The detective listened closely, taking some notes from his worn-out notebook, a small pocket sized diary-cum-notebook. Hassan wanted to interview Muljadi and Danny called him over. Muljadi's knees went weak but he was assured by Danny not to worry. He repeated exactly what Danny had told Hassan earlier.

'I will need you both to meet me at the Station to make some formal statements today and I promise that both of you will remain anonymous to protect your identity." Danny and Muljadi exchanged looks. With that Hassan walked off, now even with a slight spring in his step.

CHAPTER 8

The discussion Albert had with Dr Looi had kindled his interest in Extraterrestrials and he couldn't wait for their next meeting. However Albert remembered that they had not agreed on any particular day when he left the doctor's house. He decided to call Dr. Looi and see when can they meet up.

"Hi, Doc. It's me Albert," said Albert when Dr Looi answered his house phone.

"Yes, Albert. How are you?" said the doctor, always interested in the health of his friends.

"I'm fine, Doc. Say, how about more discussions on ETs, UFOs and life on other planets?" Albert asked, going straight to the point.

"Ha, ha! I see that you are now an ET addict!"

"In a way, yes Doc. You've got me thinking you know. Will tomorrow night be fine?" asked Albert.

"Seems OK with me. I'll be available anytime from 10.30 p.m. onwards."

"OK, be seeing you, Doc."

Albert had actually tried to do some research on the internet about UFOs and ETs but the amount of time he spent and the tons of irrelevant information made him give up. It is better to let the doctor speak. He could learn a lot in a very short time.

Albert arrived just before 11 p.m. and soon they both settled down. It was a cool and breezy evening. "So what you want to know about, Albert?" asked Doc.

"Why don't you tell me more about the Arcturians?" replied Albert, sipping his cup of coffee.

"Oh, they come from one of the most advanced civilizations in the entire galaxy, from the brightest planet in the Constellation of Bootes. It is about 36 light-years away from us. They are from the Fifth Dimension, a place where you can have contact with your soul. They do not have negativity, fear or guilt and they have been protecting Earth from hostile alien species for thousands of years.

They are short, about three feet tall and are green coloured, with only three fingers and are telepathic. They travel in starships that are the most advanced in the universe, powered by 5D crystals and can travel through dimensions."

"Ah, little Green Men," retorted Albert.

"Actually they can take any form. They who are from the Fifth Dimension and above exist with no form, just a body of light. They are truly multidimensional Beings. In fact we, too, are Multidimensional Beings but we seemed to have forgotten this." The Doc explained further.

"After the destruction of Avalon, the Lyrans set out to find a new planet to inhabit and escape from the savage Reptilians and Greys. The imbalance of Forces caused by the Reptilians and Greys stirred the Arcturians, with the permission of The Brotherhood of All, to counterattack the evil forces released. Thus it was the Lyrans who first witnessed the great battleship of the Arcturians called Athena as it appeared for them to see and announced that the Arcturians will from now seek to ensure order in the Galaxy ravaged by the greedy Reptilians and Greys."

"The Greys are also known as Zeta Reticuli, right?" interjected Albert.

"Yes, Albert and they developed without the heart chakra and emotional body, unlike us. With no heart chakra, there is no Divine spark, and you can't go into the Fifth Dimension without heart energy. So they had gone to Earth to intervene directly by trying genetic manipulation to incorporate the heart chakra into their forms but this is a very severe karmic mistake and they have thus been unsuccessful."

"What do you mean by genetic manipulation? And karma?" asked a puzzled Albert.

"Genetic manipulation means the Greys had tried to mate with human females they had abducted and yes, Karmic Law is a universal law, it is independent whether you believe it or not. Karma is a natural law of balance. Your actions determine the type of karma you create. Karma has three phases. The seed phase is sanchita karma, and the day-to-day karma that we create is kriyamana karma. Prarabdha karma is the karma that is now active in daily life and will run its course.

Karma is the seed we plant that sooner or later will sprout at some point in our life, whether in this life or the next. Our world is a world of Free Will and that is why the Arcturians or Pleidians will not interfere unless they are called, and thus permission given."

"You mentioned about us humans being multidimensional, how come and what really does it mean?" enquired Albert, now getting more interested.

"Now this gets a bit complicated but let me explain as best as I can." said Doc slowly and settling down with another soya milk drink, his other favourite drink apart from coffee.

"Many souls from Arcturus, Pleides and Sirius have volunteered to incarnate here on Earth to help in its evolution, especially so during this time of Ascension. Humans were never descended from the apes, even the Native Americans will tell you that. It is only our learned scientists that tell us so! Humans really began in Vega, 25 light years away, in the Lyra Constellation. These humans then migrated to Sirius, 8.6 light years away and finally to Earth. This is one version. Another version is the more famous Annunaki connection. Humans were genetically bred from a race of early humanoids by the Annunaki who had colonised Earth to get gold and other minerals for their own use. The geneticists of the Annunaki had created humans for the sole purpose of working in the mines for them.

Whatever the origins of humans, it is clear that we had several types of DNA incorporated into our genomes to help develop us and differentiate us from apes. I tell you, it is stated that we have almost all of the types of alien DNA that the Universe can provide and thus make us so unique. Our True Self really is Immortal. There is in fact no such thing as death, which is one of the Illusions. We are now in Third Dimension Earth which is very dense and of a lower frequency energy. Here almost everything is of dual nature like good/bad, hot/cold, male/female and so on. In the Fourth Dimension and especially in the Fifth Dimension, the vibration is of a higher frequency and duality ceases to exist as one goes into higher Dimensions. Beings have no form and their thoughts are manifest almost instantaneously. All they need is to think about something, and it happens. Responsibilities are thus greater. There is also no Time or Space/Distance in such higher realms."

Albert is fascinated and looked a bit confused.

"Higher Dimensional Beings feel very uncomfortable in our Third Dimensional world and this is why Extraterrestrials seldom manifest here. What we see as ETs are sometimes their projected forms, or sometimes we had shifted our consciousness to a higher dimension without our knowing it and are therefore able to see them. UFOs are sighted at times and these really appeared in our world but then they seem to disappear. This is because they accelerated back to their own Dimension through some wormholes in space."

"You still did not explain about us being Multidimensional, Doc," reminded Albert.

"I'm coming to that. Now be ready for some mind blowing facts. In reality, we are existing simultaneously in several Dimensions but are only aware of our Third dimension."

"What?" Now Albert is all attention.

"When we dream, many times we forget our dreams and this is because we had entered into the higher dimensions but because of the difference in frequency, we are unable to retain the impressions in our 3D brain. This is one example of living simultaneously in different dimensions. But actually even in our waking hours, our real Self resides in the higher dimensions. Ascended Masters are aware of such realities and that is why we say they are in a world of their own. They seem to be in a meditative state in most of their waking hours. In reality their consciousness is in the higher planes."

"Doc, tell me more about the Dimensions," asked Albert.

"Actually the number of Dimensions is infinite, not only the 12 Dimensions as we know them and as Quantum Physics predicts. Right now we are only interested up to the Ninth Dimension. This is because for the first time in the History of the Universe, we can Ascend along with the Planet Earth to the Fifth dimension at least within a number of years. This is our potential but in my opinion, few can achieve this."

"What will happen to the rest, then?" asked Albert.

"I suppose many will still want to be in the Third Dimension while the rest will move on to the Fourth or Fifth Dimension. Here the complexity increases because as I know, Earth will move on to the Fifth Dimension. I suppose a sort of parallel Earth will remain in 3D for those who choose to remain in 3D. Yes I admit, it gets very complicated and I don't think anyone really knows the answer. I don't."

"Why is it that Earth will cross to the Fifth Dimension?"

"This has to do with the Cycles and you must also know that Earth has a Spirit. Everything has a spirit, according to Taoist and metaphysical views. The stone, the chair that you sit on, all have a spirit. And all spirit must evolve to higher planes of consciousness. Thus Mother Earth is no exception. And she can't wait for all humanity to cross over. Several Masters had been sent to help mankind to elevate themselves to a higher vibration but as you know, basically we are no better."

"Please elaborate" asked Albert.

"Well, you asked for it! It goes very far back in time. The Atlanteans, Egyptians and a group from South America had special knowledge given by higher Dimension Beings but each time, the humans made use of the teachings and technologies for self-glorification to benefit only the few instead of the entire population. For the South American group, instead of healing, human sacrifices were propagated."

"Who were the higher Dimension Beings?" queried Albert.

"They belong to the Group called Ra, with permission from the Council. This Council oversees the running of our Galaxy and they comprise of representatives from 53 civilizations from about 500 planets and are of the Eighth Dimension."

"Arcturians, Annunaki, Ra, Council, this is getting too much, Doc."

"Want to know more? I have more to add you know. Are you in a hurry to go?"

"Not in a hurry to go anywhere! Just that I don't know what questions to ask now."

"Here, have some more coffee and I shall continue." Dr Looi poured more coffee from the pot into Albert's cup.

"I discovered that UFOs had visited Earth 18,000 years ago but there was no landing. It was just a survey. This was by the group called Ra. Later another group from Orion made several appearances in our skies and this group had no benevolent intentions, and doesn't even now. In fact I believe that most UFO sightings are crafts from Orion, which are usually cigar- shaped."

"Many of them have to travel light years in distances, do you have any idea how they are able to do it?" asked Albert.

"Well, they use mainly one of these methods depending on their level of technology. Those who are like us in the Third Dimension, use techniques of cryobiology to travel for long periods of time. Those from the Orion group usually use the light wave to be slung into our world, like a sling shot. The ones from Fifth Dimension uses thought to arrive at our skies, thus taking no time at all. They just materialize wherever they want to be."

"OK, so ETs have visited us throughout history. My question is why no confirmation from any governments yet?" interjected Albert.

"Many reasons, my friend. Basically no government wants to look like a fool in making such statements. Also people, the masses, might panic and total chaos may ensue. But things will change now." replied Dr Looi.

"Like what?"

"Like there will be mass sightings all over the world. In this way governments will have their hands so full, they are not able to cover up. I think this is the best manner the ETs will adopt. As the Americans will say, "It's shock and awe.""

"You mean to say that these ETs aim is then to colonise us? We won't stand a chance!"

"I don't think so."

'What makes you say that?"

"I admit that there are those ETs that have bad intentions but these groups of Reptilians, Greys and Orions had many of their secret undersea and underground bases captured and destroyed recently. Of course many do not know of what has been going on – the battle of Good versus Evil ETs. These battles were fought silently, without any nations knowing it."

"And can you please tell me how you came to know this?" asked Albert sarcastically.

"I told you I have several sources and means like in my meditations and channelings by gifted psychics, many of whom are in contact with me. I have even received news about a heroic deed by a Tibetan Buddhist monk who led 200 other warrior monks to do battle with a Cabal Base that had a powerful force field of several metres thickness which the monks managed to breach with their superior meditative power. There are some of the unsung heroes of humanity." They were both silent for a few minutes, reflecting on what had been discussed.

"You mentioned Earth changing Dimensions. I need you to explain a bit more Doc." Albert broke the silence.

"This Shift is what I am still researching but what I know is that we need to increase our vibration to a higher level by meditation, expressing more Love and service to others. Even our DNA has to change and start expressing more of itself, since at present we only use about 3% of our full DNA potential. Many who are sensitive will feel fatigued, have insomnia, headaches, dizziness, irregular heartbeats, hypertension or some other physical symptoms."

"How can our DNA change?" Albert looked bewildered.

"The Solar Flares that had occurred and more that will be occurring are the triggers that will signal a change in our DNAs. They send secret codes with the flares to effect the changes."

"How do we cope with such physical changes, Doc?"

"The best thing to do is not to resist them, have more rest and drink plenty of water. One will naturally find that a vegetarian diet will be most comfortable as heavy meat intake will bog down their body. Actually there are at least about 30 people in the world now that take no food at all, as they have changed into Light Bodies. They only need sunlight to survive."

"What will happen to those who don't change?" asked Albert with a worried look.

"This is a very difficult question to answer, Albert my friend. Actually I don't know the answer. But it seems to me that they have to be left behind in 3D earth though actually 3D earth may not exist anymore and so where will they be? Or they will have to disappear from 5D earth since the 2 dimensions do not mix. The other possibility is that Heaven is kind enough to allow these 2 Dimensions to exist in parallel. Those that changed their vibration to 5D will be able to shift between Dimensions but those who still have karma to work out will remain in 3D earth with the duality still in existence and see the disappearance and appearance of their 5D friends or family members when they shift dimensions."

There was a worried look on Albert's face.

"I think we should not worry too much because many of us have chosen to incarnate at this time for a purpose. Those of us who are Star seeds will remember what to do exactly when such times arrive," assured Dr Looi.

"Are you sure?" asked a worried looking Albert.

"Quite sure. And I wish to add that we are also due to meet up with our other cousins – dwellers of Inner Earth called Agarthans."

'What? As if meeting with ETs are not enough, now this? Are you serious Doc?"

"Well, since we are on this topic, I better let you know as much as I do up to now."

"Then tell me about these Agarthans!"

"It all began before the destruction of Lemuria and Atlantis. A small band of these people who are spiritual, knew about the coming destruction so they left their lands. Some went to what is known now as Egypt, others went to Tibet and China. Another group went to South America. These people started a new life and civilization in these places. Another band went underground to escape the nuclear warfare that destroyed Atlantis and Lemuria.

Thus this group are known as Agarthans and they developed an elaborate underground system of caves, tunnels and cities underground. They brought along their advanced technology and survival underground was made possible and they need not venture above ground at all."

"Not even for food?" asked a surprised Albert.

"They are pure vegetarians and they grow their fruits, nuts and vegetables with artificial light and controlled atmosphere. So everything that they need is all available in their underground cities"

"This is unbelievable!!" exclaimed Albert. Dr Looi just gave a smile and asked, "Any questions?"

"Yes, in fact I want to know how is life in 5D Earth gonna be like?"

"Oh? You don't have anything to ask about the Agarthans?"

"That at the moment is too hard for me to stomach, so I may ask later!"

"I see. Well, by then our bodies would have changed and be absorbing more Light and once fully in Fifth Dimension, we can expect perfect health with no diseases, we will not grow old for the aging process slows down and is finally stopped. In fact, we can project a more youthful appearance if we like. Then those with amputated limbs can use their power of thought to grow back those missing arms and legs or fingers. There is also no death. In fact, for the first time in the history of the entire Universe, as it has never happened before, the inhabitants of a planet will have ascended to a higher dimension without undergoing the death process. Then there is no hunger, thirst or feeling fatigued. There are no mood changes, one is constantly happy, fulfilled and in peace."

Dr Looi noticed that Albert was rather sleepy and so decided to call it a night and their chat ended. Albert left for his place, his mind thinking of the conversation they had. He was always amazed at the doctor's knowledge of things outside his own speciality of medicine.

CHAPTER 9

The investigation into the goldsmith robbery had to take a back seat as Hassan planned a dawn raid on the *kongsi* to arrest the murderer of the old lady of Lorong Selamat. He had all the facts from Muljadi when the latter went with his boss, Danny to the Police HQ to make the report and to be further questioned by Hassan who now has all the details about Ambon, the alleged murderer.

The Police had their team ready for a raid on the *kongsi*, a sort of long house style accommodation for the foreign workers employed by the construction company. The raid will take place at 5a.m. the very next morning after the interview with Muljadi so as to minimise the information of the raid leaking to the *kongsi* inhabitants.

This *kongsi* was situated not far from the ongoing construction of the high end bungalows along Batu Ferringhi's hilly terrain nearby Moonlight Bay. There is only one way in and one way out because surrounding the wooden long house is thick jungle that covers the hilly part of the island. Along with the Police, Hassan contacted the Immigration Department as they are needed to check on the work permits of these labourers as some may be illegal immigrants.

The raiding team were dispatched to the site at 4a.m. and they conducted the raid in a well planned way. The exit/entrance was blocked by two police cars and another two vans from the Immigration. Some of the police surrounded the *kongsi* while others rushed in after forcing the doors opened. The migrant workers were taken by surprise.

It was complete mayhem, chaos and confusion. The colony of workers were running everywhere helter skelter. The Police and Immigration personnel were trying to bring some order, using their loudhailers but that added to the confusion. There were also women and children and these were rounded up easily. The men were running towards the jungle when they saw their escape route blocked and quite a few managed to escape into the darkness.

After about twenty minutes of utter confusion, the situation was brought under control and the workers were contained and their documents were being checked by the authorities. This raid had caught twelve illegal workers but the wanted man, Ambon, was missing.

Inspector Hassan was furious! How could Ambon have gotten away or was he informed prior to the raid? The Operation was kept top secret!

The Police started to question the workers about their friends who slipped away and it was confirmed that six managed to run into the thick jungle. Immediately some Police and Immigration officers fanned out and went into the jungle

Dawn had broken and it made the search easier but the thick undergrowth was another matter. Hassan had also called for help from the Rangers, a company of well trained soldiers from Sarawak that was famous for their jungle survival and tracking abilities. Their Base Camp was also in nearby Batu Ferringhi, not far from the Rasa Sayang Hotel. Once the Rangers arrived, the Police and Immigration Officers were recalled, rightly so because they had not caught any of the illegals yet. Within three hours of action, the Rangers had rounded up all but one of the illegals because he was found dead at the bottom of a deep ravine. The body was not recovered yet as it was almost impossible to climb down the steep ravine walls and special equipment was needed.

It took another four hours before the body was recovered and sent to the Penang General Hospital for an autopsy and identification.

Finally it was confirmed that the dead man was the wanted man, Ambon. Now all the pieces of evidence were in place and it proved that Ambon was the one who murdered the old woman. This case was thus considered solved and Hassan can refocus on the solving of the robbery of the jeweller's shop.

Unfortunately although the murder case was considered solved with Ambon's death, more trouble brewed up and this time it was international relations between Malaysia and Indonesia. The Indonesians accused the Malaysian authorities of killing Ambon during their interrogation of the latter and did not believe what the Malaysian authorities said about finding him dead at the bottom of a ravine. Somehow the facts got twisted and now there were huge crowds of demonstrators in front of the Malaysian embassy in Jakarta almost daily. Back in Kuala Lumpur, Malaysians likewise demonstrated in front of the Indonesian Consulate and things seem to be getting worse until the governments concerned stepped in to defuse the volatile situation. In fact Malaysian students studying in Indonesia were already beginning to feel very unsafe.

The incident affected Hassan and all those involved a lot to the extent they were not able to concentrate on their daily tasks as they had to write reports after reports after being questioned by their superiors. It is now left to the politicians to mend the broken ties. In fact there had been many previous minor hiccups in bilateral relations between these two Muslim countries but in no time at all, everything was forgotten.

Ah Keat had made detailed observations of some targeted petrol stations on the Mainland and he had narrowed them down to one on the outskirts of Butterworth town. By now he knew their daily routines like the shifts of the workers, where the CCTVs were placed and their range of coverage, when the collections were banked in and how busy it was. What he thought so attractive, apart from the good business this petrol station seemed to have, were the escape routes options available and the fact that this station was especially popular with motorcyclists who pay by cash rather than by credit cards. The only thing left was to inform all the details to Ah Seng and choose the likely date for the robbery.

When Ah Keat gave the details of his observation to Ah Seng, the latter thought for a while and said that he would need to do some surveillance himself first before agreeing to his suggestion. And after two weeks of surveillance, Ah Seng agreed with his friend's observations and a date was set for the real thing. It would be on a Sunday evening as the management usually will only deposit the earnings of two days on a Monday when the bank is open.

It was at around 11 p.m. on a chosen Sunday that they struck the Shell Petrol Station swiftly when there were no customers filling up with petrol. The foreign worker at the counter was completely taken by surprise and complied with every instruction barked out by Ah Seng. It was all over in less than three minutes. The weekend collection by the petrol station is now theirs. They sped away on their stolen bikes for their freedom.

Their loot was about RM9,500 and once they divided it equally, they each went their separate ways to hide and lie low. This was far easier than the heist at the goldsmith's because they had to handle an armed guard and the loot was in kind rather than cash. Although they each went their own way, they kept in touch via their mobile phones. In this way they got closer than ever before, forming an inseparable bond.

Soon they got the itch to rob again, fuelled by the easy target of a petrol station. This time they were even bolder as they planned to hit two such petrol stations one after another in quick succession. Again, it was a breeze and the two petrol stations really did not know what hit them.

This most recent robbery had created a fear among petrol station owners and workers alike. Some had resorted to put in more CCTVs while others had employed security guards. The smaller petrol stations felt very insecure as they were not able to absorb the extra expenditures.

So far the Police had no leads or clues and the pressure was mounting on them to stop the serial Petrol Station Robbers, as the Press had labelled them.

As Ah Keat had gone into hiding, Danny had no contact with him at all for a long time and thus Hassan took Mustafa and Sobri off Danny's back, as trailing Danny did not bring in any worthwhile information and was a waste of time and resources. Both Mustafa and Sobri were relieved as the job was becoming boring and they were glad to be assigned to help in the Petrol Station robbery case where they hope to be in the thick of the investigation team. Ah Keat still had quite a sum of money from their last job but he was surveying area after area for a possible next target. Now it was more of an addiction to the "high" he gets while robbing rather than a need for money. He noticed that many petrol stations had taken great measures to deter them.

It thus became too dangerous for a strike at any petrol station around the Butterworth or Prai areas. He decided to look further and went to the thriving town of Sungai Petani in the northern state of Kedah. In the 1970s, Sungai Petani was a small town with very few supermarkets or entertainment spots but today it has grown to be the fastest developing town in the country. Traffic jams are the norm these days as opposed to the slow and laid back lifestyle of more than thirty years ago.

Ah Keat noted a petrol station nearest the exit to the North-South Plus Highway that would lead him to freedom and studied the station more in detail. He made several trips at different times of the day to observe. His partner knew of this surveillance as they had kept in contact and he agreed to the idea. Very much later he joined Ah Keat in the surveillance work and towards the end, he was alone observing the petrol station, so as not to arouse suspicions of the workers or public there.

One Wednesday evening, they both met at their usual *kopitiam,* a Chinese style coffee shop, in Bukit Mertajam for thick local coffee and some Tiger beers to go along. The waiter there knew them so well that it was not necessary for them to order their coffee or beers, the waiter knew their exact taste. Ah Keat drinks black coffee with no sugar while Ah Seng takes *teh-o* with ice.

"So what have you decided?" Ah Keat asked.

"Looks like all our demands are met," was Ah Seng's curt reply.

"Then will we strike next week?"

"If we can get a better bike, Keat. This last one, I don't like it because it is giving trouble in starting."

'This means we better start looking for another one soon' said Ah Keat. They will need to steal a better bike as they have quite a distance to travel for this job in Sungai Petani. Since the town is in Kedah State, they will need a bike with a Kedah State plate number so as not to be so prominent when they speed off from the crime scene. Stealing bikes had always been the speciality of Ah Seng, who had been doing so since he was 16 years old. It started as a prank he played on his friend but he realised how easily it can be done, he went on to steal many more. Having discussed the main issues they now enjoyed their drinks and the beer flowed continuously while smoking their contraband cigarettes. These men knew how to enjoy themselves.

CHAPTER 10

It was quite cold in the jungle at night and early morning but Jatek woke up in a sweat and breathing heavily. It was the worst nightmare he had ever had for a long time. He looked around his small hut and saw his family all sleeping soundly: his wife and the two small boys, aged 9 and 5 years old. The bright moon outside shone into the hut and it was enough for him to see that his family is safe.

He tried to go back to sleep but he could not. His mind was thinking of the nightmare again and again. In the dream, Jatek was in the town selling some honey and jungle roots he had gathered so as to buy some much needed sugar, salt, flour and rice for his small band of fellow Orang Asli. Then there was a severe flash flood occurring in the town without any warning. He was caught in the floods, all his money and goods were washed away. Many people in the town drowned. He managed to make his way back to the jungle but was taken aback by what he saw. The hills had collapsed in a landslide which was blocking his way to his people. He tried very hard to get past the landslide but it was impossible, he was very worried for his family. Then he saw several old men from his Tribe, none of whom he recognized. That was his nightmare, and he woke up from it abruptly.

Jatek was very quiet in the morning. He sat by the small river nearby his settlement and smoked his jungle stick, which is like a cigarette. He was in deep thought. He was the village chief as well as their medicine man and was responsible for their good health and safety. But now he was troubled by his dream. What truth does it hold?

He had chosen this spot in the jungle well, as it has a small river to provide fresh, clean water for their needs. If he wanted to catch fish, all he needed to do was to trek 1 km further south to a lake to fish. The small plot of fertile land also supported their daily need of vegetables and tapioca. This place had never suffered from any floods.

His wife, Som, noticed how quiet and worried Jatek was but she just carried on with her daily tasks, only glancing at her husband once in a while. She knew better than to ask Jatek at this moment. She will wait till night falls and when he is in a better mood, she will ask him.

Jatek went back to his hut and took his praying paraphernalia which consisted of a feathered cap, an earthen pot to burn some incense and a ceremonial dress made of several jungle leaves of various species but all with supposedly spiritual power. When Som saw what he was to do, she left the hut and closed its door and sat outside, making sure no one would enter until her husband had finished the meditation and prayers. No one else in the settlement noticed Jatek but they saw Som outside the hut signalling them not to disturb or make too much noise and they knew that their chief was consulting the Ancestors about something.

Jatek wore the dress of sacred leaves and feathered cap and burned some of the incense and started to meditate and within a few minutes he was in deep meditation. He was now in the world of his Ancestors in the Astral Plane. First he had to chase the pesky Elementals that tried to distract him or scare him. Some of these Elementals appeared as fierce monsters but they didn't scare Jatek one bit. All he had to do was to gather his aura into a sharp point and projected it at the Elementals, which will just run away and disappear into the vast Astral Plane.

Finally no more of the irritating Elementals were brave enough
to distract him. There was complete silence and just the darkness
of Space. It was just blackness, then slowly the stars came into his
mind's eye, first a few stars then a whole lot of them. Now the sky
was filled with so many bright stars. Then everything began to spin,
slowly at first and then at super speed. He felt like he was falling
into an abyss. After some time, the spinning stopped and he saw
several Elders approaching him. They were six Elders in all, all were
men with silver hair but their faces were bright and glowing. Their
combined auras were very bright. He could not recognise any of the
Elders but remembered they looked like the ones who appeared in
his dream.

Jatek knelt down and kowtowed three times. The oldest of the
Elders, wearing leopard skin as his attire, spoke to him, saying they
were his Ancestors and Guardians of his band of people. There here
were no actual words spoken but it was telepathic. He continued to
receive the telepathic communication. They had come to give him
some important messages from the Land of Their Ancestors. In
fact they were warning him of a very great disaster that will come
and warned him to take precautionary measures. This telepathic
communication continued for a full two minutes and much content
was conveyed, more than when speech is being used.

Jatek came out of the hut long after he had come out of his
meditative- trance. He looked more worried than before and was
in no mood to talk to his wife, who somehow knew he wanted to
be left alone. He just sat on the wooden and bamboo platform near
the river deep in thought. There were chores to do but he just lazed
around. He did not eat or drink the whole day. When spoken to, he
just kept quiet.

By nightfall, the whole settlement was very much abuzz with
talk about what is happening to their leader, Jatek. Finally they got
their second most respected tribesman to go talk to Jatek. His name
is Bambang and is actually Jatek's cousin.

At first Jatek still ignored Bambang's pleas to let the Tribe know what is happening to him but after a while, Jatek spoke as nearly the whole settlement sat down on the ground to hear what Jatek will say.

"My People, I thank you for your concern but I ask you to wait a further three days and nights. This is because I shall be fasting for this period of time and meditating, after which I shall speak. This is because I am myself very confused with the information I received in my consultation with our Ancestral Elders recently and I wish to be sure of all the facts before I speak to you all. It will be a very important announcement and I ask you to come back after the period of my fasting and meditation. I wish not to be disturbed. Bambang will act as temporary leader in the meanwhile." With that, Jatek went into his hut and closed the door.

There was a deafening silence, then all the tribesmen and women began a chatter. Bambang asked them to disperse to do their daily chores and they went obediently.

Jatek had been to school only up till age fifteen and then he dropped out of school to join his nomadic band. Now he has to deal with extremely complex information from the Ancient Elders and needed to meditate on the information given to gain some insight and understanding as well as to investigate how much of it is truth, which can be stranger than fiction.

Back in the city of George Town, Penang, Danny Ong was getting his business open for the day and today he hoped that business would be better. In fact he had lagged in paying his monthly installment for his car and it was a matter of time before car re possessors would come looking for his car to be towed away on orders of the Bank. He hoped to be able to start bank loan repayments at the latest by this month. At least he had not defaulted on his workers' pay but Danny doesn't know for how long he can afford to do that if the business is not getting any better.

The economic climate of the whole world in fact has been worrying and thus it is not Danny's bad luck or bad *feng shui* that is causing losses in his business. It started with the European money crisis. Then the crumbling of US economy did not help either. It seems that only China and India are the economic engines that are keeping the world going. Unknown to many, several countries are working on a new monetary system to stem the tide of corrupt practices and re-structure banking systems as well. With the news of a coming unification between China and Taiwan, many speculate that the Yuan maybe the currency of a new world order.

Inflation did not help the situation but aggravated the economic woes of normal people. It is no longer cheap to eat out, not even in hawker stalls anymore. Hence the poor business that Danny is experiencing. Eating out had until now never been expensive, not in South- East Asia at least. The situation has indeed changed dramatically. Price increases in basic commodities like rice, cooking oil, sugar, dairy products and vegetables have worsened the situation. With factories closing down, little or no foreign direct investments and increasing joblessness, it is small wonder that crime rates had hit an all time high, from petty thefts to rapes, murders and the list goes on.

It was not long before Danny had to think of the unthinkable: should he fold up his business as it was losing money, in fact it was bleeding his savings. Linda noticed that Danny was very quiet and moody and finally asked him.

"Dan, is there something the matter? Why are you so depressed? Have I done something to upset you?"

"No, no! You have done nothing wrong, sweet. I was just in deep thought."

"Thinking about what, Dan?"

"You see, business has been very bad and I can hardly make ends meet. So I was thinking of closing the business."

"Oh? Are you sure you made all the correct calculations, Dan? What about your two workers?"

"There is no choice, I have to let them go to find work for themselves. I really can't keep them anymore."

"Then what will you do?" asked Linda.

"I need to take a short break and look into doing some other business. But first I'll have to tell Muljadi and Hartono the bad news. I hope they can take it. Well, do you agree with my plans?" asked Danny, looking into her eyes deeply.

"Yes… I think so…if this will stop the leakage of your savings." Linda knows full well the whole situation as the firm she is working with is also facing financial difficulties.

"Then I have to tell those two workers as soon as I can. I also need to see how to sell off some of the things to minimise the losses when I close the business down. I should think that in two months I can wrap it all up." It was a sad thing to do but it must be done to stop the heavy losses every month.

The small band of Orang Asli led by Jatek was very apprehensive and it was nearing the time for Jatek to come out of his fast and meditation. He was just surviving on honey with water for the past three days and nights. Today Som had added some goat's milk to his tray. It was a signal that Jatek will come out soon after, at least before sundown. The whole settlement was getting very uneasy, they have no idea what to expect and all were puzzled by their leader's action.

Many of the tribesmen had gathered in front of Jatek's hut. The children were playing nearby and mothers were breastfeeding their smaller ones. The cry of jungle fowl was heard and singing of birds were now filling the air. The jungle was coming back to life! Every one noticed the change for when Jatek was fasting and meditating, all seemed quiet. Now even the insects were making their presence heard.

The door of the hut suddenly opened, but it was not Jatek but his wife, Som. Every one was silent and looked at her.

"I wish to say that Jatek will be breaking his fast soon and will need some rest before he makes an announcement tomorrow morning. Make sure everyone will be here then."

There were sighs and mumblings from the crowd, they had to be patient and wait for tomorrow. Reluctantly some of the crowd began to disperse.

Jatek ate his first proper meal slowly, chewing his food well and just enough to make him feel full. He was careful not to overeat after a long fast. He then walked out to stretch his body but returned quickly to his hut when many of his tribesmen wanted to approach him.

When Danny called his two workers for a short meeting, both of them had suspected what it would be about, so it was no surprise to them. This made it easier for Danny to tell them. As a matter of fact they were both more concerned about Danny than with themselves. Muljadi had decided to go back to his village in East Java to work on his small plot of land while Hartono will visit and stay with his brother who is working in the oil palm plantation in Negeri Sembilan state to the south of Kuala Lumpur, the capital. They assured Danny not to worry about themselves.

"So, Boss, what will you do?" asked Hartono.

"Well, I think I shall take a few months break and think of a new business. So keep in touch! I may need you both again!" said Danny enthusiastically.

Danny then laid out his plans about how he will wind the business up, giving notice to the Management of Gurney Plaza that he will vacate his stall in one month's time, getting in touch with the second-hand shops to sell them whatever he could and paying off his two workers. There were lots of things to settle and it was not easy to close shop which would keep Danny and his men very busy for the coming weeks.

CHAPTER 11

It was a bright day with few clouds in the clear blue sky. The jungle has come alive much earlier and while the nocturnal animals went into their hiding places, the diurnal ones were stirring into life even before the sun arose. The air was crisp and fresh.

After a bath in the river nearby his settlement and a light breakfast of roasted tapioca root, Jatek called his villagers for the much awaited and anticipated meeting. Everyone stopped what they were doing and gathered in the small clearing next to Jatek's hut. The women and children sat on the mat while several of the young adults and older men were squatting or standing further back. Som joined with the women to hear her husband talk, as she too was anxious to hear him speak of something of great importance. The crowd became quiet when Jatek stood on a small stool to speak to his Tribe. All they could hear was some birds chirping in the distance and the faint calls of some gibbons far away.

"My People, thank you for coming to hear me speak. As you know, I had been fasting and meditating for the last three days and nights and I have just come out of this with many messages for us all. Please hear me well. I will try to explain the messages for us as well as I can because there are many things and terms that I myself do not understand. Many of the messages are beyond my capability to grasp, but I am duty bound to tell you just the same. So, please hear me well and try to understand."

The crowd was even more eager to hear him.

"The messages I received are from many sources. They are from Mother Earth Herself, then messages from many Masters whom I have never even heard before but I feel their sincere Love and Blessings. So first I will tell you what Mother Earth communicated to me. As we all know in our hearts and culture, we belief in Mother Earth's Spirit.

She tells me Her name is Gaia. She will be transforming to a Sacred Planet and will be a Fifth Dimensional Planet soon. As we are made up of her elements, we too are to change into a Fifth Dimensional Human. This means that our bodies will be made of more Light and we will have extra sensory perceptions, like when I think before I speak, you will know already know what I am going to say even before I speak.

If we are able to connect with out Higher Self, then it is easier for us to follow Gaia because we then will change from what we are now, as Third Dimension human, to a Fifth Dimension human. Then we are actually connecting with our Sixth Dimension Higher Self, it is only then that we can we create whatever we wish. Those who are not able to change along with her will be removed, especially those of lower vibration and consciousness. She advises us to follow our hearts that teach us peace and love."

"What are Dimensions and how many are there?" someone shouted out from the far back.

"OK, I will try to explain this. Dimension is like what we say in our understanding of the different worlds we know that exists, a knowledge handed down to us by our forefathers The different dimensions contain the worlds associated with them All dimensions are existing in their own frequencies, not in their spaces. There are more than ten dimensions and we are now in the Third dimensional world, where the moment Now is the most important. It is the Conscious world locked in Time/ Space and Cause/Effect.

In the Fourth dimension, are all thought forms and all thoughts exist. It is also known as the Astral Plane. We navigate through it via our desires, thoughts and emotions. In the Fifth are all Time Lines, and thus all possibilities exist. We experience the Oneness with God here. Everything here is based on Love as Evil can't exist here. For the Sixth Dimension, one experiences Unlimited Space and Time. In the Seventh Dimension, all Past Lives are stored here, as all Thoughts of the whole Universe too. Everything then comes to a single point. In the Eighth Dimension, one experiences Infinity. For the Ninth Dimension, one can access any Universe at any Time Line. In the Tenth dimension, all that is in the Ninth comes to a Single Point." Everyone looked so blank."

Jatek simply went on giving his messages. "In Mother Earth's transformation, there will be movements of her body when all the 144 energy points in the grid of energy change. This will therefore result in earthquakes, volcanic activities and tidal waves. We are therefore advised to seek safer grounds."

There were a lot of mumblings and murmurs from the attentive crowd. Jatek raised his hand to signal them to be patient and quiet. He has more to say.

"Gaia also told me that there are people descended from the old continent of Atlantis and Lemuria living in deep underground cities. They have very advanced technologies and our scientists have no idea of such a group of dwellers known as the Agarthans. Mother Earth told me that when these Agarthans come out to the surface, it will be the signal for us to move to safer grounds. All of you also know that our folklore, handed down generation after generation, talked about *Orang Bunian*, and this corresponds to the Agarthans that was mentioned earlier." Every one was seen to be nodding their heads in agreement.

"How can they live underground? What about food? Air to breathe?" asked a young member of the Tribe.

"Mother Earth gave me many details. These people, survivors of Lemuria and Atlantis, had built an extensive system of cities. They occupy at least five layers, the first layer is where they stay, the second layer is for manufacturing, the third is for recreation with parks, lakes and so on. It is for the plants to produce oxygen they need. The fourth is for growing their food. They are all vegetarians and they eat nuts, grains, vegetables and fruits. Their crops are grown without the use of fertilizers and grow faster and more luxurious than those we have. The fifth is where they have their Temples. These are dome-like as well as pyramidal types with a capstone at the top that comes from Venus. Their technology is very advanced and they produce sunlight from the crystal-like walls that glow by themsleves. These are timed with day-night cycles that coincide with our daily rhythms. They use special tunnel-making machines that bore as well as melt down the rock and harden it to form smooth walls immediately."

"I have more to say, please listen." continued Jatek. The audience become attentive again.

"Our forefathers also believed that we come from the Stars above. Many of our Elders will also tell you this. This knowledge is known deep in our hearts. But soon, our Star Families will be contacting us also." This was greeted by exclamations from the attentive crowd. Excitement is running at an all time high now.

"When will this be?" someone shouted.

"Will they come in Flying Machines?" asked another.

"I don't know the answer, but come they will!" replied Jatek. "What is important is that we should not be that surprised when these things occur, unlike those city dwellers. Many of them may be so shocked that they will not believe what is happening. They will be caught out very badly. Things will never be the same again. But out of this chaos, the world will be a better place to stay, once it is fully in the Fifth dimension. Peace, harmony and unity will be established. We have to prepare ourselves for the coming events and these are the things that we must do:

One: We must eat more root vegetables like potato, tapioca, yam as these will help keep our energies well grounded, so important in this time of great changes. So we must plant more of these in our fields.

Two: We need to meditate more, to prepare our minds and to connect to our hearts. I want all of you, children above the age ten also, to do this every day from today onwards.

Three: Our best trekkers and scouts must look for new and higher grounds where we can all be safe from natural disasters. Balang, you will be in charge of this mission, as you are the best trekker among us.

Four: We must prepare dried fruits and food to help us over a period of time when we are unable to hunt or gather food. All our women must organize themselves to do this preparation.

Five: We must make more animal skin bags and bamboo containers to store water. These will be then transported to our new safe place when Balang and his men have found one. Natural things will prevail, and artificial things like plastics will disappear in the New Energies, so it is useless to buy pails, water bottles and so on.

Six : We need to get other essential items from the town nearby to help in our survival, so we need to have more money and to raise the money I suggest that we produce more handicrafts to be sold at the towns. My wife will be in charge of this project. Later I will give you a list of things to buy and what not to buy."

"How much time do we have before we need to move to a safer place, Jatek?" asked one of the crowd.

"I don't really know myself, but to wait for some signs. I believe we have about four to six months to prepare."

"What about the people in the cities? Are they aware of the coming changes?"

"I believe that some of the wiser ones will know, but the majority have no idea at all. It is a pity that we have almost no friends from the city, otherwise I would like to warn some of them. Anyway, I plan to visit our nearest neighbouring Tribe led by Tok Bubong to find out what their shaman knows."

"Will these changes happen all over the world?"

'Yes, the whole world. In fact, some changes will also happen to the entire Universe! I will now tell you about changes that will also occur in our very own bodies!"

Again, every one was all attention.

"Our bodies will change, to adjust to the New Earth. Some of these changes may result in giving us some kind of discomfort, make us feel unwell at first. We may get stomach or abdominal pain, discomfort, indigestion or feeling of bloatedness. Chest pains and food allergies will be more common to some while still others may find disturbed sleep, extreme tiredness and headaches. As we have almost all the remedies we need from the jungle herbs and plant sources, we need not fear but use these to help us overcome the discomfort."

Jatek then answered a few more questions and finally announced that the meeting was over and he would now meet with a few chosen individuals to disseminate detailed instructions for his six point plan to make sure that those in charge know what is expected of them. Jatek fears that they may actually have not much time left to make the preparations.

Thus this simple Aboriginal group went into action and became very busy with their tasks while more educated and civilised city folks were oblivious of to the coming changes of cosmic proportions. The city dwellers were more concerned with looking for a parking space for their car, making a living or picking a quarrel with their obnoxious neighbour, while criminals were having a gala time committing the most heinous crimes and politicians continued to plot how to bleed the country dry.

CHAPTER 12

In deep outer space, there was a flurry of activities that no one on Planet Earth knew of, or at least, very few did. Jatek was one of the few and that is why he needed to make a three day trek in the jungle to reach the shaman of a neighbouring tribe named Ukir. Although they could communicate when they are meditating or telepathically, Jatek needed to meet this wise old shaman face to face to confirm many disturbing visions he had and which he had told no one. Som prepared some cooked tapioca roots and dried deer meat for her husband's long journey but Jatek also took along his weapons comprising a blowpipe with poison darts and machete in case he needed to hunt for food. He set off early the very next morning as there was no time to waste, it was that urgent.

Although it seemed he walked slowly, in actual fact it was a half-run by Jatek. The jungle path was still easy going but it will get tougher by the second day. His stamina was incredible for he kept going for hours, only chewing some of the deer meat if he felt hungry. But usually on such journeys, he needed little food.

It gets dark early in the tropical jungle because of the thick tree canopy and so Jatek had to look for a safe place to sleep soon. He noticed some pug marks of a grown tiger nearby a small stream. He was happy and not worried because to him, it meant that the jungle ecosystem is still sustaining plenty of life. There were also the other usual prints of other animals like mouse deer, honey bear and tapir.

When travelling alone in the jungle, Jatek will not be bothered to build a shelter for the night but selects a good tree and climbs up to settle in for the night. Before that he would collect some special herbs and tie a bunch of them to his body to prevent mosquitoes and jungle ants or insects from bothering him. The only thing that could bother him was the cold, for temperatures may drop drastically during the nights.

It was only during the third and last night in the jungle that he was bothered by a herd of wild elephants that tried to shake him down from the tree but gave up after a while. In the morning, Jatek went to the nearby stream for a drink. He had no more food and if he could not reach Ukir's settlement by noon, he would have to hunt for food to sustain himself.

Although it had been three days of running, walking, wading through streams and cutting new paths, it conditioned his wiry body and he in fact could travel faster than the first day. His adrenalin was still flowing at full throttle, for he was one with the jungle.

Telepathically, Ukir knew Jatek was looking for him and he sent a small team of three trekkers to welcome him. This team finally located Jatek about five km from their settlement and provided Jatek with refreshments of drink and some food.

Soon they were at the settlement and Jatek was welcomed by Ukir and then he was ushered into Ukir's hut. After exchanging the usual polite pleasantries, Jatek started the discussions right away.

"I wonder if you know of some danger that may come from the sky?"

"Yes, I know why you are here and I tell you I am as worried as you are!" replied Ukir. "But tell me what you saw in your astral travel while meditating."

"I discovered this very huge and gigantic Cube high up in the astral plane. I was chased away by some of the evil Beings of the Cube. But I felt that there are more bad things about this Cube. It felt very frightening and threatening for our very existence!" said Jatek.

"Hm, I had a similar encounter. But I was bounced off by a very great force field. I sense a very Dark Force from the Reptilians."

"What do you think are their intentions? I know Reptilians are always trying to conquer and occupy planets and they have been doing so for aeons. What are we to do, Ukir?"

'While you were making your long journey here, I had contacted telepathically with a Buddhist monk friend of mine who is in Beijing. He too confirmed the Cube's presence. He told me that another yogic hermit in the Himalaya mountains also discovered the Cube's presence in the astral dimension. Although both of them joined forces to try penetrate the force field, they were unable. Then they were set upon by the Greys and Archons and they managed to escape just in time to come back into their physical bodies. However both of them were injured by the space parasites and they are now quite ill. They believe that there are many human souls entrapped inside the Cube."

"If none of us can deal with the Evil Reptilians and their allies, then Earth will be doomed as none of even the most advanced countries can ever handle them."

"I know, Jatek. I am as worried as you are. As my friends are recovering from the ordeal and are under going a purification ritual, they are not available for further consultation. However before they went into that ritual, the monk asked me to seek help from the people of Inner Earth!"

"How? I have never made contact with these Inner Earth brothers, also called the Agarthans," replied Jatek. "What about you, Ukir?"

"I too never made any sort of contact with them. However in my investigations, I learned that there is one elusive Taoist hermit who had been in constant contact with these Inner Earth People.

He is our only hope if we are to save Earth from the evil plot of the Draco Reptilians."

"Who is this mysterious one? Where does he live?" asked Jatek.

"Oh, he lives somewhere in Penang. I only know he is called Cheow Chek, The Bird Uncle, as he is well known to be able to communicate with birds."

"Then we must waste no time to get in touch with him!" exclaimed Jatek.

"This is the problem. I tried telepathy, I tried meditation, but he is elusive or refuses contact."

There was a deep silence. They both knew how big was the task that lay ahead of them.

"I am quite old and frail, Jatek. It is only you who must go to Penang and find him," suggested Ukir.

"Then I must. Give me as many details as you can and I will leave for my village today before it gets dark. Then from there I will leave for Penang." The two men looked at each other. Ukir knew Jatek well, he could do it. In fact taking three days and night to reach here was an achievement as even the most experienced trekkers needed at least four and a half days.

Ukir gave orders that Jatek is leaving soon and that he should be given ample provisions of food and water for his tiring journey back. A quick ceremony was done to appease the jungle spirits and to protect Jatek in his return journey and to ensure the successful mission to locate Cheow Chek. Jatek had a few cuts and scratches over his body, which is quite unavoidable when travelling through thick undergrowth in the jungle and so he was given some herbal rubs to ease the discomfort. After a quick meal prepared by the women of Ukir's tribe, Jatek left the settlement. Just as he was about to disappear from Ukir's sight, a beautiful, multicoloured jungle fowl appeared from nowhere and flew out of sight. Ukir smiled, this was a good sign! He felt that somehow the Bird Uncle already knew Jatek was looking for him!

Jatek literally ran as fast as the terrain allowed him for he wanted to cover as much ground as possible before nightfall. However this time it rained heavily, making progress much harder and due to rain clouds, nightfall was setting earlier. Tropical rainstorms are hard to predict, sometimes they last for a few minutes but it could be for hours as well.

Jatek had to settle in for the night and found a good tree and climbed up to make his make-shift shelter by weaving the branches together. He was thoroughly soaked and had to eat as much of the dried wild boar meat that he was given because once wet and in the humid conditions, mould will grow rapidly to spoil the meat. It was just impossible to sleep during the entire night as it was just too cold and wet. Fatigued as he was, Jatek had to continue his journey back. He set out as soon as dawn broke by which time the rain had stopped. He had to be extra careful as the ground was soggy and the mud made it very slippery. The last thing he needed was to get injured in a fall. As it was, he had several small slips which gave him small cuts and bruises over his shins and knees.

Finally Jatek reached his settlement on the seventh day after he left. He pushed himself really hard and was totally exhausted and covered in new and old bruises and wounds from cuts and falls but no major injuries. He was nursed back to perfect health by his wife, Som. While he was resting and recovering from his wounds, he told them of his trip to consult with Ukir and what he needed to do. Many then donated some cash for his journey to Penang. It will be Jatek's first trip to the North and to a big city. He is more worried and apprehensive about this trip to the urban jungle than to anywhere in the tropical jungles. He will be like a fish out of the water.

CHAPTER 13

Both robbers are now ready to strike. That is what they are now, robbers of petrol stations. Ah Seng had done a good job of stealing two motor bikes as their getaway vehicles. Actually they only needed one getaway bike but Ah Seng couldn't resist taking the brand new Honda bike. This now calls for a different plan of action and it will be to strike two petrol stations, one at a time and each will take their turn. After the second strike, they will each go on their own way to reduce chances of being spotted or caught by the authorities. In this way there is no need to divide the loot, each take all from the station they rob while the other acts as a look out. So now they toss a coin to decide who takes the first station and it turned out that Ah Seng won the toss.

The day for action then arrived. Ah Seng left his bike running near the end of the targeted petrol station while Ah Keat acted as lookout, next to the running engine of his friend's bike. They stationed themselves at the blind spot of the CCTV they had noticed during their surveillance work a few weeks ago. They will do the same at the next station they are to strike. In less than two minutes, Ah Seng came out of the petrol station's office walking briskly and acted real cool. The next minute, they were racing out into the North-South Highway heading towards Prai town, forty minutes away, for the next target.

This time they have to be even faster and waste no time. When they reached the station, and without taking their full-face helmets off, Ah Keat rushed into the office of the petrol station and took out his machete, and shouting out orders at the same time walked towards the cashier menacingly. Even though there were three other customers near the counter, they were frozen in fear. Again, Ah Keat barked the order to empty the cash machine's drawer into his bag and the money that is in the safe as well. Within a minute, everything was over.

Now they will run separately and they took off with their bikes fixed with false number plates at full throttle to separate directions. It is not known where Ah Seng had headed for but Ah Keat headed for Taiping, a town in Perak state about 120km south of Prai. It is a small town where nothing much happens and Keat deemed it a safe place to hide out.

On his way, and keeping to the speed limit of 110km/hr, he witnessed a horrendous accident near Bukit Merah. A Kancil car with a family of four burst a tyre with a loud bang, and the driver could not control the car which then hit the central railing and burst into flames. It happened about eight hundred metres in front of Ah Keat.

The family was trapped in the wrecked car which is burning, the occupants were yelling for help. Keat was simply shocked to the core by the horrific sight. At that moment, there were no other vehicles on the highway. He was running away from a crime, now should he stop to help?

He passed by the burning wreck,. but he just can't carry on as if nothing happened, so he turned back to help. He saw two kids yelling and crying at the back of the car and the flames were getting bigger. The driver was slumped across the steering wheel while the front seat passenger was moving slightly, as if just recovering from the shock. It was a woman. Keat made a quick phone call to the Plus Highway Patrol to inform them of the accident and told them to call for the ambulance. He then approached the car and tried to open the car doors but they were stuck fast, due to the misshapen car. He could see the fear in the eyes of the two kids and the woman was groaning in pain while the male driver lay still. The flames got bigger by the seconds and all the doors were stuck tight. Keat thought that the car would explode any minute now, yet he was helpless.

He looked for a stone or something to break the windows but there was nothing available. Keat then proceeded to hit with his bare fists but he could not break the glass. He saw the woman had stopped moving and groaning now. The children too were quiet. He had to do something fast. The heat from the burning car was getting unbearable.

Then he remembered his machete that he used in the robbery— did he throw it away? He was supposed to toss it away when they left the robbery scene. He ran to his bike: there it was! He retrieved it and ran back to the burning car and smashed the windows with his machete. Then he half climbed into the back seat to get the two kids who were now unconscious. He got the smaller girl first and then ran back to get the older one. By now, there were some travellers who had stopped, but only to look and no one went to help Ah Keat. All were just too afraid as the flames were really consuming the whole car and the heat was intense. One man was seen catching the action on his mobile phone.

Keat now smashed the car windscreen to get at the two adult passengers. He struggled to get the lady out and just then, the Plus Highway Patrol car arrived and two men went to Keat's aid. They got the woman out and now they were attempting to get the male driver, who was completely unconscious. They discovered that he was trapped inside his seat as they could not free him at all.

The driver of the Highway Patrol had taken the fire extinguisher from the 4WD and started to extinguish the fire. However the fire was just too fierce and continued to burn the car still with the driver inside. They had to retreat.

The ambulance arrived and took the woman and her two kids and rushed to the hospital. A huge crowd had gathered and a major jam had developed on both sides of the highway. The man who was filming the action on his mobile phone went to ask a few questions to Ah Keat, who was exhausted and felt depressed that he could not save the driver of the ill- fated car. Keat just said a few words and quickly got himself lost in the crowd and then took off in his bike. He slipped into Taiping quietly and unnoticed.

As he no longer had any friends in Taiping, he had to check into a hotel and he chose Hotel Panorama. It was only now that he realised that he had sustained some burns over his arms along with numerous cuts obtained from the rescue. He was really tired out by the day's events and fell asleep on the bed as soon as he laid down to rest. He did not even count how much his loot was. Unknown to Ah Keat, he will be famous all over the country by 8.00 p.m. this night. The man who had filmed the rescue by Ah Keat had sold the footage to TV3, a private TV station. At the 8.00 p.m. news hour, the daring rescue by Ah Keat was shown not only over TV3, but snippets of it were also aired by all other TV stations. They called him 'The Unknown Hero' and 'The Mysterious Good Samaritan'. This was because nobody knew his name. Reporters also mentioned about a machete being found at the scene.

Ah Keat was still sleeping in the room.Then his mobile phone rang and Keat woke up with a jolt. He now remembers he is on the run. He looked at the number displayed and answered it for it was from Ah Seng.

"Hello?" answered Keat.

"Ah Keat!! You are on TV News did you know?" asked Ah Seng.

"What? What news? What about it?" Ah Keat is now fully alert and sitting up on the bed.

"You mean you don't watch the News, especially after what we did today?"

"Oh, I fell into a deep sleep…what was it about?"

"I hope you will not get into trouble with your heroic act, Keat! They showed you rescuing some people trapped in a burning car!"

"What?? How come? Someone….oh no! That idiot who asked me to say something about the rescue….it must be him!"

"If I were you, Keat, I will be very careful from now on as people want to know the name of the hero! Take care!" and with that, the conversation ended.

Keat's head was reeling now. What has he done? He reached out for his cigarette, puffing away and thinking deeply. In all the robberies that he had committed, he had worn his helmet with the visors covering his face, surely no one could see and recognise him. However he must not take chances. He needed to buy a cap and also he was hungry and it was time for dinner. He went out of the hotel, walking quickly and then looked for a shop that sells caps. He found one easily and bought it without bargaining with the old lady owner. Next he bought some dinner and packed it back into the hotel to eat. He also bought some buns and biscuits for breakfast as he intended to just stay in the hotel room until he thinks of something. So far no one even took a second look at him. However he did not sleep very well that night, especially after catching the 11 p.m. news on TV, making him look like a hero.

The morning newspaper that was delivered to Keat's room made him even more worried as it was headlines on front page. Now he read the details about his rescue. The children he pulled out were Mohammad Arif, aged 9 years as outpatients and discharged. Their mother was Zaiton, a housewife aged 38 years and is still being warded for broken ribs. The dead man was Azahar bin Alaudin, aged 42 years who worked as a Security Officer. Keat got even more depressed that he failed to save the man, who was the sole breadwinner of the family. A large part of the report was about 'the unknown Good Samaritan' and his rescue, without which the entire family could have died.

Unknown to Keat, one of the goldsmith shop sales assistant, a Ms Pang, saw the news on TV with the footage of Keat saying something to the man who filmed his rescue and she instantly recognised the voice. She was shocked. The more she thought about it, the more certain she was about him being the robber who robbed the shop, as Keat was the man who gave the most orders to hand over the jewellery and cash. She is in a dilemma. That man, although a criminal, had risked his life to save some folks in a burning car.

Meanwhile, the Police was curious to know why a machete was at the accident scene and took it back for Forensics to investigate and results were pending. They had established that it did not belong to the family in the accident car and the kids and the woman had confirmed that it was used to break the windows of the car as well as the windscreen to facilitate their rescue.

Keat decided that he had to leave town, but where can he run to? The newspapers had put up a photo taken from the video footage showing his face, with a message for him to meet up with the relatives of the accident victims who wanted to thank him for saving the lives of their loved ones. Meanwhile the Police were puzzled as to why and who this person was, carrying a long machete that is usually associated with gangland weaponry.

CHAPTER 14

Keat is packing up to check out of the hotel as he has decided to run to Kuala Lumpur (KL) the capital city simply because it is the largest city and it is far easier to be lost in such a place. He quickly made a count of his loot and it amounted to over RM 12,000, not bad at all. He wondered how much his accomplice Seng had from the first petrol station they hit. After checking out, which was a breeze, he headed to the bus station, abandoning the stolen motorbike as it has no further use and would in fact be a liability. There was no problem in getting a bus ticket as it was not the school holidays and thus he managed to leave Taiping within 45 minutes in the next bus.

The journey will take about 4 hours and he has plenty of time to plan. The bus was not new but was at least clean with comfortable seats and the air conditioning was good. What he hated most was poor air conditioning which one can get. in such long distance buses He managed to get a seat near the front, on the left side of the driver, as it seemed to be the safest place in a bus. If he were to get a seat right at the back, he will get travel sickness.

Keat has no more good friends in KL and so he will not be able to put up with them. He will be looking for some cheap, nondescript hotel so as to be really "lost" in the city. It has been quite some time since he has been to KL as he hates the place for its traffic jams and always getting lost there as new roads and highways seem to be springing up all the time. And food is not as tasty nor as cheap as that found in Penang.

The bus must have been speeding because it was overtaking many cars on the highway. Bus drivers, whether in city roads or the highway, are well known to be drivers from Hell and this one was no exception. They had only one stop, at Sungai Siput, and reached KL more than half an hour earlier than scheduled and Ah Keat found himself at Puduraya Bus Station.

As it was around his lunch time, Keat decided to hang around the Complex to find something to eat before heading out to look for a hotel. This place has plenty of hawker stalls selling all kinds of things from fruits and titbits to all types of Asian food. The whole Complex is always full of travellers catching out-station buses or making connecting journeys and so is never quiet for 24 hours. Being so crowded with people from all walks of life makes this place unique in KL. One has to be in Puduraya to understand what KL is all about.

Puduraya Station is well known for ticket touts, snatch thieves and pickpockets and thus Ah Keat was very cautious walking around looking at the food stalls that he just located on the second floor. The air lacks good ventilation and he could smell the mixed aroma of food and smoke from the many smokers who light up after their meals and the noise was quite unbearable. With so many travellers walking about, the floor cleaners still were able to sweep or mop the floor almost unhindered. It is amazing how the public was able to sort of dance around their mops and brooms.

Keat saw a stall selling Hainanese chicken rice and as it was his favourite food, he sat at a long table that had the only empty seat and a young pretty girl came to take his orders. Beside him on his left was a young man who looked like a college student type while on his right was a man who looked quite lost and also worried at the same time. Keat thought he looked like an East Malaysian.

After a while, the East Malaysian gave Keat a half smile and Keat just nodded his head and this was enough for the stranger to start a conversation with Keat.

"Hello, can you please tell me where do I go to buy a bus ticket?" asked the East Malaysian.

"Huh? Oh, you need to go to Level 1." Keat thought to himself that this guy really must come from the deep interiors of East Malaysia, as anyone would have located the many ticket counters easily.

After some time, the food came and Keat started to eat. He want to find out how this hawker here compares with Penang's chicken rice, made famous by the man known as Fei Loh. After the first mouthful, Ah Keat thought it was way below Penang's standard. Before he could take the second mouthful, the East Malaysian spoke.

"I am going to Penang for the first time, can you advise me where can I get a cheap hotel to stay? Do you know Penang well?"

Keat turned to have a good look at the stranger and then said, "Go to Chulia Street and you can find a lot of budget hotels there." And he continued to eat, hoping to be left alone.

The man made an effort to remember the name. Then, "Are you from there?"

Keat began to feel a bit irritated for he was in no mood to have any conversation with anyone. He took another mouthful of chicken rice, chewed a bit before he answered, "No, but I know the place." Keat is now on the defensive mode, having to lie when necessary.

"Sorry to bother you again, brother, but can you help me with my most important job? You see, I need someone to help me look for a very hard to find Taoist hermit called Cheow Chek."

Keat nearly choked on his food when he heard the legendary hermit's name. He scrutinised the East Malaysian carefully and then asked, "Why? And how do you know of this hermit? Who are you?"

The 'East Malaysian' was excited for perhaps this man knows a lot more of Penang and about Birdman than he may like to say!

"My name is Jatek and I am the leader of my small band of Orang Asli in Pahang. I have a very important mission to accomplish, I have to find Cheow Chek as soon as possible!"

Keat could not believe what he heard. He asked, "Why? And how do you know of Cheow Chek?" Most folks in Penang could have heard of this strange man but very few have ever met him.

"It is a very long story. If you know how to locate him, then please help me find him! It is very urgent!" pleaded Jatek.

"However long the story is, I want to hear it. You will have to explain things to me and why this is urgent, not that I will not help you."

There was silence, then "You must help me! Little do you know the whole world depends on this Cheow Chek!" answered Jatek boldly. Then he went on to relate to Keat the whole story, only leaving behind the minor details. Keat was mesmerised. He did not know what to say. Is this man from the jungle crazy? If it is the truth, then it is real scary.

"Please help me find Cheow Chek! There is really no time to lose."

Before Ah Keat could say anything, his mobile phone rang. He looked at the number displayed, then he answered.

"Where are you now?" asked Seng.

"In KL,why?"

"Don't you know the Police are looking for you?"

"What? How?" Keat's face changed suddenly. He quickly scanned around the Complex to see if there were any policemen around.

"The girl from the goldsmith's shop recognized your voice when she heard you saying something to the man shooting the video recording on your heroic deed that was shown on TV! She then told police and now the police is releasing your photo from the video shoot to the Press and by tonight, all the Newspapers will have your face in the front pages!"

Keats face went pale

"I just got this news from Yu Toh of Kheng Hoe Bar. Get lost, Keat! Don't let the police get you! And if they do, don't you ever tell them about me!" Then the line went dead, leaving Keat still holding the mobile phone to his ear, and his mind was racing.

Keat then quickly finished his food and not saying a word. Jatek saw the sudden change and knew something bad was brewing for Keat. However, he kept asking Keat to help him locate Birdman. Keat then picked up his sling bag and started to walk in a hurry. Jatek was surprised by this action and took off after Keat.

"Please leave me alone!" Keat told Jatek.

"Look Mister, do you understand that the whole world's survival depends on us contacting Cheow Chek who is the only person here who is able to contact the people of Inner Earth to counter the imminent attack by the Dark Extraterrestrials! At least explain to me your sudden change in behaviour, maybe I can help you."

Keat stopped walking and turned to look at Jatek with eyes glaring. "Mind your own business!"

"OK, remember I've told you my mission, and should I fail, the whole world will not stand a chance against the Greys and Reptilians! You will bear the karma!" With that, Jatek went to look for the ticket counter, wanting to waste no more time. He had to track Birdman down with or without help. And time is running out.

Just as Jatek moved off and got lost in the crowd of people, Keat saw two policemen. Perhaps these two were just doing a routine round there, which is a hotspot for pickpockets and thieves but he is taking no chances and had to move away from the cops. Keat walked slowly so as not to get any sort of attention and blended with the crowd. Then his mind got an idea. What if he give some contacts for Jatek in exchange for some help?

Keat walked in the direction which Jatek took, looking for that aboriginal. He suspected that Jatek would be heading for the ticket counters and so he proceeded to Level One. The place was very crowded and noisy, and it made walking very difficult and slow.

He then spotted Jatek in the queue to counter 41, which was selling bus tickets to Penang. He made his way to Jatek.

"Hi, Jatek!"

"Oh, it's you."

"Look, I am sorry but can I make a deal with you?"

"What is it?"

"If I give you a contact of mine in Penang to help you find this hermit, will you let me stay in your settlement for as long as I need?"

Jatek thought for a while, then he said, "You are running away from the…"

"Sh! Not so loud!" Then he continued, 'Yes, my friend. I made several mistakes in my life. I just need a chance to sort it out. So what is your answer?" Jatek knew he has to seize the opportunity.

"OK, it's a deal."

"Good! Let me make a phone call first." Keat dialled a number on his mobile and waited for the other person to answer. It took quite some time for Johnny Santiago to answer his call.

"Hey Johnny, It is me OK. Now listen I need some help from you…" Keat went on to explain briefly about helping Jatek to find the hermit. Then he turned back to Jatek. "OK, he has agreed to help you. When you reach Penang, call Johnny and he will help you." He gave Jatek the mobile number of Johnny. In return, Jatek gave him instructions of how to get to his settlement.

"Thanks! Now take some of this" said Keat, and thrust some cash into Jatek's shirt pocket. "Now, don't argue. You will need this in your trip." With that Keat rushed to locate the counter that sells bus ticket for Rompin, Pahang, which is the last stop before getting into Jatek's small remote jungle fringe settlement. "And good luck!" Keat turned back to say as he hurried to look for the counter.

CHAPTER 15

The bus journey from KL to Penang took less than four hours and as expected it exceeded the speed limit throughout the journey. After crossing the scenic Penang Bridge, the old one, it stopped at several places in town to let off passengers before ending up at the Bus Terminal in Sg. Nibong on the Island. Jatek's eyes were wide open for he had never been to such a big city. The cars, motorbikes, lorries and wail of passing ambulances really disturbed him very much. The noise to him was unbearable. In the jungle it was so quiet, and if there were sounds, they were from Nature, like the melodious chirps of birds of all sorts and the howl of the monkeys. The polluted air was another thing that disturbed and astounded him.

He alighted from the bus and looked around the new surroundings. There were so many people, and they all looked so unfriendly, bored with a don't-disturb-me attitude. The bus fumes choked him a lot. He looked for something to eat and found it upstairs. It was crowded and noisy. Jatek decided just to buy a bottle of mineral water and thought how ridiculous this can be. Water should be free and cool with a sweet taste to it, like from the stream in his settlement. He found a quiet spot and started to make the call to Johnny Santiago.

"Hi, is it you Jatek?" asked Johnny.

"Yes, yes!..."

"I had been expecting your call. So where are you now?"

"I just arrived and am still at the Bus Terminal"

"OK, wait for me there and I will come to fetch you, OK?"

With that, Johnny jumped on his trusty and rickety old Honda bike, starting it in two kicks. As he sped off happily, his bike letting out the most polluting black smoke from the exhaust pipe, but he had to turn back because he had forgotten to carry an extra helmet for Jatek.

It was very lucky for Jatek when Ah Keat managed to get Johnny to help. Johnny is the kind of guy who will help anyone but he is hard to get. Most of the time he will be off exploring someplace quite far away and he always uses his old, rusty bike to get there and get there it does. Once Johnny decided to see the Perak Man exhibit in Lenggong, a small town off Grik, right in the middle of nowhere. Perak Man was the famous 8,000 year old skeleton dug up by local archeologists. He used his old Honda bike and it took him there and back without incidents. Due to his roaming about on his bike, he is heavily suntanned and so looks very dark. No one knows what he does for a living, yet he is never short of cash. And Johnny is a big spender. Right now he wants to settle Jatek into a cheap, liveable hotel along Chulia Street, in the heart of George Town.

With Johnny zooming in and out and between traffic in the polluted air, it was enough to scare the daylights out of this jungle expert, so Jatek held tight to the side bars near the bottom of the seat. His helmet was not strapped because Johnny had not showed him how and thus the strap was flying around in the wind, flapping across Jatek's face occasionally. With the wind beating into his eyes, Jatek could hardly open them and he wondered how could Johnny see in this situation. The motorbike ride seemed to take a very long time for Jatek, for he was counting the seconds before they could stop and be off this contraption. He felt very uncomfortable with this machine.

When they reached Chulia Street, Jatek had to open his eyes to absorb the scene. This is the backpacker area and within the enclave of the UNESCO heritage site. Jatek had never seen so many

Westerners walking along a street, some of them were even barefoot. This amazes Jatek because the road is hot, hard and was not like the cool, soft earth of jungle paths.

The street is full of life. There were so many old style hotels, Tourist Agencies, Travel Agents, Money Changers, secondhand bookshops, cafes and shops with motorbikes and cycles for hire. In fact the street sells almost anything for both locals and tourists alike

They stopped right in front of Blue Diamond Hotel and Johnny helped Jatek to check in. Johnny had made a booking earlier on as otherwise it would be difficult, if not impossible to get accommodation in the much sought after hotel. Jatek indicated he was now hungry and so they went downstairs to eat at the coffeehouse, referred to as *kopitiam* in the local dialect. They settled in a comfortable place under the ceiling fan and waited for their orders.

Now they have a chance to talk, but actually Jatek need not explain anything to Johnny because Johnny is the sort of guy who is not a busybody. Anyway Jatek carried on, giving him only a very brief reason as he felt that Johnny need to know the importance of finding Cheow Chek, the Birdman. Johnny just shook his head in disbelief – that now he and Orang Asli are crucial in saving Earth? That's a great responsibility!

"Let me now brief you how difficult it is to find Cheow Chek.,"said Johnny. "No one really knows where he stays and there are only rumours about his whereabouts. I will try my best to help you, nevertheless." Jatek just listened attentively.

"The first place we will check out is a pet shop in Air Itam. I hear that once is a while he will be found there. Maybe we may get more accurate information for his whereabouts by the people who hang around there."

This pet shop that Johnny mentioned is no ordinary pet shop because there are always certain group of men sitting by the corridor apparently doing nothing but chat and smoke. Many of them are heavily tattooed but one particular man with a dark complexion, has tattoos even on his face. He looked fierce and usually keeps to himself and quite separate from the others. There are also strange on- goings in the pet shop, which should be called a bird shop as there are more birds for sale than any other pets. It was perhaps for this reason that Cheow Chek was known to frequent this bird shop. But usually he keeps to himself while he plays or communicates with the birds, occasionally buying them and setting them free in nearby forests.

When Johnny and his new friend arrived at the bird shop, those men were there and they all stared at them, looking especially at Jatek. Johnny then approached the fat one sitting among the group and asked if he had seen Cheow Chek.

"Oh, he has not been here for many weeks now. Why?" asked Fat One.

"Well, my friend wants to meet him. Can you tell me where else does Cheow Chek hang out?"

"No idea. He seldom talks to any of us but to the birds only." All the while the men were staring at Jatek, and the heavily tattooed man was there, sitting apart from the others but throwing fierce looks at Jatek, who was clever enough not to make any eye contact with this man.

"OK, if he comes, can you please call me on my mobile?" and Johnny gave Fat Man his number. Jatek was relieved that they were leaving the place because the heavily tattooed man gave him bad vibes. Johnny was not dumb, he noticed the cold blooded stare from this mysterious man. They jumped on his old bike and off they went, leaving more black smoke from the exhaust. There was no conversation between the two and Jatek had no idea where Johnny was taking him to. They passed several areas before reaching some place with a steep winding road with forests on both sides. This time Jatek had learned to fasten the helmet strap properly by watching Johnny closely and so he is not bothered by the free and flying strap any more. It seemed to be a long time before they stopped by the road side.

"Jatek, this place is called Paya Terubong Hills and is where many people had seen Cheow Chek along the road, presumably walking out or to his forest hut along here. But I really don't know where to start. We need to ask someone that knows this place well."

"Who to ask? There is no one around this lonely road!" replied Jatek.

"I know, we have to go further on to see if there is anyone around." With that Johnny kept going for another 2 km of winding road now going downhill and then he spotted a makeshift shelter selling some local fruits like durian, mangosteens and bananas. He stopped near the shelter and went to the fruit seller to ask about the whereabouts of Cheow Chek.

:Never heard of this man," was the old fruit seller's short and curt reply and since Johnny was not buying anything from him, he showed no further interest to talk to Johnny. This behaviour is not new to Johnny, he had seen it several times before.

They kept moving on for another kilometre or so and stopped at a stall selling soya drinks. It was just the right thing to do, as the day was hot and sunny and they were sweating and needed some fluids badly. However the hawker could not help them either. This is strange, thought Johnny. Cheow Chek was so well known but over here where he is supposed to be found, almost no one knows him. What a paradox!

There is no giving up and Johnny continued to ask as many hawkers, cyclists, bikers as he could but none was able to tell him anything. This is proving to be an almost impossible task. However, soon it will be nightfall and they reluctantly abandoned the quest. Jatek was disappointed but ever so grateful for Johnny's assistance, while Johnny promised to track down this Bird Man. They will resume the task tomorrow. Jatek could see that it is after all not easy to trace this man and tomorrow may well be the same story. After

Johnny left him, Jatek went to his hotel room to meditate, hoping to establish some contact with Cheow Chek mentally or in the astral realm. The street noise was indeed just too much for Jatek to concentrate in his meditation. It is so different when in the jungle, so quiet and cool. Nevertheless, he continued his meditation and made some progress.

CHAPTER 16

Although they had agreed to meet at 9am, Johnny was there to pick up Jatek by 8.15am. This time Johnny had brought along a few bottles of water to drink and some biscuits packed neatly into a small sling bag. He thinks today they will make some progress, thus the small preparation for a jungle trek.

Jatek too was up and ready early himself. He told Johnny he was given a vision in his meditation last night and in the vision a bird showed him a statue of the Buddha and that is where the path will lead them to Cheow Chek's little hut on the jungle fringe. Johnny's eyes went wide open and nearly popped out.

"Then this is it! Last night I went round asking plenty of people and one old lady mentioned that we needed to look for a Buddha statue by the roadside near the Paya Terubong Hills that will lead us to Birdman!" exclaimed Johnny. "And I was also told that many of those who knew where to get Birdman would not let strangers know because they were protecting Birdman's privacy! No wonder I thought it was odd that those whom we asked didn't know and yet they are from the area. Let's go, what are we waiting for?"

Jatek jumped on Johnny's bike just in time as Johnny took off in great excitement. Jatek held the side bars tightly in his grip as otherwise he would surely fall off the speeding bike, Johnny was that enthusiastic today. The wind again hit Jatek's face and instinctively his eyes were closed as much as possible. The ride was always a blur for him.

It took a good 45 minutes ride of zigzagging around the heavy traffic to Paya Terubong and Johnny's control of his old motorbike was that of an expert rider. Although he has an old Toyota car, he seldom uses it except on rainy days. However even when he wants to use the junk of a car, the battery would be dead due to lack of usage and he always has to ride his trusty old bike.

They passed by the hilly area and kept their eyes open for the Buddha statue. As Johnny was going slow now, so as to spot the statue and also because the old bike was straining to go up and down the hilly rural road, Jatek could open his eyes and look out as well. But to their dismay, and after two rounds, they still could not spot the statue anywhere along the road. Johnny stopped the bike to think what to do now. He lit up his own home-rolled cigarette.

"How come we can't see the statue?" asked Johnny, drinking some water from the bottle.

"We need to extend the area of search I think," replied Jatek, wiping some sweat from his forehead.

"Let us rest for a while first."

They just sat down by the roadside, each thinking hard, for a full 20 minutes when Jatek 's eyes went wide open again.

"Look, at the bird on that tree!' shouted Jatek in excitement. Johnny was puzzled, they are looking for a Buddha statue, not bird watching, what's got into this Orang Asli, Johnny thought. "That is the same bird I saw in my meditation! It is flying off now, follow the bird!" shouted Jatek. They scrambled onto the bike and followed the bird which flew in parallel with the road for some distance before disappearing into the nearby forest.

"The Buddha statue!" they both shouted out as they spotted it at the same time. The Buddha statue was that of a Laughing Buddha but it was so small, only about 20 to 25 cm high and nearly covered by the undergrowth. No wonder it was so difficult to spot it.

"I am going into the forest, you wait here and pick me up later." With that, Jatek was as fast as a deer and ran into the small pathway into the jungle, leaving Johnny speechless. Johnny wanted to follow but a look at the terrain and jungle gave him the shudders. He will never be able to catch up with the aborigine and besides he is sure he will get lost easily in the thick jungle on his own. So Johnny Santiago just sat down and lit another of his cigarettes.

Jatek could not see the bird anymore, it seemed to have disappeared although he was quick to follow it into the jungle. Then he saw some tracks of barefoot human footprints. They were not fresh, about a few days old, thought Jatek. He followed the tracks and they led him to a steep ravine. He climbed down and then up again, still following the tracks, which were harder to locate now as the grass was thick again. His instincts then took him further in and then he saw an abandoned small Taoist temple build on a slope!

Jatek went to the temple and looked around. There was no one. The fallen leaves were scattered all over the temple, making it looked dirty and abandoned. The altar was bare, no statues of the Taoist Gods, only an urn with incense sticks already burnt long ago. There was only very sparse furniture and it looked badly weatherbeaten. The whole Temple was painted red but the colour too had faded with patches of paint peeling off. Jatek knew somehow that Birdman will not come and so he made his way back to where Johnny was.

He caught Johnny sleeping on the ground and woke him up. "Oh, sorry. Did you meet Birdman?" asked a startled Johnny.

"No. I may have to come here daily until he appears. But I know he will come."

For the next two days, Johnny would leave Jatek at the same spot and to pick him up by dusk. Although Jatek looked disheartened, he always had some kind of telepathic message that indicated Birdman is on the way.

It was almost 4 p.m. on the third day of waiting, and in another 2 hours or so, Jatek would have to leave as Johnny will be waiting by the roadside. Then he heard birds singing suddenly. It was always quiet there. He knew that Birdman is quite near. Finally all the waiting will be worth it. He felt so excited and apprehensive at the same time.

Cheow Chek almost startled Jatek when he just appeared behind him. There was no sound at all, Cheow Chek was so silent in his footsteps or is that he "just appeared"?. It is creepy because not even a leopard could take Jatek by surprise, much less a human.

"You must be tired of waiting?" asked Cheow Chek, with a wry smile, speaking perfect Malay.

"Oh, you must be Cheow Chek!" replied Jatek, and he then dropped to his knees, saying, "Master!" Jatek could see that the aura of this hermit was unique and he had never seen any body with such clear and bright aura before. Cheow Chek was taken by surprise and invited Jatek to sit with him on the temple floor, as the stools were too unsteady.

Jatek studied the mysterious hermit closely. He must be not over 60 years old, thought Jatek. The clothes he wore were simple, with smudges of dirt and partly torn here and there. The hermit had slightly greying, long hair tied by only a rubber band into a pony tail. He stood as tall as Jatek but a lot slimmer. He was also barefoot.

"I know why you are here and I must thank you for taking such trouble. I must also apologise for keeping you waiting for so long but I had to do something far away."

"It is no trouble, Master!" Jatek was thinking what does far away mean? This man could mean physical distance or into the realms of the unknown too!

"Let us not waste time but let me tell you the details. Both you and Ukir were right about the huge Cube in the sky, actually in the Fourth Dimension of the Astral Plane. It is a military Base for the Reptilians and their ally, the Archons. They were making final preparations to invade Earth before Mother Earth Herself ascends to the Fifth Dimension, by which then would make it very difficult for them to invade. Many of us Lightworkers who are bound by the code of Service to Others rather than only Service to Self, tried individually to penetrate the Cube and sabotage their plans, but we were all unsuccessful. In fact, many of us were hurt badly and I was lucky to escape unscathed. We then realised that we needed much help and I was given the task of contacting our brothers who live in Inner Earth."

"You have already done so?" exclaimed Jatek with glee.

"Yes, and the Mission had been accomplished!" said Cheow Chek, flashing a smile.

"Can you tell me more?" pleaded Jatek.

"Yes, but come tomorrow at 2 p.m., and come alone. I am afraid what I am to tell you is not meant for the ears of your good friend with the old motorbike. He has a big mouth!"

Jatek was surprised that this Taoist knew so much. He thanked the man and as he was leaving the place, the hermit shouted out,

"I am afraid you both will have to walk quite a distance as your absent-minded friend has not filled his petrol tank!' The hermit then gave a good laugh as he turned towards the forest. When Jatek turned round to look at the hermit again, Cheow Chek was nowhere to be seen!

"Oh, you are already here?" asked Jatek when he emerged from the jungle path leading to the road when he saw Johnny sitting on his bike smoking away.

"Yes, and you look very happy. Did you meet him?" asked Johnny.

"No, but I had made telepathic contact with him while meditating and I got the impression that he will be coming tomorrow after lunch." Jatek had to tell a lie to Johnny, although he is now his fast friend.

Johnny started his bike and they zoomed away. Jatek thought to himself, "No petrol? This man is speeding away!" He held on to the bike with a tight grip on the side bars. However after a few minutes the motorbike spluttered, coughed and choked with jerky movements and they came to a stop.

'Shit!" cursed Johnny. "No more petrol!" This is followed by a long list of profanities. Then he kicked the bike and hurt his foot, like a classic clown act. But Johnny is Johnny, he has to do it.

CHAPTER 17

Jatek had asked Johnny to leave him at the spot that leads to the hidden Temple early. Secretly he wanted to see how Cheow Chek could sneak up to him if he is there early to prepare himself by sitting with his back to the temple wall. In this way, anyone will have to approach him from the front and there is no way he can be surprised anymore. But Jatek was really surprised a second time because Cheow Chek was there before him! How do you outwit this hermit?

"I see you are early, Jatek!" greeted Cheow Chek with a mischievous grin.

"Good afternoon, Master. Yes, I thought it was a good idea not to keep you waiting but looks like I did."

"Never mind. Have a seat and I shall begin. Ask me questions if you do not understand what I am to say. You may be an Orang Asli but I know you have far greater intelligence than many city dwellers."

Jatek gave a smile and settled himself on the floor covered with dry leaves. He offered Birdman some water from his bottle along with some local cakes he brought along.

"When we knew we could not handle the situation, it was up to me to ask for help from the people of Inner Earth, some of whom are known as the Agarthans. It is a Law of the Universe that the Divine will not intervene if no permission is granted, as we are all Beings with Free Will. Some of the UFOs surface people see are actually those of the Agarthans when they fly their machines to our world for various reasons. UFOs that are really unknown are very few because those with evil intentions are chased away by the Agarthans.

However, this time the Agarthans too needed help from other Sources as the foe this time has a very formidable Force. Imagine, the Cube has a side of 60km in diameter each side. It is a gigantic ship, with a force field that surrounds it, to protect it that has the size of the Planet Pluto. It is almost impenetrable! All of us were bounced off when we tried it. But the Agarthans had a plan. They discovered that the Cube Ship's force field is powered and connected to the Earth's Grid of Energy, which is in turn connected to the Ley Lines. The Venus Transit date of 6th June, 2014, the brief moment when the Ley Lines will be disrupted, is the only window of opportunity to attack, as the force field will be weakened by a few cracks appearing on that day. But still that weakness is not enough to breach their defence shield. We needed 144,000 meditators to meditate at the same time to force the shield to break down and we got these critical mass of people meditating on the day of Venus Transit, and you and Ukir were among these people!! You follow so far?" asked Birdman.

"Yes, Master."

"Then I shall continue." He took some of the local cake, chewed it slowly and Jatek just had to wait. Taoist masters will chew their food well to extract the essence of the food, not only the food.

"They also discovered that it was the Cube Ship that was beaming false information to many mystics, channelers and shamans to confuse the Earth population with false information and cause chaos before they strike. There were also 5,000 trapped human Souls in the Cube Ship."

"Why, Master, do the Reptilians do that?"

"The Evil Beings thrive on the energy of sufferings, chaos, pain and sadness. So they captured the Souls and contained them in secret chambers of the Cube to torture them to take their Life force and feed on them. So apart from an imminent attack on Earth, we had to rescue these trapped Souls. Yes, Reptilians feed on human souls' sufferings and so it was the tradition of such Reptilians to kidnap humans, sometimes known as "Abductions" to us. So our Agarthan relatives contacted the Special Forces, who also reside in Inner Earth. There are only 250 elite Special Forces available to combat more than 100,000 elite soldiers of the Reptilians with their 100 battle ships. So we were greatly out-numbered."

"Who are these Special Forces, master?"

"These are Incarnates from the various Star worlds, highly evolved Souls with humanoid bodies that were sent to Inner Earth and to be used in times of imminent danger to Earth. They form the Silver Legion and together with ships from the Galactic Federation, were the nucleus of our attack Force, which was still far out-numbered by the Reptilians! And five among the Galactic Federation forces were originally from a planet that were destroyed completely by the Reptilians!"

"How did the Silver Legion and the rest do it?"

"Ah, so they came up with a plan! But first I must tell you where the Cube Ship of the Reptilians was situated. It was outside the Kuiper Belt, exactly 15 degrees to the North of Ecliptic of the Star Alpha Centauri. So the Agarthans sent a false message that they were unable to attack the ship the size of the Cube, and instead we were to attack a sister ship, far smaller than the Cube, at another location! Of course the Reptilians intercepted our message and took the bait! Of their 100 battleships that had in the Cube, they sent out 10 to intercept some of our Galactic Federation ships that were sent there. It was a much smaller force sent out than what we expected, nevertheless, it helped to reduce their battleships to 90; it was better than facing their full force of 100.

At the moment we got the 144,000 meditators from all over the world focussed on Love and Compassion, and at the crucial timing of Venus Transit, we teleported our Special Forces into the Cube Ship. Our elite soldiers wasted no time, they planted bombs and managed to locate and rescued the 5,000 human souls and all we teleported back into our Base. The bombs we planted were special ones that will implode first and then explode simultaneously to destroy the Cube Ship. This had to be done and timed precisely because their Cube Ship was able to do self-repairs as the Cube has an Intelligence of its own. With the special bombs, the Cube Ship was destroyed completely."

"So all the Reptilians were destroyed?" asked Jatek in excitement.

"No. Of the 90 ships, 70 were destroyed while 19 of their Battleships managed to escape while one was captured by us. We suffered casualties too. We had seventy-five of our elite Special Forces returned to Source."

"Meaning?" asked a puzzled Jatek.

"In human terms, these seventy-five died. Their physical bodies suffered great injuries that were beyond repair and their souls were sent to Source to recover from the trauma. They are now waiting for new physical bodies to be incarnated into and for the time being, their only complaint was being bored! The rest are now recuperating in our Andromeda Hospital Ships as they were all infected with the Space Parasites developed by the Draco and Hydra Beings of lower Fourth Dimensions. These parasites were programmed to destroy all Non-Reptilians when contact is made, and is impossible to avoid them as they inhabit the very space inside the Cube Ship."

"Will they recover?"

"Yes. They are all in the best facilities to be healed. The Agarthans are now left with the task of clearing away the nuclear debris in Space before these cause harm to any Life forms. There is still a lot of work to do, ….wait, sh!.." Birdman listen attentively, 'Wait here, your nosy friend is trying to sneak around, let me teach him a lesson not to eavesdrop!"

Birdman took off so fast, it was unbelievable and in a moment he was out of sight. This really surprised Jatek because first he did not hear anybody approaching and he is not a city dweller, he is among the best trekker from his tribe! A good trekker not only sees tracks but hears and smells well also.

Johnny had been waiting near the spot where he left Jatek, at the place where the small Buddha statue is. Tired of waiting since running out of tobacco to roll his own cigarettes, he decided to see if he can find them and join them. He was also very curious to know who this Cheow Chek was and what he looked like, since he was so elusive. Johnny hadn't even ventured more than a few metres when Birdman knew he was coming! He decided to play a trick on Johnny and he projected the image of a roaring tiger prowling nearby. Johnny heard a loud and fierce tiger's roar and after a second frozen in disbelief, he turned and ran the fastest 20m in his entire life. He wasted no time to take off on his trusted old bike, leaving the back wheel kicking up sand and gravel as he sped off full throttle. Jatek even heard the loud roar of a tiger but did not react because he thought it was too near the fringes of a jungle for a tiger to venture here, besides he suspects that it must be due to Birdman playing his tricks.

When Birdman came back, he was laughing away and Jatek joined in the laughter. "You better not laugh so much because he may not come back to fetch you!". Then they both laughed out loud again. It was time for Jatek to bid farewell to Cheow Chek, his mission being accomplished. The two men looked at each other deeply into the eyes with a sense of camaraderie.

"Go back to your people, Jatek and lead them well, which I know you are able to!" said Cheow Chek.

"Thank you so much, Master. Especially in the work you have done!" replied Jatek, with a lump in his throat.

"In the months to come, listen to the forest, see the signs that Mother Nature shows and you will be able to lead your people safely into the future. I know you will. Remember, listen to your heart, Jatek!"

"What about you, Master? What will you be doing?"

"Me? I always have some work to do, if not this, it is that!"

They both laughed, and parted. Jatek was so happy that a heavy burden and responsibility had lifted off his shoulders. His mission has been accomplished successfully. He felt greatly indebted to Johnny. He was surprised that Johnny was waiting for him by the roadside and not abandoned him after being frightened by the roar of the "tiger".

"Jatek! You are safe. Thank God!" Exclaimed Johnny when he saw Jatek emerging from the jungle fringe.

"Yes, how are you, my friend?"

"You know, I tried to go inside the jungle to see what is happening but when I heard the roar of the tiger, I ran for my life. Did you know a tiger was prowling nearby? It is very strange, when I was much more calm, I thought how come there are tigers on this island?"

"Yes, it is strange, but I heard the roar too, however I had Master Cheow Chek with me and we were safe in his temple." replied Jatek, half concealing his smile.

They talked for a while longer and it was time for Jatek to take the night bus to Kuala Lumpur.

"I will be so indebted to you, Johnny."

"Don't mention it, my friend. It is my pleasure. Keep in touch."

CHAPTER 18

This time the bus to Kuala Lumpur was much more comfortable. It was a bigger and more modern bus, the air conditioning was cool and drinks and food were served during the journey. The concept was to make the experience very much like that of an aircraft flight. The ticket was sponsored by Johnny and Jatek felt much indebted to him. Although Johnny looks like a drifter and good-for-nothing type of person, he has a good heart, thought Jatek. Now he settled down to have a much needed rest as the journey will be quite a long one.

However Jatek's mind began to think of his wife and kids, his people, and wondered how Keat was doing: did he manage to locate his settlement? Can this city dweller be comfortable in a semi-jungle environment? As there will be no mobile phone signal in the remote place, he will not be able to call Keat to find out how are things with him. It was not long after when Jatek fell into a deep sleep.

Actually Jatek need not worry because Keat managed to make his way to the settlement as Jatek's description was accurate and all the landmarks were easily found. Keat's sense of direction and orientation was also good and that helped a lot. The taxi left Keat nearest to a path that leads to the Orang Asli settlement. It was almost in the middle of nowhere and is the best place for being out of police radar. Keat had not walked more than 50 m into the path when he was met by some Asli children and an adult man. They were going back into their settlement after an outing to collect honey from the forest across the road.

After a brief exchange of greetings and some questions, Keat discovered that they belonged to Jatek's tribe and so he showed a headband that Jatek gave him as proof that they had met. The adult Orang Asli, named Pandik recognised it at once and became friendlier. Keat told him that he was being invited by Jatek to stay with them for some time and Pandik asked him to follow them as they were about to return to their settlement. Keat felt a great relief because he was getting worried because he had never stepped into a jungle before.

Pandik and the Asli kids had to slow their pace for Keat to be able to catch up. The path led to some hilly tracks and the climb was giving Keat lots of perspiration, he was actually drenched in sweat but Pandik and the kids hardly had any trace of sweat on their skinny but muscular bodies. And they were carrying bee hives draped in a cloth bag at the end of bamboo poles. When Keat slipped and fell a few times, the Asli kids laughed so loud it frightened the birds that flew off from their hiding places. The Orang Asli also noticed that the macaques were making noises up in the trees because they had spotted a stranger in Keat. Usually they were quiet and would not show any interest when the Asli people were using the path.

It took at least an extra 40 minutes and several falls by Keat to reach their settlement and Keat was surprised to see a clean little settlement with five huts on stilts. There were four other smaller huts at the periphery. The three mongrel dogs gave a bark to warn the villagers of a stranger among them. Many of the women were at a nearby stream washing clothes and utensils and they all wore their *sarong* up to their armpits, thus covering their breasts. Almost everyone was barefooted.

Keat was introduced to Bambang, the acting Headman in Jatek's absence and then to the rest of the community. The children gathered near Keat and giggled among themselves. Luckily Keat had managed to buy several packets of sweets at the bus station in Rompin and he distributed them to the eager kids, feeling like a

Santa Claus. Keat was then shown a small bamboo hut next to some durian trees as his living quarters. No, he is not lucky, as there are no durians at this time of the year.

When Jatek arrived, the whole settlement got very excited and welcomed back their Headman. They held a celebration that night and Keat joined in the merrymaking. Jatek saw that Keat was beginning to be able to fit in. After the feasting and drinking of the sweet rice wine, *tapai*, they all sat by the bonfire to hear Jatek tell his adventures in the city of George Town and how he met a most mysterious Taoist hermit. Everyone was attentive, even the noisy and mischievous Asli kids were quiet. You could hear a twig drop! Even Keat, half drunk from the rice wine, was suddenly attentive and spellbound.

Back in Penang, Danny had finally disposed of all the things he no longer has any use for since closing down his business and he had paid off his two workers. Finally the big headache was gone and a heavy burden was taken off his shoulders. Now he finds that he has a lot of free time as he has not thought of what to do next. He just planned to take a break for the time being to relax while thinking of his next move, either to get a job or start another business. The next day Danny decided to do some fishing, a hobby he developed when still at secondary school. He had accompanied his cousin, Jerry Ong on many fishing trips and finally he got hooked on it too. Jerry was the spoilt one, always skipping school to go fishing and Danny had also begun to play truant to go fishing with Jerry. The cousins were very close but fate has it that Jerry died quite young of a heart attack and Johnny really missed his cousin very much. They had lots of good memories together- be it fishing or to "paint the town red' as Jerry always said.

Since Linda was at work, Danny decided to go on his own, besides, the solitude will let him think about his future without any interference.

Gathering his old and trusted fishing rod and other fishing gear, Danny drove first to Tanjong Tokong beach to buy some worms as bait from some boys. Then he picked up a newspaper, cigarettes, some snacks and two bottles of mineral water and headed towards Bt. Ferringhi beach, his favourite spot. On the way, he noticed he had forgotten his cap but it was not his habit to go back just for a stupid cap. He will have to do without the cap to shield his face from the sun.

After parking his car by the winding roadside, he collected his gear and bag with all the things he bought and headed to the beach below. The road is actually very close to the beach on a sort of cliff all the way round the island. There are some spots where it is easy to climb down to the beach while other spots are just too steep. The spot he chose was away from the swimmers and is a more secluded spot but has huge rocky outcrops that jutted into the sea. To the locals, this means a habitat for fish to hunt for food and so increases the chance of landing a catch, especially the groupers that like this sort of environment. The negative point is that one is more likely to get his fishing line stuck at the rocks in the bottom which means losing hook, line and sinker. However, experienced anglers will know the knack of freeing the line with a special kind of manoeuvre they all learned by following what others did.

Danny noticed he was the only angler there today. The sea breeze was there and sky was clear with the sun shining down mercilessly. He really missed his cap now. The smell of the sea is still strong and reminded him of the days he and the late Jerry used to fish. Nowadays Danny noticed very few anglers below the age of thirty. Most teenagers are now found loitering at shopping malls or in internet cafes playing games or gambling on the casino websites. Seems like fishing by the sea will be a dying sport soon with fewer and fewer of the younger generation showing any interest.

Settling down to his familiar spot, Danny started to fish and cast his line far out with an expertly executed throw. Then all he has to do is to wait and be with Nature. The mid-day sun was hot. It was glaring. The only relief was provided by the occasional sea spray from a big wave hitting the rocks and the breeze dispersing the droplets onto his face. He had plenty of time to think about his future, about Life.

It was almost an hour and he has yet to land a catch. He had checked his hook several times and there was no bait left. Either the fish were able to nibble away the bait or it just slipped off in the strong waves as the tide was coming in. Danny spotted a hawk flying around, or was it a kingfisher? He wished he had brought his binoculars along. Hawks have curved beaks while kingfishers have a long, straight beaks and are smaller than the hawks.

It was another 30 minutes before he got a bite, now the excitement starts. It was quite a strong, sudden tug at the line, followed by three more tugs in quick succession. Danny reeled in the line – it was a small puffer fish, worthless as it is very poisonous. He released the fish back and prepared a new bait and threw the line into another spot to avoid the family of puffer fish. This is odd, Danny thought. Usually he would have caught at least two or three fish by now. Anyway he is prepared to carry on fishing, to kill time, as there is still some bait left and his supply of water has not gone.

Then something caught Danny's attention. Something very bright flashed across the cloudless sky very fast and stopped in mid-air. There was no noise at all. Danny looked at the object in disbelief. It was quite huge, bright, made no noise and was shaped like an elongated object with smooth, rounded ends. It remained suspended in mid-air for a few seconds and then zoomed out of sight at incredible speed, still making no noise.

'What the Hell was that?" thought Danny. He looked around the place and found no one but himself. Can he believe his own eyes? Could this be a UFO? Danny felt a tinge of fear and decided to quit the fishing and go home to rest or ask some friends if they had seen what he saw. In his haste to leave the place, Danny slipped on a rock and fell, hurting his right ankle with a twist and a cut. The pain was quite unbearable and he had to stop for a while, grimacing in pain. Although the cut was not too deep, it was bleeding and Danny knew he needed to see a doctor to get this wound dressed up.

Although there are plenty of clinics around the Batu Ferringhi area, Danny preferred to see his old GP and thus he drove all the way back to Dr Looi's Clinic. The old doctor is far better and more experienced than all these young doctors these days.

"Danny Ong!" announced Alice, Dr Looi's nurse, now getting a bit plump. Danny was then showed to Dr Looi's consultation room.

"Danny!" said Dr Looi.

"Hi, Doc" replied Danny. "Need you to have a look at this," and showed Dr Looi the cut.

"Oh, hm, let me see..., OK, this will only need some dressing, no need to stitch!" Danny was relieved to hear this. As Dr Looi was doing the dressing, Danny said, "Doc, do you believe in UFOs?"

Dr. Looi raised an eyebrow and looked at Danny. "Belief in UFOs? I think they are real! Why?"

"I just saw one today while out fishing in Batu Ferringhi." This time Dr Looi not only looked at Danny but stopped the dressing for a moment.

"No kidding?"

"Serious, Doc! I was out fishing when suddenly a bright flying object flew across the sky and then stopped in mid-air for a while before flying off in great speed!"

"Did you manage to take any photos?"

"No, I don't carry a camera around, especially when I am fishing." Dr Looi then finished the dressing. "Well, Danny do inform me if you ever see any such UFOs again as I am very interested in them."

"OK, Doc. I'll be on the lookout since I have more free time now as I have closed my business."

"Oh, sorry to hear that. What plans do you have then?"

"Oh, I am still in the planning stage, Doc. OK, bye then."

"Take care Danny, Alice will give you an appointment for wound check, OK?"

Not long after Danny left, Dr Looi had a phone call from Albert.

"Doc! Do you know that several people had called the newspaper offices to report on strange flying objects that flew over their houses?" said Albert with full of excitement. He knew this because he has some reporter friends.

"Really? Strange, you remember this guy Danny Ong? Well, he just left. Anyway he claimed to have seen the UFO while fishing at Batu Ferringhi!"

"Wow! OK my mobile is ringing again. I'll get back to you once I have more news."

Dr Looi by then was thinking fast, and he decided to switch on the TV in the next room to catch any news but there was not any so far. Then he got onto his Notebook and signed into his Twitter account to check for any news on UFOs being sighted in Penang. What he got in Twitter, he can't believe his eyes! There were many people in Penang who had described what they saw at about the same time that Danny saw. There was a lot of excitement and chatter in Twitter. People reported seeing the bright object in Tanjong Tokong, Gurney Drive and Air Itam areas, and more people are still writing about it. Traffic almost came to a standstill in congested Air Itam areas which resulted in a few cars being involved in minor accidents as drivers lost their concentration on the road, stopped their cars suddenly and looked up into the sky.

This also meant busy times for people like Kim Heng, Mokhtar, Ramu and Ah Boey. In fact their walkie-talkies were crackling news almost non-stop, telling each other of the location of an accident that they were rushing to. Albert had by now received enough information from his sources to call Dr Looi back.

"Hey Doc! Listen, It is confirmed that many people saw the UFOs in Penang, but not only that, there had been sightings in many other parts like in Sungai Petani and Alor Star too!"

"What? I am now looking at Twitter and many are still writing about the UFO they saw! What is happening? It's like the UFOs are no longer afraid of being seen." said Dr Looi excitedly.

"Looks like it. Doc, let us keep in touch and maybe tonight I'll drop in your place, OK?"

"Yes, good idea Albert. Bye."

People were still talking about the daring appearance of the UFO in coffee shops, markets and almost every where when they meet, even strangers will join in the conversations when the word 'UFO" is being mentioned. The news was mentioned but only briefly on all TV and Radio stations and that was a disappointment to those who had witnessed the sensational phenomenon. At about 10 p.m., Albert dropped in Dr Looi's Condo.

"So, Albert, any thing new? There was no more UFO sighting, right?"

"Yeah, and I have done some research myself and I dug up some very interesting facts."

"What did you discover?" asked Dr Looi, very curious to know.

"Before I tell you what I had found out, let me ask you something first. Were you disappointed with the way this was handled by the Press and the Government?" asked Albert.

"Yes! The Press was a disappointment in their very brief report and no word from the Police, Army or the Government at all."

"Correct! All of us felt the same way. In fact every Government has reacted in the same manner wherever UFOs were reported. But what I had dug up is even far worse and it happened in the USA!"

"Really? Now, what had happened in the USA?"

"In the Roswell Crash of 1947, the US government covered up the story but still it somehow leaked out that a flying saucer had crashed and alien bodies were recovered for autopsy. This is well known in the UFO circles."

"Correct." Dr Looi interjected.

"Now this is new and not many people know about it, so far that the former US President Dwight Eisenhower had a top secret meeting with Aliens and even signed a treaty with them?"

"What?" said Dr Looi, in great surprise.

"Yes! And here are the details. In the early hours of February 20th, 1954 while on vacation in Palm Springs, California, he was whisked to a secret meeting in Edwards Air Force Base. The whole Nation was told that he had an emergency dental treatment and the Government even produced the dentist who treated him at a function later.

When the President was missing, it was speculated by the Press that he might be ill or even have died, hence his Press Secretary had to allay the fears by announcing his dental emergency. However many journalists were sceptical because the President's vacation was hastily announced and he went missing for several hours purportedly for emergency dental treatment. Then a certain Gerald Light became a whistleblower and in a letter claimed he was part of the delegation who accompanied the President in a meeting with Aliens. He described the panic, emotional impact and utter confusion to all those who were in attendance. He believed an announcement would be made and he thus jumped the gun by making his own statement. Of course no such announcement was ever made.

He mentioned some other names of those who were allegedly present with the President. One was Dr E. Nourse, economic advisor to the Government, to gauge the economic impact this may lead to. Cardinal James Macintyre, head of Catholic Church in Los Angeles was there to represent a Religous point of view and another member was Franklin W. Allen, a former senior reporter, to represent the Newspaper communities.

Another whistleblower was William Cooper of Naval Intelligence who had access to top Government documents and disclosed that a prior meeting had occurred and the meeting at Edwards Air Base was a planned one with an Agreement already worked out for signing."

"This is just too much for me!" declared an amazed Dr Looi.

"Wait, there is more that I found out. Before meeting with this group of Aliens, believed to be those from a red planet called Betelguse in the Constellation of Orion, and these are the big nosed Greys, another group according to Cooper, had warned the US government about signing any Agreement with the Greys. This group, more humanoid-looking, had warned about our being on the path of self destruction, that we must stop killing each other, stop polluting Earth and live in harmony. They had demanded that US dismantle their nuclear weapons and said that they will not exchange technology but instead focus on spiritual development as a condition for meeting. The US however did not want to comply with these conditions and these Aliens were never heard of thereafter.

Originally the US government had planned a slow release of information as regards their meeting with the Greys but it was soon apparent that many of the conditions in the Agreement signed had been violated many times, especially in the case of forceful abductions of humans by the Greys that amounted to millions. It was due to this embarrassment that no disclosures were ever held."

"Well done, Albert! Your account had filled up a missing link." commented Dr Looi.

"What is it?"

"There was a theory about President Kennedy's assassination was due to his intention to disclose about Alien contacts!" Albert was dumb struck.

They talked a bit further and when Albert noticed a storm was brewing, he decided it was time to go and left.

CHAPTER 19

When the local press were not reporting in full the several sightings of UFOs in the Northern states of Penang, Kedah and Kelantan, many went to the internet to look at the foreign news which gave a much wider coverage and details, with interviews of those who had sighted them and even videos were uploaded by those who managed to catch the phenomenon. It really made the authorities looked childish in trying to downplay the mass sightings. Internet chats, coffee shop talk and housewives' tongues were wagging non- stop on this mass sighting of UFOs.

International News also reported on several UFO sightings in several parts of the world a few days later, in Vietnam and China. The latter country was more open and allowed their press to publish detailed reports of the several UFO sightings. To Dr Looi, it was a signal that the so called Galactic Federation had executed their plan of a mass appearance with the aim of disclosing their presence to humanity. Well, he hoped that it was the more benevolent Galactic Federation and not those that belong to the more sinister groups from Orion, that comprise the Greys, Archons and Reptilians and other more hostile alien groups.

The local weather had been very unpredictable, in fact bordering on being rather strange with gale force winds and heavy torrential rains. This led to several states in the country to experience unprecedented floods. Flood mitigating projects carried out years ago were just unable to cope with the deluge. Although the country was not affected by hurricanes or tornadoes, the winds were very strong and roofs were blown away, trees toppled and several landslides occurred throughout the country. Due to the scale of natural disasters, the populace had forgotten about the UFO sightings and concentrated on repairing their homes and bracing for more storms. Those not affected directly by the fierce storms were fearful after witnessing the ferocity of the storms that any time the destruction could land at their doorsteps..

In the midst of all this mayhem, Jatek the Aboriginal had led his small band of people to safer higher grounds a few weeks before the weather turned ugly. Keat had remained with the Tribe and blended well into jungle living and they seem to like him. He also proved to be very helpful to the tribe and contributed a lot of his energy in helping them prepare for the big move to higher grounds. Jatek had even given Keat an Orang Asli name and calls him Suntek. hey had prepared their new settlement well, with new makeshift huts that were able to keep them dry and cozy.

Jatek looked up at the dark skies and said, "It is so lucky we moved well ahead in time. This weather will not be gone for several more days, in fact, it can be worse!"

"That is why you are our leader!" replied Som, his wife.

"With the heavy rains, it will be next to impossible to walk in the jungle!" added Keat. With his mobile phone battery dead and no power source to recharge the batteries, Keat is now non- contactable to the outside world. He is more lean and has a darker complexion now and is as quick footed as the next Temian. His hair has grown long and he looks really like a jungle man while remaining rather handsome. Keat now has somewhat of a hero status in the tribe because one day he rescued a young Temian boy of 6 years from a wild boar attack. The wild boar, one of the most dangerous animals in the Malaysian jungle, suddenly appeared from the bushes and came charging at the boy. Keat who saw the danger the boy was in, quickly managed to push the boy out of harm's way by inches. Keat managed to shout for help and some of the Temian men came to the rescue and managed to kill the wild boar with their weapons.

"Yes, even hunting and gathering our food will be next to impossible as long as the heavy rains continue. But we are well stocked with food," added Som, looking lovingly and so proud of her husband. Keat nodded in agreement. He has blended well into the jungle community. However ever since the tribe had moved much deeper into the jungle, they noticed many changes in their small community. The first change was that many more of their children from nine years old onwards had joined in their morning rituals. Usually these kids will be playing rather than joining the adults in the prayers. There were fewer petty quarrels among the adults and more cooperation in their daily tasks. This led to a very conducive environment that radiated more happiness among the tribesmen and women. There was more laughter and more smiling faces everywhere. Many of them too noticed that they had developed a heightened sense of taste while others reported to have a more acute sense of hearing. Still others were surprised they could see vivid colours of the human aura.

Quite a few had complained of dizzy spells, tingling sensations over their bodies or having vivid and lucid dreams. But the dizziness was temporary and soon disappeared. Everyone seemed to be healthier too. Many minor ailments likes body aches, pains and headaches disappeared. The Elders had noticed these changes and consulted their shaman, who was not as puzzled because he had felt that some positive energies were evident in their new village site and explained that what he called the 'Golden Light' was strong in the area and that is why they were experiencing the phenomena.

Unknown to Keat, Hassan has managed to obtain very important leads in his investigation into the robbery at Wing Onn goldsmith shop.

It was the taxi driver who took Keat to the spot which leads to the Orang Asli Settlement. In all his 18 years as a taxi driver, Syed

Arrifin had never had a request from anybody to go to the remote place where the Orang Asli Settlement is. So naturally he had a good look at the stranger and when he saw Lim Ah Keat's police photo on TV and news papers, he contacted the nearest Police Station. The diligent officer there made contact with the Police HQ in Penang. It did not take long for Inspector Hassan to be informed and to travel to Rompin to meet the taxi driver and interview him. The police dragnet is closing in on Ah Keat.

Hassan left Penang with his team of Police Officers that included Mustafa and Sobri. When they left Penang, it was in heavy rain and many roads were having some flooding, but nothing of a grand scale. He was surprised that it was also raining heavily in Rompin. Hassan got to work immediately when he was at the small Police station in Rompin by interviewing the taxi driver to get more information. It now seemed to Hassan that it was difficult terrain to track Keat down as he is wandering with the aboriginals and no one in Rompin knows how deep into the jungle the aboriginal's settlement was. What the public sees near the roadside was just a temporary shelter where the aboriginals display their jungle produce for sale. And the rain went on unabated, making the hunt more difficult and perhaps even dangerous.

Back in Penang, Kim Heng and his boys were busy towing cars that had got stuck in flooded streets like Rope Walk, Jalan P. Ramlee and Jalan Thean Teik. They had not seen anything like this before, the almost non- stop rains that pelted the island. Flooding is even made worse when the tide is high as the waters meet the incoming tide and drainage is thus compromised. Luckily so far there were no reports of any drowning cases, unlike in Kelantan state. There the victims were both young and old, being swept away by the swift and swollen rivers as they either played near the river banks or while crossing with their small boats.

It was almost 5 p.m. but because of dark clouds and the rain, it was like night is descending upon them. It was really an exhausting day for Heng and the boys and they had not eaten any lunch even.

"What is happening to the weather?" complained Ah Boey to Heng. He was totally drenched, cold and hungry.

"Ask your grandmother!" replied Heng for he doesn't have the slightest clue.

"Even my grandmother has not seen freaky weather like this before!" interjected Mokhtar. They all burst out laughing and that was the only joke of the day. They each went back to their homes but none was in a good mood although it was a good day of earning commissions from the many cars they had pushed, towed and saved. Although exhausted, they were all deep in thought. So far none of their houses were affected in the flooding but as the weather still didn't look good, they all wondered if they too would have to face the dreaded floods themselves.

The freak weather had kept Dr Looi and his nurse Alice busy with patients needing treatment for coughs and colds, cuts and bruises sustained from falls and motor vehicular accidents on the wet and flooded roads, diarrhoea from drinking contaminated water and a myriad of other complaints. This kept Dr Looi away from his hobby of researching more about the UFOs. His mind is also kept occupied about the fear of his clinic being flooded at the rate the wet weather is going on.

Danny had more than bad weather to worry about as he had not found a job or a new business to start and his savings looked like they will not last long. He got involved in a scheme that promised quick returns of investment and it looked like a very good deal. It has something to do with investments in a joint venture involving New Zealand cows and milk production. Unfortunately after a few months it looked as though the high returns would not materialise. His friend who introduced him to the scheme had been avoiding him and not returning all his calls. This had put a strain on his relationship with Linda who had marriage on her mind. Poor Danny, he has to think of something fast, the least is to get a job.

Luck was smiling down on Hassan because finally, after so many days of rainfall, the sun broke out and the drizzle evaporated away. Time to act fast, thought Hassan. In fact the wily Inspector had not wasted time during the rains but had contacted and assembled a team to track Keat down. Apart from Mustafa and Sobri, he had permission to get the help of trackers from the world famous Sarawak Rangers, an Army Battalion from Sarawak State of East Malaysia that have the native Ibans in their crack tracking team. They were brought in from Kuala Trengganu. The hunt begins.

CHAPTER 20

The Police jeep dropped Hassan and his team at the spot they knew would lead to the nearest suspected Orang Asli outpost. The team, now comprising three policemen and another three Rangers who are expert trackers all had backpacks with life support that can last them up to a week. The trackers had also brought along the Army radio telecommunications to be in touch with their Head Quarters as there were no mobile phone signals deep in the jungle. They all had their standard Police or Army issued fire weapons. The Rangers carried 2 tents and wore their Army outfits while the policemen wore civilian clothes.

They had started very early in the morning for many reasons—the most important being that the less the public come to know of this Operation Code named "Orang Utan", the better and besides they needed many hours of daylight to do the trekking. Although the rain had stopped, the jungle track was partly flooded, slippery in many places and the urban policemen had a hard time keeping up with the Iban Rangers from Sarawak. This slowed the team down considerably. Ibans were the former headhunters in the jungles of Borneo. They were feared warriors of the jungle. Today many of their men have joined the Rangers to serve the Nation and are natural jungle warfare experts. They are also well known for their loyalty and bravery. So this Team is a formidable one, they are bound to get their man.

Although they had food provisions in their backpacks, the Iban Rangers will collect edible jungle fruits and roots as they go along. Soon Hassan and his subordinates followed suit. They knew their provisions would last 3 days into the jungle and they will have to turn back by then if they had not collected extra as it will take another 3 days to get out. This leaves only spare rations of one day, which is not a comfortable margin. Thus the Rangers were preparing for a long haul until they get their target. This pleased Hassan very much. Ranger Joseph anak Johan was the leader and the most experienced. He had his two assistants – Ranger Robert anak Juga, who is very stout in his build and full of Iban tattoos over his body. The other was Ranger Mike anak Sam. Mike was slim and looked more like a Chinese because of his Chinese ancestry. These Ibans were all third generation Christians.

Their plan was to reach the suspected Orang Asli settlement according to what the Orang Asli Affairs Office had in the old records. They hoped to get further information from those that live there. It was the only lead they have. The hike was difficult even for the experienced Iban soldiers, made worse by the struggling policemen, who were also not as physically fit. The mosquitoes and leeches seemed to attack the policemen more than the soldiers.

The posse had to clear away jungle foliage to make almost every inch of the way and this puzzled the Ibans because if the Orang Asli were nearby, there must be some sort of a cleared path from their frequent use. However the other possible explanation would be that from the almost one week of continuous rains, jungle foliage could grow very fast or that the aboriginals were sitting out the rains.

The Ibans indicated that they were making camp at a specific spot as it was getting dark soon. Due to the overcast skies and thick jungle canopy, it gets dark by 4 p.m.. The policemen were only too happy to rest their aching bodies. They settled in for the long night in their tents. It was cold in the jungle and the policemen found it hard to sleep, tired as they were. It is the first time they had spent a night in the jungle.

The next morning the Iban soldiers woke up the three sleeping men. All three of them had only fallen asleep near dawn, so they only had a few hours of sleep. After a quick breakfast of tea and biscuits found them clearing camp, the hike is on again. The Ibans made sure their camp was cleaned of anything that would give away their presence.

It was good weather now and Jatek led his people to collect fresh jungle produce of wild tapioca, fruits and edible plants. Although they had ample supply of dried food, collecting fresh fruits and edible plants and herbs will extend their supply longer. So they too had set out early with their woven baskets and this time even the women and children were allowed to follow. It was indeed a merry affair, with the kids running around and babies still being carried piggy back tied to the sarong support or breast feeding. The men were in front but the rear of the group which was walking in a sort of single file was being guarded by two males, who happened to notice that the jungle birds and macaques were rather silent for the last 10 minutes, which was out of the norm. They thought perhaps they were in a large and noisy group thus it frightened the jungle birds and insects.

There was a lot of talking and playful banter when all of a sudden it was broken by some screams from some where in the middle of the group. This broke the serene atmosphere and everyone stopped for a moment but the rear guards recovered from the shock and were among the first few who ran to investigate. They arrived almost at the same time as Keat, who also sprang into action when he heard the screams.

What they saw was shocking. A jet black panther was mauling a 14 year old boy named Akun, who was fighting back the animal with his bare hands. Keat, who arrived just a few seconds ahead of the two guards, began to hit the panther with the stick he had but the animal ignored the blows and sink its teeth into Akun's left shoulder and shook the boy up and down as it did so. The big cat had wanted to sink its teeth on the boy's neck but at the last moment Akun managed to swerve his body in the nick of time and the panther's jaws landed on his shoulder. This quick reaction saved the boy's life as the jaws of the powerful animal could have broken his neck.

In the next few seconds, one of the guards took out his blow pipe, inserted a poison dart and took careful aim at the panther. He could not shoot the dart because it might hit Akun or Keat. Then the second guard took out his dagger and went in to the rescue. He stabbed the panther a few times. By this time Keat's stick had been broken by the hard blows he gave to the panther and Keat threw the useless stick away and tried to open the big cat's jaws that had locked so hard on to the boy's shoulder. Sensing it was being outnumbered as more of the men arrived, the panther released its jaws, gave a huge leap and disappeared into the jungle foliage.

Akun was lying on the ground, covered in blood all over his upper torso and writhing in pain. Jatek and Keat took a closer look at the wounds and what they saw was an ugly sight. There were deep fang marks with lacerations over the left shoulder and claw marks over the left cheek and numerous other places on the hands and fingers.

They had to think fast as the boy was bleeding. While the rest were all talking and discussing what best needed to be done, Keat tore his shirt to pieces as a makeshift bandage and began to bandage up the wounds as best as he could. The others did the same as they knew more bandages were needed.

"We will need to take him to the hospital!" exclaimed Keat to the others.

"I will make some herb mixture first! This will help stop the bleeding at least. Give me a few minutes to collect the herbs!" their Chief and shaman said, and he disappeared into the forest. By this time Akun's parents were by his side and giving him some water to drink and trying to comfort their traumatized son. Jatek moved the crowd further back to give space for the rest to attend to Akun.

While awaiting the herbal paste to be made, the other men went to look for two strong branches to build a makeshift stretcher. The Chief came back within 15 minutes with a bunch of herbal leaves known to him that will help stop the bleeding and infection and proceeded to make a paste out of it and in no time the wounds were re-bandaged with the herbal medicine.

Keat volunteered to accompany the boy to the hospital, a good five days' journey from where they are. He told them he had to accompany them as he knew the 'civilised' world better than them, especially in dealing with hospital admissions and the sometimes seemingly rude staff. Jatek nodded in agreement. They had picked two other strong volunteers to carry the boy on the stretcher. The others gave the parents some of their emergency food supplies and water cans as the boy will would need his parents by his side for moral support. Keat will risk being arrested should the police recognise him but still he had to do his part as the Orang Asli had accepted him, a total stranger, into their community.

This small party of five and the injured boy set off and Jatek wished them a fast and safe trip to the hospital in Raub. Since the panther is now a threat for any human as it had attacked the Orang Asli boy unprovoked, and could have been injured by Keat, Jatek gave the order to hunt the animal down and he sent three of his best hunters to track the big cat. The hunters knew they had to bring back the carcass of the animal before they can go back to their village. The rest of the group will continue in their original task of collecting food and jungle produce like honey, rattan and other items useful for them. They can not lose the opportunity of good weather by abandoning their original plans. So the group has now broken into three smaller bands, each with its own mission.

They proceeded at a trot, the strong stretcher bearers were sure footed as well as fleet footed. They had a long journey ahead of them. The aboriginal boy never cried but his eyes betrayed his fear. When the terrain was difficult, they slowed down, especially when there were slopes and small hillocks to climb. At times Keat volunteered to relieve one of the bearers and so did the father of the boy. It was a tough journey. They intended to carry on until nightfall.

So far the boy had not developed any fever but one can never know, the Orang Asli were aware of the dangers of animal bites as a few of them had succumbed to animal attacks over the years and not all survived their horrific wounds even with the best of care. Finally it was time to make camp as night was fast creeping in. They had pushed to the very last moments before nightfall. All were exhausted and they made just a simple camp with a small fire and slept in the open, Keat volunteered to do the first watch, to allow for the others to have a longer rest as they had carried the stretcher most of the time. Dinner was just some dried meat and cooked tapioca root.

CHAPTER 21

Although Hassan and his men found it difficult to keep up with the Iban soldiers, they some how tagged along quite well and soon the Ibans signalled that they must be near the Aboriginals 'settlement. The policemen couldn't see anything and wondered how the soldiers knew. They went silently. In fact, the Ibans had spotted old tracks left behind by the Orang Asli and in an hour, they spotted the abandoned village.

'There is no one!" whispered Ranger Joseph. They looked at each other in amazement.

"How did they know we were coming?" hissed Hassan, full of disappointment in his voice.

"These Orang Asli! They have supernatural powers!" said one of the policemen.

They went to explore the abandoned settlement. Soon the soldiers said it was strange that they had left many weeks ago! It was even more puzzling. They looked at each other in a bewildered manner. How did the Orang Asli come to know of the Police party weeks ago? Or did they abandon the settlement because of some other reasons? The Iban trackers immediately went to look for tracks that would lead further on their search for the Orang Asli.

"Boss, how much deeper do we have to go into the jungle?" asked Sobri, looking worried.

"Don't know, but we need to go wherever it takes to get this man," replied Hassan, with an even more determined look.

Mustafa noticed the Ibans signalled them to follow and alerted the other two men. They hurried to catch up with the Iban trackers, who had located tracks that led to another direction and looked likely to be leading the whole community away to a new place. To Hassan it seemed there were no tracks left behind but he trusted the Ibans. They forged on.

By this time the hunting party for their part had been following the tracks of the wounded panther but had yet to catch up with the animal. This could only mean the animal was not badly wounded and still very fit. Soon it dawned on one of the hunters, Adek Tun, that it seemed the panther was tracking the party with the wounded boy! This was because the tracks were heading out of the jungle and most big cats would have rather escaped into deeper jungle. The others thought it was too early to tell since they had not found any of the tracks of their friends and maybe the animal might even turn away later. But they kept the suggestion of Adek Tun in mind. They had to hasten their tracking, just in case.

Keat felt the forehead of Akun, the wounded boy and he felt it rather hot, so some infection had developed in spite of the herbal concoction. They had better put more speed in their journey to the government hospital. The look in his eyes told the others the bad news and they put their best efforts into getting help for the boy fast. There will be fewer stops for rest now. The boy's mother gave him more water to drink to keep the fever down. Akun's father and Keat took turns to relieve the stretcher carriers more often, to keep up the speed. They pushed on until it was too dark to continue and they all rested their tired and hungry bodies. Akun's fever is now making him weaker and his appetite is gone. Septicaemia is developing, thought Ah Keat. Tired as they were, it was difficult to sleep for all were worried about the boy. It will take another 3 days and Keat hoped that if they are able to maintain today's pace, they might make it earlier. Something was bothering Keat, but he told no one. In the last few days, he had very disturbing dreams. In the dreams, he felt so aware of things that it was as if he was not dreaming at all! He could see so many things in great detail, and even seemed to have some control over the dreams, especially where he wanted to go or who he would meet in the dreams. It was surreal. More than this, even during daytime and while carrying the stretcher or just following the Asli ambulance party, he would suddenly have flashes of memory coming back. It was the memories that troubled him the most.

He remembered about his previous lives. In Egypt he had been a lowly slave worker in the time of Tutankhamen. It was a hard life. In fact flashes of another life earlier on in Atlantis also came back to him. Then he was a geneticist experimenting with the creation of abnormal life forms. However the most disturbing past life remembered was as an Alien! And it was not only this, it seemed to him, his brothers and sisters (from that time?) were now trying to make contact with him! His memories are coming back fast, his name is Votek, from the Pleides Star System. He wondered whether he was going mad from the many months in the jungle.

He remembered he had agreed to be incarnated as a Human with a certain mission. However, try as he would, he could not recall what the mission was. That is, if he believed he is actually Votek. At the moment, he feels his mission is to seek medical help for Akun, even at the risk of being arrested by the Police. He also somehow was given the impression that his other mission had failed due to his wayward life and that his Star relatives had wanted to call him back to re-evaluate the situation. Keat was thus very confused and disturbed by these revelations.

The Ibans were getting excited, one of them, Ranger Mike, had picked up some solid trails of the Orang Asli which they believed would lead them to their new settlement. In their excitement, they automatically went faster, leaving the policemen to struggle to keep up. However, Hassan was lagging behind further and further but he signalled his officers not to worry about him and asked them to catch up with the Rangers. He had painful toes as the damp had seeped into his boots and caused a blister to develop. It was not a lack of stamina as he was quite athletic, being an ex- Rugby player. Soon it was too painful to walk fast and he slowed down further and was trailing further behind until he was out of sight..

It was Akun's father who stopped the group in their tracks and signalled them to be quiet for a while. He looked puzzled and concerned at the signs he was getting. They all looked hard at him, trying to decipher the look. In whispers, he told them he could feel something was not right and told them to proceed slowly until he gave the all clear signal. Again the normal jungle sounds disappeared. Danger must be lurking somewhere. Keat had already drawn out his machete. They waited in complete silence, ears and eyes alert.

Then they heard the cries for help from a man far away and they looked at each other in surprise. Who could it be? Keat took one of the stretcher bearers along with him to investigate, leaving the rest to guard Akun and giving the instruction that if they did not return in two hours, to continue taking the wounded boy out of the jungle to the hospital. With that, Keat and Tobeng disappeared into the jungle foliage.

The cries for help became louder as they got nearer and to their amazement, they saw the panther attacking a Malay man. Keat slashed at the panther with his machete, accompanied by Tobeng. The animal however just continued to maul Hassan, who had his left arm in the jaws of the panther. Tobeng managed to drive his bamboo spear into the furious animal's chest, piercing its heart and killing it.. At the same time, a rifle shot rang out and a bullet hit the animal in the body. The Ibans too had heard the commotion and returned to help Hassan. They were so fast that they left the other two policemen far back. It was the sharpshooter Ranger Mike who shot the panther just it it fell from the spear of Tobeng.

Hassan was relieved that he is now out of danger but worried about his wounds. He looked at Keat and muttered a word of thanks. By now the two policemen had caught up and looked at Hassan's bloodied arm and body. Then they all looked at the two strangers, but mostly at Keat, because he really didn't quite look like an Orang Asli of these parts, although at a first glance, he did resemble them. Keat became uncomfortable, not knowing what to do now, but he had guessed they were looking for him. He quickly moved closer to Tobeng and whispered something into the latter's ear. Tobeng looked at Keat in disbelief and stood rooted to the spot. To break this awkward moment, Keat quickly shifted attention to Hassan, who was still lying on the ground moaning in pain and holding his injured arm. It was bloodied.

Keat tore up his own shirt to make a bandage and proceeded to bind up Hassan's bleeding arm, all the time avoiding eye contact. Hassan was too worried about his injuries and shocked by the turn of events to think of anything now. Keat then made a sling to rest Hassan's badly mauled arm.

"You will need to be taken to the nearest hospital as soon as possible." Keat said to Hassan, in the Malay language, without looking at his face. By now Keat's accent is almost like an Orang Asli. Hassan just nodded his head. Ranger Robert was looking hard at Keat. He thought although this man sounded and looked like an Orang Asli, something about him made Robert a bit suspicious. He thought Keat was too tall for an Orang Asli and his features also did not look quite like one of them. This puzzled looked was caught by the sharp eyed Tobeng, who now knew the gist of Keat's background.

"Can you walk?" asked Keat to Hassan, trying to break the silence and hoping none of the armed men would question him. "We need to take you to hospital now'. He helped Hassan up on his feet as Hassan was struggling to get up. The other two policemen also lent their helping hand to their injured boss. Hassan was able to steady himself and walked a few steps to test his own strength.

"Careful, Boss," said Sobri. Hassan was quite unsteady on his feet and Sobri held him.

"You are bleeding, Boss," chipped in Mustafa. Indeed blood was oozing out of the bandage that Keat tied.

"We better make a stretcher to carry your boss, he will not be able to stand the journey out of here on foot," suggested Keat to the two Policemen. Sobri and Mustafa looked at each other.

"So the Police Force never taught you how to make a stretcher?" said Keat sarcastically as he went to look for suitable branches nearby. Tobeng immediately took the chance to help Keat. The Rangers and Policemen gathered closer together in a close circle.

As Keat and Tobeng were cutting down a strong branch, Keat whispered to Tobeng.

"Tob, listen. If any thing happens to me, you ran and look for our group carrying Akun and make sure Akun gets to hospital. Later only let our people know. Do not worry about me. Make sure Akun gets treatment, OK?"

They then finished what they had set out to gather and made their way back to the group. All eyes were on them. However Keat and Tobeng continued with making the stretcher silently, tying the branches across the two larger branches for the jungle-made stretcher, using vines as ropes. They worked silently and in a matter of minutes, the stretcher was ready. Keat signalled to Hassan to lie on the stretcher.

"What is your name?" asked Ranger Joseph, looking straight into the eye of Keat. There was complete silence, but the jungle sounds continued as before but more distinct now due to the human silence. All eyes and ears were on Keat.

"Why do you ask?" replied Keat without any signs of fear.

"Just answer the question." said Joseph. Both men are staring at each other now.

"I am Suntek.."

'Don't lie!" interjected Joseph.

"...to the Tribal people here. To the outside world, I am Lim Ah Keat," replied Keat.

There was silence, the Rangers and Police looked at each other.

"Then I must arrest you," said Inspector Hassan, almost in a whisper, for he finds it hard to arrest a man who just saved his life. The Rangers pointed their rifles at Keat. When Tobeng saw this, he ran as fast as he could into the jungle in a flash.

"Leave him alone!' shouted Hassan to the others. "I will have to handcuff you," he said to Keat.

"Arrest me for what?"

"For the robbery you and your gang committed in Penang. I am sorry but I have a job to do,"

said Hassan apologetically.

Sobri took out the handcuffs and locked Keat's hands roughly behind his back.

"But first let's get you to the hospital." said Keat. The answer surprised all there. "You are about 2 days' trek from here to the nearest hospital and I suggest you get onto the stretcher as you are still losing blood."

Fast as he could, Tobeng backtracked his way to where they had left the group carrying Akun. Then he realised that he may have to alter his plan because the group would have moved on without them as ordered by Keat when they did not return within the stipulated time. So he changed direction and tried to intercept the group heading towards the town. There will be no rest for him until he catches up with them.

Meanwhile the Policemen and Rangers took turns to carry Hassan on the stretcher. Keat followed with both hands handcuffed behind his back. Lots of things were on his mind, but not the idea of escaping because somehow he had changed tremendously. He is more calm and has managed to control his hot temper. He also noticed that almost all of a sudden, he has more knowledge about his past lives, Universal Laws and Human history. He just seemed to know and he could not explain this phenomenon He accepts the fact that he had committed crimes for which society needs to punish him and he will meet his fate. That was why he had not been afraid to tell his full name to them.

Then Keat's mind wondered about the wounded boy, Akun, for he was very concerned for the him. A vision of Akun flashed in to his mind! He saw that the group had followed his orders, they took off for the hospital when he and Tobeng did not return after two hours and they had made good progress. The boy looked ill and had fever, being given water to drink every now and then by his parents. But Tobeng was not yet with them. The vision vanished as suddenly as it appeared. He was jolted out of this surreal experience by the detectives who shouted at him, ordering him to walk faster.

Although Keat had his hands hand cuffed behind his back, he was still as fleet-footed and was in better physical shape than the urban policemen, who had to stop several times and let the Rangers help with carrying Hassan's stretcher. The group intended to cover as much distance as possible before making camp for the night. The going was tough.

Tobeng did not stop to rest or eat but he travelled as fast as he could to try rejoin the group. Although he is a good tracker and knew the jungles well, still it would be an awesome task to try to intercept the group carrying Akun. Although this group was carrying a wounded boy, they were still very fast on their feet. He was thinking hard whether he would be able to do it as he had not picked up their trail yet, While he was thinking, he suddenly had a an idea flashed into his mind, or some thought was inserted t into it from outside. It told him to change direction and keep going to his left. He was puzzled, but also it seemed to have come from Keat. Tobeng, being an Orang Asli, did not question this but took the advice. And another image came to his mind- it was Keat's face and he was smiling, letting Tobeng know he was fine!

Indeed the thought was inserted by Keat, who now was using his new abilities of telepathic thought transfer and remote viewing. Ever since he was arrested by Hassan and his group and was being led out of the jungle, his mind had been free to think and he discovered he could do remote viewing. This enabled him to a locate Tobeng and see that Tobeng was heading the wrong way and quickly send him the thought of a change in direction. He was glad Tobeng responded, hence the smile. Mustafa noticed Keat's smile and he hit Keat on his right shoulder with the butt of his AR15 Assault rifle. It sent Keat flat on the ground. Hassan, lying on the stretcher, saw the act and shouted out at Mustafa, who answered that the criminal was being rude, smiling and thus ridiculing them.

"How can he smile unless he must be thinking something bad about the police and the Rangers!" said Mustafa in defence. Keat managed to get up on his feet again saying nothing. They plodded on trying to cover as much ground as possible before nightfall.

With the change in direction, Tobeng managed to catch up with the group carrying Akun but it was nightfall before he spotted the fire made by the group to cook some meal. First he smelled the burning wood carried by the soft jungle breeze. He knew they were near and like a tiger, he followed the scent until he saw a glimpse of the fire and headed in that direction. Tobeng was cautious not to be mistaken for a wild animal and risk being shot with arrows or impaled by the spears the group carried so he whistled a tune known only to the tribe. The group welcomed him and gave him some food cooked over the fire and Tobeng ate like a hungry animal. They waited for him to finish his meal and without prompting, he told them what had happened. There was a bit of discussion among themselves after what Tobeng told them.

Tobeng then directed his attention to Akun, who was sleeping.

"He is weak, and now has not much of an appetite," said Akun's father.

"How are the wounds?" asked Tobeng.

"Looks rather bad. He has a fever, too. We are leaving very early in the morning and can reach the hospital tomorrow."

"Then let us all get some rest."

CHAPTER 22

The three hunters, led by Adek Tun finally found the animal they were tracking, but it was dead. They examined the carcass and were surprised to see it had been killed by a spear and bullet as well. They recognised the spear as one of their men's but who shot it? They tried to read the tracks found around the animal and although it was very confusing, they came up with an accurate account. The hunters then tied the animal to a long pole to carry it and started the journey back to their main group. As they needed to relay the events that took place to their chief Jatek, they knew they had to hurry. In fact they virtually did not stop at all except for taking several five to ten minute breaks.

Adek Tun kept turned an eye towards the sky whenever the jungle canopy was breached, as he noticed dark clouds forming. This time it did not look good, something is brewing. It was his sixth sense that told him so. The others saw what was bothering Adek Tun and without needing to say a word, they all had the same idea- they had better hurry if they want to re- join the main group soon. Once the downpour starts, it will be very difficult to travel in the jungle. They thus increased their speed and would take fewer breaks.

Throughout the night there was thunder and lightning but not a drop of rain. The police team with Keat in tow had long made camp and they took turns to keep watch. However those that were supposed to sleep were bothered by mosquitoes, except the Ibans and Keat, who was still in handcuffs. His wrists were now bruised and sore from the friction of the handcuffs. But this was his least worry. In the quiet of the night, he focussed his mind on the Orang Asli boy as he was very worried for him.

Keat was surprised that the group had not rested and continued in their journey to get Akun to hospital. The group were really exhausted, he could tell by their faces and slower pace. Keat then raised his sight high above the jungle canopy and he saw the lights of the town not far away. He was delighted! Akun will receive urgent medical attention soon! A feeling of relief came over Keat and as he too was exhausted, he fell asleep, only to be jolted awake a few minutes later. He was not sure if it was a dream or some Voice was warning him indistinctly that there would be some kind of natural disaster by morning. Keat was confused. He looked around him and saw the others were now fast asleep, including the sentry. They were all overtaken by exhaustion and even the attack by mosquitoes was not enough to keep their bodies awake. Since everything looked so calm and peaceful, he went back to sleep.

It was around 6 a.m. when the party carrying Akun reached the small Government Polyclinic. Akun's father went to look for the staff in the empty clinic and found them sleeping in one of the rooms at the back. The rest of the party just slumped on the floor exhausted. One of the nurses stirred slowly from her slumber and when she saw the condition Akun was in, she became wide awake and went to phone for the doctor, who was sleeping in his own house. They had to wait for a further 45 minutes for the doctor to arrive. The young doctor then examined the boy and decided to send him to the General Hospital in Raub, a bigger town, as he needed specialist attention, and the staff arranged for an ambulance. Only Akun's parents were allowed to ride in the ambulance while the rest of the party stayed on to rest before returning to their Tribe.

Keat was the first to awaken, as was his usual habit. His hands ached as they were still handcuffed behind his back. The others were still sound asleep and if he had wanted to escape it would have been easy but he decided not to keep running anymore and face his destiny. As he was reflecting on his life, suddenly he heard the Voice again and it was very clear:

"Votek…you must get to higher ground soon…there will be heavy rain, flooding and landslides… the same message is also relayed to Jatek, be alert for more messages later…"

Keat was still dumbfounded as to whom the Voice belonged, but nevertheless he was relieved that at least his Tribe will be safe if Jatek really had received the same message. He then looked at the morning sky and noticed dark clouds were gathering and shifting shape as well. The wind was starting to blow stronger, rustling the leaves of the jungle trees. By now the three Ibans had woken up. Ranger Joseph then woke up the rest of the group and within a few minutes they were all ready to continue their trek out of the jungle and bring Hassan to the hospital.

They were not gone more than half an hour when large drops of rain began to pour down and within a few seconds there was a torrent of rainfall. Despite the heavy rain and windy conditions, the men continued bravely on without a word. Keat was getting worried for their safety and as the rains got heavier, it reminded him of what the Voice had warned him, so he told the men it would be better to seek shelter on some higher ground fast. All of them really looked worried and each looked at the other for some sort of agreement. The winds howled loudly now and branches that were weak broke and fell around them. There was no need to persuade the group anymore. The men hurried to look for a safe place but in the dense jungle, it was like the blind leading the blind and with the heavy rains, it made visibility worse, and impossible to see almost anything.

The men were struggling with every step, even worse for those carrying Hassan, in the wet and slippery conditions. Pools of water were forming on the jungle floor and this could only mean that the downpour was really heavy and the surface water could not be drained in the usual manner. The Ibans and Keat knew this sign, and they were really worried. As Keat was still in handcuffs, he really found it hard to balance and fell down on numerous occasions, sustaining bruises on his knees and elbows.

It was apparent to Keat that the group would not make it out if they could not find higher ground soon. Keat thought hard, he had to do something to save himself and all the others. He noticed that the jungle floor was just starting to be waterlogged, and this increased his worry. They were still just wandering about, and nowhere near any higher ground.

Then a movement in the thick under growth caught Keat's eye, and he saw a jungle fowl with it's brightly coloured feathers. The bird flew up from branch to branch and perched each time, repeating this several times and it seemed to Keat it was a message to follow it so he shouted to the group to follow the bird. Although all of them were puzzled at the strange instruction, the Ibans were quick to understand and nodded their heads in unison.

Once they followed the jungle fowl, it flew from tree to tree at a faster pace but just enough to let the struggling group to keep up. Within an hour, they noticed they were struggling to follow the fowl as the gradient became steeper. Keat and the Ibans looked more relieved. Even now the other policemen understood it better. Then just as soon as they were feeling better, the fowl gave a cry and flew off into the dense jungle foliage and disappeared from sight. Keat knew that the jungle bird somehow knew they were going in the right direction and so had left them. The men continued in their struggle uphill as it was really tough, with mud, water and more rain, plus the weight of the man on the stretcher.

To their amazement, even a small deer and some snakes were seen hurrying in the same direction, with the deer overtaking them in a flash. Now Keat started to look worried again after seeing these wild animals hurrying to higher ground. This could only mean that something big is in store for them as animals have a sixth sense for danger. But what? They really had to hurry and so the group quickened their pace on their already weary legs. Keat was still in handcuffs and it was even harder still for him. Then he had an idea and asked for his handcuffs to be to be taken off so that he could help relieve them in carrying the Inspector. It seemed a reasonable and logical request under the circumstances and the policemen agreed after consulting with Inspector Hassan.

The party struggled on for another hour in the heavy downpour and now Keat was helping them carry Hassan's stretcher. They had a few more metres to go before the hilltop and they pushed on. Now even more animals were racing past them, a family of wild boars, foxes, mouse deers and the like. It took the men another hour or slightly more to reach a sort of plateau and they had to stop the ascent as they were all completely exhausted. It was high enough and they felt safer. All of them except Keat and Ranger Joseph were stretched out on their backs. The two fitter men looked around them from this vantage point to see what they could make out amidst the deluge that made even the wildlife flee. However due to the heavy rain, visibility was rather poor but they could at least make out the treetops. As there was nothing to note any more than the heavy rain, they too went to lie down but something caught Keat's eye. He stood up quickly and then he gave a yell, which alerted everyone and they all started to stand up to look, except Hassan, who was being weakened very much by the infected wounds

Far off on the blurred horizon, they saw a section of the trees topple down and disappear from view.

"Wow! A landslide!" shouted out Keat. The rest could only look in utter amazement and shock. They were beginning to feel unsafe and looked at each other. The wind was strong and rain kept falling heavily. It did not look too good. Heavy dark clouds blocked out the sun and no birds were seen flying at all. Keat was very quiet, thinking of his jungle family. Where were they and how safe was everyone, he wondered. Then he had a vision which showed him that they were safely huddled in their new place. Had they not moved from their original village, they would have been in serious trouble as it was too close to the river on low-lying land and must be terribly flooded by now. Keat felt better. He looked at Hassan who was very ill from the infected wounds and looked weaker than ever.

"Can I go look for some jungle herbs for your Inspector? He looks pretty bad. We will not get out of this place anytime soon. No, I won't run away."

The rest of them gave him a funny look.

"OK, one of you may accompany me, while for the rest, I suggest you go and build a shelter, start a fire and cook something. At least boil some rainwater." After a few minutes of silence, they looked at Hassan, their superior.

In a weak voice, Hassan gave out his orders, "What he said is correct, I am feeling very bad, with a fever and my wounds are getting worse. We don't know how long this storm will last. Sobri, you accompany Keat. And you Rangers can build a shelter faster and better than us policemen."

Thus Sobri accompanied Keat to look for jungle herbs and to gather some food if possible while the Rangers with the assistance of the other policemen went to make a small shelter. All the while the bad weather continued unabated.

Although Keat was looking for healing plants, he also kept an eye open for gathering some food. After wandering for almost 40 minutes, and leaving a trail of knotted branches behind to act as markers so that they would not get lost, Keat spotted a jackfruit tree with some huge ripe fruits. He told Sobri to help him bring one down and leave it on their trail to be collected on the way back, as these fruits are big and heavy. They also harvested some jungle *petai*, a long fruit with a hard covering but soft seeds inside. After another 30 minutes of wandering, Keat could not find any further edible fruits nor the required herbs for Hassan, and made the decision to return. At least he had some fruits for the party of wet, cold, weak and tired hungry men.

By the time they got back to the place where they had left Hassan and the others, the soldiers and policemen had built a reasonably adequate shelter. One of the soldiers had killed a snake and they were building a fire to cook it by roasting it over the flame. The skill of the Iban in getting a fire started in wet conditions was tested to the limits and now all eyes were upon them.. However, all were disappointed that Keat could not find any herbs to treat Hassan's infected wounds. Keat promised to keep looking as they went along the next day and they began to prepare for the long, cold, wet night. The Iban soldiers finally managed to get the fire going and they settled down for their jungle meal.

The men did not speak much, each of them thinking of their families back home and how glad they would be when they get out of this mess. Soon fatigue overcame all of them and they fell asleep. Little did these men know that although they are in the jungle and exposed to the storm, they were in fact far safer than anyone else in the cities and towns. It was a heavy downpour in Kuala Lumpur for the last 36 hours and serious flooding had occurred throughout the city. The capital reported flash floods after only two hours of downpour. Cars were stalled on the flooded highways, some even washed into the monsoon drains, people were stranded, the trains and LRTs were not plying anywhere and trees were uprooted by the strong winds. The Fire and Rescue Units were severely stretched and in the mayhem, many motor vehicular accidents occurred, adding to the confusion and casualties.

In the states of Johore and Pahang, landslides had occurred and severe flooding was almost everywhere. The Northern states of Penang and Perlis had, for the moment light rain only. However just across the Channel, Seberang Prai area had floods that were chest high especially in the more rural areas of Laboh Banting, Padang Menara, Paya Tok Akil, Desa Puri and Merbau Kudong villages.

It was not only Malaysia that had suffered. Many parts of the world had recently been experiencing abnormal weather conditions.

Further north, in China, torrential rains had caused heavy flooding in the Xinjiang Region damaging over 12,300 ha of crops and killed over 2,300 head of livestock plus the destruction of almost 300 houses. Economic losses were estimated at 104 million yuan. In Shanxi Province a hailstorm caused havoc and destroyed 28 houses, killing at least one person. Elsewhere, severe drought had been reported in Western Australia, with temperatures above 43 C. Forest fires were burning in great stretches of Western Australia and were last reported approaching the suburbs of Perth. Weather conditions had gone berserk all over the world. Only a few weeks ago, gale force winds lashed southern UK, and were billed as the storm of the decade. Wind gusts of up to 160kph occurred in Europe and in France 75,000 homes were without power supply. London's Heathrow Airport, Europe's busiest, had cancelled at least 130 flights and express trains between Central London and Gatwick and Stansted airports were suspended.

In areas where weather was more moderate, earthquakes had shattered their peace. The quakes registered from minor ones of 3 to a devastating 6.2 on the Richter scale – the latest being reported in Southern Alaska (3.1), Central California (2.8), Greece (3.6), Kermadec Islands, New Zealand (5.6) and Oaxaca, Mexico (6.2). So far none had occurred in the seabed and thus there had been no tsunami dangers as yet.

Volcanic activity too had been more frequent and dormant ones were getting active lately. None as yet caused any need for the evacuation of the residents nearby. The lesser known Zhupanovsky volcano recently erupted, throwing an ash plume 5 km high (16,000 feet). It is situated about 70km northeast of Kamchatka and it last erupted in 1959. The Sakurajima Volcano in Japan too exploded, sending ash and rock debris to an altitude of 5.4km but since then it had calmed down. Another volcano to watch is the Langila in Papua New Guinea. From satellite surveillance, it showed increased lava flows and a danger of full scale eruption.

A few days before, six other volcanoes erupted within a quite unprecedented twenty-four hour time period. This was happening all over the world, from Nishino-Shima island in Japan, producing a new island, to Mexico seven thousand miles away where the Colima volcano blew its top. In Guatemala another one oozed out lava. In Indonesia Mt Sinabung came back to life, causing panic among the villagers and in Italy Mt Etna rumbled and spewed out lava and rocks. The Yasur Volcano in Vanuatu gave out ash continuously causing a huge concern to the government and farmers whose fields were buried in volcanic ash.

The men and women of the jungle knew only of the heavy rain that was making their lives difficult at this point in time. How could they know of Mother Nature's wrath in other parts of the world? And with their. traditional way of living that took only from the jungle what they needed, how could they know that the rest of the world had infinitely more and worse problems than they did? Perhaps they were fortunate that their simple way of life was not yet affected by the increasing ills of modern society: increasing inflation, joblessness, greed of huge multinational companies that swallow up small businesses and crime rates soaring almost every where. What did the jungle folk know of large-scale robberies, carjackings, kidnapping, human trafficking, drug wars and murders? Inspector Hassan could have told them that nowhere can be considered safe anymore. And underneath all these lie racism, religious intolerance, extremism and rampant corruption so widespread that benevolent Aliens would hardly know where to start.

CHAPTER 23

Danny Ong could hardly wait to tell the good news to his girl friend Linda and so he reached for his

mobile phone and quick-dialled her number. And as is always the case when you have some urgent matters, he could not reach her as she was in a lift and there was no cell phone signal. It was frustrating for Danny. Nevertheless, he tried several times and finally her phone rang.

"Linda! Listen, I have very good news!" said Danny excitedly, almost shouting.

"Yeah? What is it?"

"I've been offered a job"

"Wow! That is great. What job is it?"

"Well, it was Johnny Santiago's contact who wanted a van driver to ferry the cigarette promoters to various outlets and it's a 9 to 5 job and pays well."

"Cigarette promoters? You mean those sexy sales girls?"

"Oh Darling, don't worry, I am just their van driver. Besides, it pays well and is such an easy job. Please!"

"Just testing you, Dear."

"Yippee! How about a celebration dinner tonight?"

"It's a deal. Pick me up at seven then"

Danny was overjoyed, as he could sense that Linda is being more receptive and perhaps now things will go smoothly for both of them. They both looked forward to an agreeable evening at the least.

Linda wore a bright yellow blouse with denims and she really looked stunning and she was ready even before Danny arrived. Danny boy came five minutes earlier than agreed. Like most young couples, they headed for a western food restaurant along Bagan Jermal road. They used to go for hawker food, usually by the road side, and Linda had no issues with that but tonight is special. As they were early, parking was no problem right in front of the stylish restaurant. Although the weather was fine, there was a stronger than usual evening breeze blowing. They hardly noticed it. They settled down at a table for two in a corner and ordered their dinner. Danny ordered Black Pepper Chicken while Linda opted for the Baked Fish.

Soon the Restaurant was being filled by many young couples as well as groups of teenagers. There were some families with their young kids running all over the place and grandparents walking slowly. However Danny and Linda were oblivious to their surroundings as they were engrossed in their own world. To them, the rest of the crowd did not even exist. The evening flew by fast and when they had finished their order, Danny asked for coffee for himself and a milk shake for Linda.

"Dan, when will you be starting your new job?" asked Linda.

"Oh, the HR man told me to report by this Friday for a short period of orientation and briefing."

Linda noticed Danny looking outside while answering her, so she asked 'Dan! What are you looking at?"

"Uh? I just noticed that the wind is blowing stronger outside and yet there is no rain."

Linda looked and saw the branches of the potted plants outside all swaying and shivering in the gusts of wind. The decorative lanterns at the veranda were swaying wildly.

"Linda, I think we better leave because I really don't like the look of this storm that for sure will be coming," continued Danny. So instead of waiting for the waitress to bring the bill, Danny went up to the counter to pay. Although their evening was rather cut short, Linda was still in a great mood as they left the restaurant and headed home, making it back safely to Linda's place and then Danny continued on his own drive back. By then it was beginning to rain cats and dogs and Danny was happy he had made the right decision. The night being rather early still, Danny decided to catch up on his DVD movies.

Albert had dropped in at Dr Looi's place, eager to discuss with the doctor about what he managed to find out about strange noises being heard in many parts of the world and other strange occurrences. As it had been quite some time since they had met up, the doctor was pleased with the visit from his old friend.

"So what is it that you said you have to tell me, Albert?"

"Doc, did you know of people reporting about hearing strange noises in many parts of the world?"

"Like what?" asked Dr Looi.

"Well, a sort of deep humming noise as heard in Canada. And also others in Europe reported about a machine-like chugging noise."

"No, this is news to me. Sure they don't have an explanation to it?"

"None whatsoever. They can't even pinpoint where exactly it comes from, and the place there has no factories or logging activities. Some geologists explained it as the vibration that resulted from some earth movements in the area but could give no further details.'

"This is strange," replied Dr. Looi.

"This is even more strange – it was reported that in San Diego they have found the carcass of a strange looking creature on the beach. It looked like a serpent, about seven metres long"

"Do you have a picture of this?"

"Yeah, wait a second while I open my iPad." After a few seconds, Albert showed the photo to Dr Looi. The photo revealed a very long dragon-like creature with an ugly looking head full of long filament-like tentacles. It also had some very large, sharply pointed teeth.

"Wow, what a creature. Have never seen anything like it before! Do you know anything more about this funny giant fish?" asked Dr Looi.

"It is found in very deep waters, mostly in tropical seas and they can grow up to fifteen metres in length."

'That is even longer than the arapaima of S. America, which is a river fish there. This must be the fish in the legends of sailors long ago about sea monsters that look like serpents that attacked them," said the doctor.

"Yes, and the modern legend is that when they are found, a huge undersea earthquake is bound to happen."

"Yeah?"

"There was another carcass found, also very recent, in the village of Villaricos in Spain, at the beach called Luis Siret Beach. This specimen was smaller, about three metres long," Albert announced.

"Do you know it's scientific name, Albert?"

"Yes...I have it somewhere here..OK, it is *Regalecus glesne*. So Doc, any news from your side?"

"Ah, yes! I was looking into the question of sun flares and I had dug out quite a bit of information. As you know NASA had reported about the increasing amount of sun flares of late. Luckily most of them occurred on the surface of the sun that is away from our planet and so not much interference can be felt. But by their calculations, they expect a huge sun flare to occur anytime soon and if by chance it is directly opposite our planet, then the solar storm created can cause a lot of damage to us," explained Dr Looi.

"How does it affect us?"

"Solar storms are electrical in nature and the blast will knock out first the satellites and thus all our telecommunications like cell phones, internet and GPS. Then our electrical grids system will be blown apart and so cause total darkness at night as there will be no electrical power. Depending on the damage and resources of the country concerned, it may take up to two or three weeks before some power lines are restored. And in that time, Banks, ATMs and all our electrical appliances will not work. As water pumps are needed to supply water to many high-rise buildings, there will be no water in the taps and our flushing systems will not work. In fact, nothing that needs electricity will work.."

"This is scary, Doc."

"Yes, I can imagine total mayhem all over. Food and water will be greatly sought after and within days all supermarkets will be ransacked by crowds and so you will not be able to get any supplies."

"And no telephone line, radio nor TV," added Albert.

"Also debit cards and credit cards are useless," continued Dr. Looi.

"Petrol pumps will not work, so cars will come to a standstill and airplanes can't fly and travellers will be stranded!" said a worried-looking Albert.

"People will be jobless as no work can be done, so lay-offs will happen, commerce will come to a standstill and the stock markets will close due to no trading being possible!" lamented the Doctor, and he added after thinking, "and some hospitals will have to suspend operations :think of the plight of patients!"

"So what do you suggest, Doc?" asked a worried looking Albert.

"I've been thinking that one needs to stock up on some essential supplies," replied the Doc.

"Like canned foods and stuff?"

"Actually I made a list of essential items to get, I mean I got it from the internet and made some of my own modifications. It's in my Notebook." And Doc got up to retrieve the list from his Notebook. Yes, he is still using the old Notebook and old hand phone with no touch screen, he doesn't think much of the iPads or smart phones of today. After printing a copy, he gave it to Albert.

"Here, take a look and see if you can improve on it. I had also just sent a copy to your email while printing it."

Albert took a long hard look without saying a word. The Doctor's list is as below-

ESSENTIALS:

Flashlight
Battery-operated radio
2-way radio or other form of communication (who gets the other end?)
Extra Batteries
First Aid Kit (one for your home and one for each family car)

WATER:

3 gallons of water per person, minimum, in a food-grade, plastic container.
Water purification tablets
Additional water for sanitation

FOOD:

Minimum 5-day supply of non-perishable food that requires no refrigeration or preparation and little or no water.
Dry cereal
Peanut butter
Canned fruits
Canned vegetables
Canned juice
Ready-to-eat canned meats
Ready-to-eat soups (not concentrated)
Quick energy snacks

SANITATION:

Disinfectant
Household chlorine bleach
Soap, liquid detergent
Toilet paper, towelettes, paper towels
Personal hygiene items
Cloth towels (at least 3)
Feminine supplies
Plastic bucket with tight lid
Plastic garbage bags, ties (for personal sanitation use)

CLOTHING:

Plastic garbage bags, ties
Rain gear
Sturdy shoes or work boots
Blankets or sleeping bags
Complete change of clothing and footwear per person

TOOLS & SUPPLIES:

Whistle
Aluminium foil
Mosquito coils
Compass
Paper, pencil
Plastic sheeting
Needles, thread
Signal flare
Matches in a waterproof container (or several lighters?)
Pliers, screwdriver, hammer

Plastic storage containers
Heavy cotton or hemp rope
Cash, traveler's checks, change
Map of the area (?)
Non-electric can opener, utility knife
Cell phone with charger (not much use unless solar-powered)
Mess kits, or paper cups, plates and plastic utensils
Tape, duct tape
Patch kit and can of seal-in-air for tires (but need stock of petrol if electric pumps are not working)
Toiletries stuff

FOR BABY:

Formula
Diapers
Bottles
Medication
Powdered milk
Baby food

IMPORTANT DOCUMENTS:

Important telephone numbers
Record of bank account numbers
Family records (birth, marriage, death certificates)
Inventory of household valuables
Copy of will, insurance policies, contracts, deeds, stock and bonds
Records of credit card account numbers and companies
Passport, Identity Card

FAMILY MEDICAL NEEDS:

Prescription drugs in original containers
Heart and high blood pressure needs
Denture needs
Extra eye glasses
Contact lenses and supplies

"Well, what do you think?" asked Dr Looi.

"It is impressive, you've covered almost all the essentials." replied Albert after a short pause.

"Can you improve on it?"

"It will take time to think and I shall let you know later, via email."

"Yes, and once the list is finalised, we should try to spread it to all our contacts."

"Good idea, Doc."

"A better idea is to get as much of this stuff as soon as possible ourselves! I've just started to get some lately. Actually there is yet another thing that worries me even more."

"What's that?"

"It's the MPR or Magnetic Pole Reversal." explained Dr Looi.

"I don't have the faintest idea about this!" exclaimed Albert excitedly. That is why Albert likes to visit the doctor as he always gets to know something new.

"You see, the Sun does this thing every 11 years, that is, the North Pole turns or flips 180 decrees to occupy the South Pole and vice versa."

"So what's the big deal?"

'The big deal, my friend, is that our Earth too will do so anytime now. In fact there had been a very slight Pole shift already and aircraft GPS computers needed to be recalibrated or otherwise the planes will fly off course and land somewhere else than intended."

"How do you know about this?"

"Well my cousin is a F16 Fighter pilot and he confirmed it."

"Pole Shift or not, it didn't seem to affect us."

"That is because it had been slow. But imagine if the Pole Shift flips suddenly."

"I see…" replied Albert, in deep thoughts. 'Then it's scary"

"Indeed. I just can't imagine what kind of a scene it will be like. I guess total chaos, total mayhem, Armageddon."

"What can we do, Doc?" asked a worried Albert, clearing his throat at the same time.

"Nothing! Nowhere is safe."

After a few minutes of silence between them, Dr Looi continued, "Maybe…prayers may help. That is the least anyone can do."

"You mean pray so that this MPR thing will not occur?" asked Albert.

"No, pray that it goes slowly and there will be minimal casualties because it is bound to occur."

Dr Looi made another cup of Vietnamese coffee for both of them as it seemed they are in for a long conversation. They both loved the Vietnamese coffee and Dr Looi had enough supplies to last for a long time as he bought a lot in his last trip to Ho Chin Minh City. Settling back into his favourite easy chair, Dr Looi continued.

"Now hear this, Albert. There is something even more mind boggling to tell you."

"With a new cup of coffee, I am ready, Doc."

"It seems that there are at least 12 holographic types of Earth in existence now."

"What?!" interjected Albert.

"Just listen because I myself am totally out of my league here. I am just conveying to you what I had found out. OK, where was I?"

"Holographic Earth"

"Yes, we have now 12 Holographic Earths in the lower Fifth Dimension. And a massive MPR has already occurred in two

Timelines of the Holographic Earth resulting in massive destruction and the loss of up to two billion lives."

"Whoa! This is too much." exclaimed Albert.

"You and I did not experience it is because it was not our destiny or karmic lesson, yet or ever."

"But things seemed to be like befor and everyone we know is still around. So how can 2 billion people have died?" asked Albert.

"That is why I say this is beyond even me. Anyway, to answer your question, it seemed that many had met their karmic destiny and their soulless clones are still around in the other remaining holographic Earths. Perhaps that is what it means to say that Humans are actually Multidimensional Beings."

"Doc, I'm getting very confused," and Albert sipped more coffee, presumably to calm his nerves to try to make sense what is being discussed.

"Actually what this is all about is the time for Humans to Ascend to a Higher Vibration to usher in the Golden Age and live in Upper Fifth Dimensional World along with Mother Earth or Gaia. The making of several Holographic Earths is one way to spare many souls the trauma of the MPR, culling those of low vibration each time. There are souls who are very recalcitrant in their ways who *for* their own good need to be removed and settled in a world of the old Third Dimension to live out their karmas, in a dog eat dog world," explained Dr Looi further.

'What is this low vibration you are talking about?"

"Low Vibration encompasses behaviours like hatred, anger, envy, jealousy, fear and deeds like rape, murders, robbery, kidnapping, drug dealings, corruption and so on., while Higher Vibration means clean in thought, words and deeds, as well as compassion, unconditional love and forgiveness. Being in a state of joy is also of a higher Vibration. Sadness attracts the negative energy and so is of lower Vibration."

"Does doing meditation help to raise our level of vibration?" asked Albert.

"Yes, it does. This is because when you are quiet in the mind, you make contact within where all the answers lie. Then you open up channels to re- connect with your Higher Self."

"Doc, I think it's time for me to leave and moreover I hear the winds howling outside and some rain too." said a tired Albert.

"Oh, how time flies. Sure, I'll see you out."

CHAPTER 24

For the men in the jungle, it was a horrible night as the rains never stopped and all were drenched and cold. Hassan was shivering not from the cold but due to his high temperature and he really did not look good at all. Sobri, one of the Policemen that went along with this group, now is also not feeling well, with a slight fever, body aches, running nose and bouts of sneezing with a typical coming common cold showing up. Stress and strain is now showing up among the men also. The Iban Rangers were tough, and they are several shades better off than any of the urban policemen, except with Ah Keat, who now has adapted well to a tough jungle life.

Keat then suggested that they try working on their radio transmitters to get help. The transmitters did not function because they were out of range or had become faulty in the wet, humid conditions. He told them he would try find some jungle herbs and this time he is prepared not to come back without any. This startled the rest of the group but when they looked at their boss, Hassan, now moving in and out of consciousness, they agreed.

"Do not worry, I will not run away from my crimes. I have to face my destiny but it will not stop me from doing an even more important task- to save the Inspector's life. I may be back before nightfall or even earlier if I find those herbs. Do not move away from this location or I may waste precious time in tracking you people. If you have to move to a safer site, leave a trail behind or some indications,' assured Keat. With that he disappeared into the jungle and the rest set about what needed to be done. All of them are beginning to look worried. This time Keat made a simple prayer in his heart, asking the Jungle Spirits to lead him to the healing herbs or reveal them to him and not keep them hidden from his eyes. This he learned from his Tribe.

Keat moved like a jungle cat, swift, sure footed and with both eyes and ears attuned to the jungle. He just allowed his instincts to lead him, unlike the last time when he used more of his human intellect, which led him nowhere near to finding the herbs. It was surreal: his body no longer feeling fatigued, he felt that he was floating effortlessly although it was more like gliding along. The rains came again but he could not feel them hitting his body.

It has now been three hours since Keat left the group. Ranger Robert tried to get some signal from the transmitter but to no avail. They were getting anxious, what if they can't get out fast enough to save Inspector Hassan? Will Keat return at all- even with no herbs? And their rations are fast disappearing. How long need they wait?

Keat kept moving and he just seemed to know where to turn or go, so he let his intuition do the work, not his brain. He became one with the jungle, he was with the Tao. And he seemed to get images in his mind's eye also – that Jatek and the rest of the Tribe are on safe grounds as the rest of the world is in turmoil. That he need not worry as he will be guided by his Star Family. Then, something caught his eye. Something like a ball of light to his left. He followed the light and then, right in front of him was a small, indistinct plant. He did not recognise the plant, nor recollect that his jungle friends had ever showed him it. Just as he stood there puzzled, he received a thought in his mind! It seemed to say, "I am here for your friend." What? Is he going crazy, a plant communicating with him telepathically?

"What do you mean?" Keat thought back.

"I will cure your friend of his fever," came back the message.

"But I don't know you- I mean my Tribe has never used your type in their jungle medicine"

"They have not known of our existence."

"Then I may use you? How?"

"Just take all my leaves and chew them."

"What will happen to you then?"

"I will re-grow."

"Then I thank you and the plant kingdom, the Spirits of the Jungle and all devas and angels that guide me, and take these healing leaves of yours! Thank you!"

Keat gently plucked the leaves off the little plant and put them safely into his trouser pocket and clasped his hands in thanks before he ran off. With renewed energy, he traced back his route and reached Hassan and his band in a little over two hours.

Ranger Mike heard some noise coming from the bushes and raised his rifle to take aim.

"Don't shoot!" shouted Keat, for the Ranger already had his finger on the trigger and had almost pulled it. Keat appeared from the bushes and dived to the ground as a precaution. They were all glad he had returned, empty handed or not, and luckily Ranger Mike withheld his fire.

"I've found the herb!" shouted Keat.

Many in the group gave a yell, they were very happy to know this. Keat went to work immediately on Hassan, who was getting weaker, running a high fever and just barely conscious.

"Inspector, you must chew this, it will kill the germs and bring your fever down!" said Keat.

Hassan opened his eyes and looked at the leaves in Keat's hand, then at all the others.

"Eat it!" almost every one said in unison.

Keat took the smallest leaf and placed it in Hassan's mouth who chewed it slowly at first and then a little faster. There were smiles on everyone's faces. Then Keat did a wonderful thing, he gave each man a leaf and asked them to help feed Hassan. Everyone gave a cheer, even Hassan managed a broad smile. Keat was very smart, he wanted each member of the Team to have a go at helping their Officer so that he will not get all the limelight to himself, and besides it boosts the morale of the men and gave Hassan reason to finish the leaves.

As the men were taking turns to feed Hassan with the herbal medication, Keat stood aside to take a breather and to consider the next move for the group. They are still about three to four days' hike from the town district hospital as they had detoured while escaping the flooded jungle plains. His mind then turned to Jatek and the rest, and when he did that, Keat instantly had a picture in his third eye. He saw that they were safe, but huddled together on higher grounds. And he saw that Tobeng and the group of Orang Asli had also joined up with the rest of the Tribe, so they had completed their mission to bring the boy Akun to the district hospital and even Adek Tun, sent to hunt for the wounded panther, had also returned to the Tribe. So they were all united again, he gave thanks to all the Gods of the Taoist pantheon for these blessings.

His thoughts were disrupted when Ranger Joseph came up to him and asked "When can we leave for the town hospital?" as if he was now in charge.

"Oh, I think the sooner the better, now that it is only a drizzle. How is the Inspector?"

"He looks slighter better already. The leaves must be doing their job now," replied Joseph.

"Good!"

"While you were looking for the herb, we had looked at our map and plotted out the best route to take us to the town," said Joseph in a much friendlier tone now. He is starting to trust Keat and thinks that this guy is quite OK, unlike many other criminals.

"That is good. Then you lead the way. Let's go!"

With better weather and renewed energy and enthusiasm, the men started their journey out of the jungle. Hassan's fever seemed to be abating, he looked more alert and less in pain. Sobri was still having a running nose and his body is aching more and more but he trudged on. Joseph was leading the way, with the map and compass in his hands, while Keat is helping to carry the stretcher.

They had gone for about two and a half hours when Keat heard the Voice again, "You are heading towards danger, turn to the left! Get out fast!" It jolted Keat out of his day dreaming. For a moment he was not sure whether to follow the 'advice'. Then he realised also that so far the Voice had never been wrong.

"Stop!" shouted out Keat. The party stopped in their tracks and all eyes were on Keat.

"I think we better turn left."

"What? Why?" asked Joseph, in surprise.

"We could be heading to danger if we go on this way." replied Keat.

"How do you know?" asked Mustafa.

"I…I just know it." Answered Keat, not wanting to reveal the reason for his sudden outburst.

"Hey! Remember you are a prisoner here, OK?" said Sobri, raising his voice.

They were now arguing back and forth and Keat was warned that they would put the handcuffs back on him if he insists on this. The policemen were just being cautious and suspicious. They felt they could not fully trust Keat yet. The three Rangers just kept quiet and out of the argument. Anyway Keat could give no good reason for suggesting the change of direction. For all they know, he could be leading the party into a trap as he knew the jungles well and then escape for his freedom. Keat knew he could not convince them and so he kept quiet but always keeping a look out for impending danger as this was the least he could do.

They continued, but you can sense that all of them are on the alert anyway. They had hardly gone more than two hundred metres when there was a loud sound followed by the movements of the jungle trees and other foliage. The men froze in their tracks as none could make out what was happening. However they could feel the ground trembling under their feet.

"Run! Run to the left!" shouted out Keat as loud as he could. "The ground is giving way!" The men reacted very fast and the four of them that carried Hassan struggled to keep pace together and it was not easy; Hassan was nearly jolted out of the bouncing stretcher as the men ran for their lives.

None of them dared to look behind but they could hear trees crashing down, the sound of tree trunks breaking and an eerie sound of earth movements. Keat was the last of the men to go as he stood around a few seconds more to see that they had all started running, so he was closest to the earth that was giving way behind him. Sobri was struggling to keep up with the rest, he was weaker and his throat was very dry and sore, plus a cough was also developing. He tripped on a dead branch and he fell flat. Lucky for him, Keat managed to scoop him up and they continued to run, with the earth giving way not more than two metres behind. Again, Keat had saved another life

After what seemed like eternity to the men, suddenly the jungle became quiet again, the huge sinkhole that developed behind them had stopped expanding. Feeling whatever the danger might have been was over, they looked behind them while still running and realised the danger was no more. They stopped to get their breath and try to make sense of what had happened. They were shocked to the core by what they witnessed. There was a huge hole in the ground, at least twenty metres in diameter and because it had swallowed up the trees, it must be at least thirty to forty metres deep. They looked at each other, their faces pale and sweating, in disbelief and many shook their heads. For a few minutes the men were quiet. Then Mike said, "What is happening? Oh, Lord!"

"We must get out of here fast!" shouted Robert, his face all tensed up.

"But how? I have lost the compass. It must have dropped while running." said Joseph.

"Now we are all done for!" cried out Mustafa. This got every one more worried than ever, except for Keat, who strangely, was very quiet. He seemed to be looking at the sky and far away in his own mind. The men then turned to Keat and noticed his strange behaviour.

"Lim Ah Keat! What's the matter now?" asked Hassan, who was sitting on the ground. Keat just waved his left hand at Hassan and put his finger of the right hand to his lips, signalling them to keep quiet. Every one now was all ears, trying to make out what Keat was listening for. They could not hear anything at all, just a quiet jungle and wind blowing and rustling some leaves. No animal, insect or bird sounds either. They were all puzzled, looked at one another and then strained their ears to listen.

Keat was actually receiving telepathic messages and visions. He was told that a Great Change is about to occur in the world, something like a Pole Reversal is taking place. He was advised to lead the small party in a certain direction to avoid more craters that will appear in many places in the jungle, and the direction was away from their intended path towards the nearest town. He then was given a vision of Jatek too leading his Tribe to another place for safety and he was thus reassured of the safety of his jungle friends. However Keat froze when his next vision was shown to him. He tried to blot it out of his mind but he couldn't. It was then he was shook out of his meditative state when Hassan shouted out his name.

"What…what is it, Inspector?" answered Keat.

"What are you listening to? We can't hear anything after the stupid earth gave way," said Hassan.

"Oh, I…..er….am looking for more signs of danger….and…for a way out of here. I've been with the Orang Asli long enough to be able to read what Nature tells us," replied Keat, keeping the visions to himself. How can he tell them the whole world is going to be topsy turvy soon?

"Well?" asked Hassan, who looked much better; the herbs must have been working their magic, or the excitement and near death experience they all had a moment ago had the adrenalin running.

"We must get out of here fast.." said Keat.

"Where?" every one said almost in unison.

"In that direction" Keat pointed East.

"But this will lead us away from where we are going!" protested Ranger Mike. There was a short silence as everyone except Keat looked confused.

"There is no choice, it is the safest direction to take," replied Keat.

"How do you know? How can we trust you?" answered Mike.

"I don't want to argue with you, but we better…" and even before Keat could finish what he intended to say, the ground shook again, accompanied by an eerie sound never heard before by human or animal ear.

"This way!" shouted Keat, and he grabbed one of the poles of Hassan's makeshift jungle stretcher. The rest of the men followed to get Hassan's stretcher and took off, allowing Keat to lead the way. They could feel the trembling grounds under their running feet.

As they ran for their lives, and with Hassan grabbing the edges of the stretcher poles with terror in his eyes, he was the only one looking in the opposite direction to those fleeing as his head was at the further end when his stretcher was picked up. Hassan saw another sink hole appearing within a few feet behind the last of the running and panicked men, Sobri.

It was amazing how fast they could run, while carrying Hassan, and in the jungle terrain. And the wonderful part was that none of them slipped in the uneven, wet and muddy grounds.

In the commotion, Keat was able to keep a calm mind, always asking for more advice from his unseen Guide. He was not to be disappointed, for he received a telepathic message to "turn right." Keat saw a small opening among the heavy undergrowth and used it. He was not a second too late as towards their left, a sink hole opened up without any warning and the bushes, shrubs and a few trees were all swallowed up. This time everyone witnessed it. And Hassan had the best vantage point of course. Keat had once again saved their lives and this should leave Mike with no more doubts about Keat's sincerity. The shell-shocked men continued running, their adrenalin was still pumping into their veins.

After struggling for another twenty minutes or so, Keat signalled them to stop. The rest were quite willing to do so as they were now feeling very tired but all were still worried as hell. The jungle again became quiet, only their heavy breathing could be heard. They discovered all of them were suffering from gashes and bruises to their bodies as they had rushed on through the foliage where exposed branches, thorns and prickles had cut their uniforms right through to the flesh. The tall grasses also contributed to tiny cuts all over, as the edges of the grass leaves were sharp. They were covered in blood in most places, and even their faces were bleeding.

Keat recovered his breath somewhat faster than the rest and then again he stood still, closed his eyes, hoping to get further messages. The rest of the men did not disturb him now. They now realised that their lives depended on this prisoner of theirs.

"I am not getting any messages now, nothing." said Keat at last. "Maybe we are safer for now."

"Are you sure?" Robert asked.

"Quite sure. But we shall move on in this general direction until I get some messages," replied Keat.

"Let us get our strength back for another five minutes," said Sobri as he sank down to the ground exhausted. The rest followed suit.

CHAPTER 25

Danny reported for duty early the next morning. Finally the rains had stopped in the early morning hours while it continued to drizzle in other places on the island. When he arrived at the Office, his new Boss Mr. Leong, was already there, although Danny was ten minutes early.

"Ah, you must be our new driver?" asked Mr Leong.

"Good morning Boss," replied Danny, happy he was early rather than late on his first day at work. Good impressions are important on a new job. Danny looked at the older man and noticed this Mr Leong was shorter than him but weighed much more, in fact he was rather round with a huge belly along with a rough voice.

"OK here is the list of Promoters and their addresses, so you pick them up and then you bring them to KOMTAR where we have a stall at the Doom. Then after their work, you transport them back, OK?" and Mr Leong passed to Danny the printed list of names and addresses.

"And here are the keys to the van."

"OK, Boss." Danny pocketed the keys and walked over to the van parked outside. He had to fetch eight girls and be at KOMTAR by ten o'clock. He sat at the driver's seat and put on his sunglasses but decided to take them off as it was very cloudy and besides he needed to study the list to plan his route. Having worked out his route, he started the van and looked at the fuel gauge, which showed the tank was only half full. Or half empty as some would say. He decided to get the fuel tank filled up first at the first petrol station he sees.

Danny looked at his watch to keep an eye on the time and by now he had fetched six of the girl promoters and two more to go. He seemed to have plenty of time still. The girls were very young, most were not over twenty- three and they chatted among themselves. All were well dressed and had their makeup on and looked pretty. No wonder, they were very successful in promoting the cigarettes.

As Danny drove to Mt Erskine road, it had started to rain heavily again. To make matters worse, the van's windscreen wipers were hopeless and ineffective, making visibility even worse in the pouring rain. Danny wondered if he should have tested the wipers before driving. Traffic too was bad as everyone was slowing down. Some stupid drivers would put on their hazard lights and this irked Danny very much. It would have helped if only the sidelights were on. Danny was heading towards Fettes Park. There seemed to be a jam now and he had no choice but to inch his way forward. He glanced at his watch and thought he might be late if this got out of hand.

Unknown to Danny, Fettes Park area was building up a flood of rising waters and motorists were crawling gingerly along the inundated roads. It was still pouring cats and dogs as they say. He switched on the radio to ease the tension in him but as usual the stupid banter of the DJ was very irritating to Danny and he switched stations over and over again until finally he switched the radio off. There were no CDs to play and he thought he would try to get the Boss to fix a player in future, or he would have to bring his own MP3 player next time.

The traffic lights turned green and when he noticed the cars in front of him edge forward slowly he realised there was some flooding ahead. The girls behind stopped their gossip when they saw the flood waters but only for a moment, and then they continued with their chatter, much to Danny's irritation. As he edged forward, the car ahead made the mistake of slowing down too much and that got the flood water to choke the engine and finally the car, an old Proton Wira, stalled. Danny gave out a short curse and some local swear words too as he slammed on the brakes while the chatty girls behind screamed as they were thrown forward. The girls were not hurt and to Danny's surprise, these cute and young Chinese girls also burst out in dialect profanities and Danny was not sure whether it was directed at him or the driver of the car in front.

As they sat in the van waiting for the car in front to restart, the rain became heavier and Danny noticed that the flood waters seemed to be rising, as he noticed currents being formed. He got very worried because he knew if the waters rose further and they got stuck, it would mean real trouble. He made a quick phone call to the last girl he was going to fetch to tell her of the situation and he was shocked to learn from Alice Chew that the front of her house was already flooded with about ten inches of water. Danny asked her to wait for further instructions while he phoned up the Boss. He learned from the Boss too that they were having a mini flood in front of the shop. He then made another phone call to Linda to tell her not to go to work as there was flooding in many places. He just got her in time as she was about to leave for work, not knowing the mayhem outside.

In the next instant, Danny saw the car in front being pushed by the flood waters and the water was up to the number plate. The driver, an old man, was seen trying to get out but was unable to open the door. And then Danny realised he too was in trouble. The chatter at the back of the van stopped and then turned to screams. They too were trapped in the van with the waters rising fast. Danny tried to open his car door and was unable to do so due to the water pressure outside, which by now was just under the door handle. He pressed the window button to wind it down and luckily it worked but stopped just a quarter way down as the electrical system was short circuited by the waters. He looked for something to break the window but there was nothing in sight. The girls at the back screamed even louder. He then decided to kick it but that too proved useless. Danny remembered about the head rest and he yanked it out from the seat back rest and used the two steel prongs and that was able to crack the window until he managed to break it enough for an adult to get through. Danny beckoned one of the girls to climb over to the front seat to get out of the van via the window on the driver's side while he went on to break the other window to create another route for a faster evacuation as the waters kept rising.

Scared as they were, yet the girls were able to scramble out via the windows and climbed to the roof of the van and that surprised even Danny, who was the last to get out. Many of them, in their haste, had small cuts from the window's broken glass edges. Danny was unscathed. While safe for a moment on the roof of the van, it was a frightening moment, and they saw the old man's car now almost submerged in the raging flood waters with him inside still struggling to find his way out of the car.

Then they saw three men swimming towards the partially submerged car to rescue the old man inside. It was Kim Heng, Mokhtar and Ramu. They knew of the floods and were there to make some money for their company, the car repair workshop. They knew there would be accidents and cars needing to be towed away when the cars got stalled in the flood waters. Nevertheless, after they spotted the trouble the old man had got himself into and saw that he would be unable to wade through the chest high flood waters even if he did get out of his car, they started to swim as it would get them to the car faster.

When they got to the car, the three men tried to open the door but were unsuccessful. Danny then grabbed the head rest he still was holding and jumped into the waters and swam to them himself. The strong currents nearly swept him off course but he struggled harder to get to them. Mokhtar saw Danny with the head rest and knew at once that was what they needed now and so he swam to get Danny, who was struggling. Danny was relieved that Mokhtar managed to get to him and together they helped each other to reach the others. The girls on the van's roof top then broke out into a cheer. Heng then took the head rest from Danny and started to break the car window to save the old man. He used all his strength and broke the window after three hard blows, making a gap enough for the old man to escape. The cheering squad, the Promoter girls were now shouting to encourage the old man to get out, but he was too slow and so Ramu grabbed the old man's hand and eased him out, helped by the others. Now they all stood on the roof of the old man's car, with the waters rising up every minute.

The men knew that they were all far from safety because the flood waters would soon cover the whole car and van. They would have to work out a plan fast. Danny told Kim Heng to help the old man struggle to safety while he would go back to the stranded girls and try to get them out of harm's way, so he asked Mokhtar and Ramu to accompany him in case some of the girls were too scared to swim or could not swim at all. Many other people had been successful in getting out of their stalled cars and they Danny and the others were the only stranded ones out there.

The plan was agreed and Kim Heng helped the old man to leave the almost submerged Wira. The old man held onto his side and they both swam to safety, encouraged by the spectators on the edge of the flood. Then the rest swam to the stranded girls. The men reached them with no difficulties, Ramu reaching first.

All the girls wanted the men to help them as they were too scared to swim out unaccompanied, and although they all knew some basic swimming they were gripped by fear. Danny knew it was useless to argue at this moment, as every second could change their situation, so he told the girls they would all be accompanied. This meant the men had to make two trips after Heng and the old man had made it safely.

Gingerly, like a slow motion movie, the first girl went into the flood waters closely accompanied by Ramu. When they were halfway out, Mokhtar encouraged the second girl to get into the waters, after asking her to take of her shoes, which she reluctantly did. This one was a good swimmer and Mokhtar needed not to do much but just swam beside her. Ramu was catching his breath and taking a few moments of rest before getting the remaining girls. Danny had a tough time coaxing the third girl to get off the roof of the van. The remaining girls too were encouraging their timid friend to do it. It was some time before she took the plunge and in her panic, she nearly went under the water and Danny had to grab her and used the life guard's method of towing a drowning person. Danny was glad he had learned this well as a part- time lifeguard in the Chinese Swimming Club in Tanjong Tokong. Thus one by one, all the girls were brought safely through. It was tough work and all the men were tired out. By then the van was totally submerged and the swift currents swept it away. The girls had been very close to a disaster had they remained at the top of the doomed van. Now all the girls were chattering again, lamenting their ruined clothes and make- up and their lost possessions in the van. None of them thanked any of the men who risked their own lives to save them. The old man was different, he thanked Heng and the rest of the men profusely. It is only then that the rescuers got to know each other.

"Thank you guys for helping out," said Danny.

"Oh, it's nothing." replied Heng.

"Luckily you had the head rest and let us use it to free the poor old man," chipped in Ramu.

"OK, now we need to go and see if any other people need help," said Heng.

"Good luck then. I have to be around these girls as they are still my responsibility. Keep in touch if you need my help anytime," said Danny. He had to memorise Kim Heng's mobile number as all their mobile phones were soaking wet and could not be used. Danny wished he could join these men but he was stuck with the girls. He watched as Kim Heng and his friends went to bystanders to get more information about the situation. They were engaged in serious information gathering to get an idea from several people about what had been happening.

Danny borrowed a mobile phone from one of the crowd that had gathered to contact his boss and briefed him on the situation. He discovered that many parts of Penang had been flooded, even those areas considered "safe". His boss told Danny to wait at a safe place and await rescue by the civil forces that would go into action. Then he called Linda and learned that she was safe in her apartment, but she told him how extensive the floods were at her place even. The rain just kept pouring down.

Dr Looi could not leave for his Clinic and he had told his long time nurse Alice Lim not to open the clinic and take the day off instead. He then went to his computer to try get some sense of the weather. What he stumbled into shocked him. The reports were still sketchy but enough to tell him of the bad situation in the whole country. It was unprecedented. The whole country was having torrential rain and floods were everywhere. It seemed that Kuala Lumpur was the hardest hit. Reports of massive traffic jams, stranded motorists, power failure and simply panic and chaos reigned all over. It was much the same in other major cities like Ipoh, Kuala Kangsar, Teluk Intan, Malacca and most places in Johor state. Penang seemed to be less hit by the mega floods.

He read that in Terengganu state, Kemaman faced a worsening situation as the number of evacuees had risen from 36 to 10,898 and twenty 10-ton lorries, twelve excavators and an additional five lorries had been dispatched to deal with the floods. And University Sains Malaysia Hospital in Kubang Krian had sent twenty-five volunteers comprising doctors, paramedics and nurses to help those in affected areas. Then in Pahang state, Pekan town reported 3,241 flood evacuees, followed by Kuantan (924), Maran (670), Temerloh

(404), Bera (305) and Rompin (113). The authorities had sent 500 bags of rice, 350 cartons of mineral water, 1,000 cartons of instant noodles and 600 dozens of T- shirts along with six water tankers and three lorry- trailers loaded with various food items to the relief centres.

Knowing the situation now, Dr. Looi braced for the floods in Penang, although his area was still holding out. He then made a phone call to his good friend Albert and discovered that he too was at home and monitoring the situation via news report by the local radio stations and TV. He is not very much into the internet. Both had decided to keep each other informed if either received any important news about the flood situation. Dr Looi then went back to his internet to look at what was happening in other parts of the world. He was shocked with what he discovered.

He discovered that much of Thailand too had heavy rains and Bangkok was hit with flash floods. Vietnam was preparing for a very strong typhoon that would hit its coasts by the morning and many were preparing to be evacuated. Then he turned his attention to Mt Sinabung in Sumatra, Indonesia. This volcano had been spewing ash for the last three weeks and now suddenly molten lava was flowing down and the villages were being evacuated. However many still remained to tend their fields and watch their properties thus exposing themselves to serious danger. Freak weather was also reported in the USA which was having a severe winter, with temperatures in the Mid-West falling to minus 44 centigrade, this being colder than in the Arctic. It had caused considerable damage from falling trees, electric cables snapped in the severe cold and countless motor vehicular accidents from the slippery conditions, not to mention deaths from both the accidents and cold weather exposure, where an exposed body part can be frozen in five minutes.

Dr Looi kept searching the internet for more sinister news and chanced upon the mysterious mass fish deaths reported all over the world – like twenty acres of fish ponds full of dead fish in

Shandong and five thousand kilos of dead fish in a lake in Nanjing (China), hundreds of dead stingrays washed ashore in Veracruz (Mexico), large amount of fish washed ashore in Lake Michigan and hundreds in Holter Lake, Montana, more dead fish in a creek in Madison County, Montana (USA), 2,000 dead fish found in a lake in Vollsmose (Denmark), tons were scooped up in Lake Tondano (Indonesia), massive numbers washed up in a lagoon in Venice (Italy), about thirty thousand fish dying per day in fish farms in Ratchaburi (Thailand), masses found floating in River Lea (England), seven tons were scooped up in Keelung (Taiwan), hundreds were dead in a creek in Laille (France), there were hundreds of thousands of dead fish in a 'red tide' in South Korea, large number of fish deaths in a river in Skane (Sweden), three tons of fish died in a river in Pilsen (Czech Republic), hundreds of dead salmon in Port Coquitlam (Canada) and tons washed ashore in Karachi (Pakistan) just to name a few places. All these strange mass fish deaths occurred within three months, from August to October of last year. Besides this, Dr Looi also knew of mass bee deaths in many parts of the world and heavily reported in the USA, whales and dolphins beaching themselves in USA, Canada and New Zealand. In the USA dead birds had been reported falling from the sky.. Scientists just could not come up with a satisfactory answer to these phenomena. The latest report came from Australia where thousands of bats dropped dead due to a heat wave, where temperatures had risen almost to forty-eight degrees centigrade.

Then he discovered about the occurrences in the USA of huge sink holes that swallowed up highways and even houses. Many people from several countries reported strange humming sounds that had never been identified and seen fireballs in the sky which were not comets. Even increased UFO activities were reported almost daily and the footage was posted in YouTube. Dr. Looi was trying to cover as much ground as possible so he skipped the YouTube videos which take too much time to view and practically, it also saved his internet bandwidth quota as well.

The doctor's eyes were now glued to his Notebook and now he was looking at sunspot and sun flares activity that could have some connection to the Earth's weather going crazy. There were several huge sun flares that had occurred in the last few weeks. Many were of M- Class types. So the space weather had been extreme too. So far ninety- nine percent of the sun activities were not facing Earth's direction, thus avoiding a direct impact of the magnetic storm. If one had recently occurred, then it had yet to be felt. He learned that these solar flares direct special coded energies to activate the human DNA and transform it from the double stranded types to the twelve strands that are required for the crystal- based new human blueprint, thus changing from the carbon- based types that will no longer be functional when the entire solar system shifts to the Fifth Dimension. Dr Looi could hardly believe what he had read. Looks like he will be spending lots of time doing this research to grasp what really is going on.

It is still raining outside but Dr. Looi felt he would be safe as his Condominium unit is on the ninth floor and so he went on with his research via the internet. Now he stumbled upon the possibility of a magnetic pole reversal (MPR) of Earth, which scientists say is long overdue. In fact many airports and airline pilots were informed to recalibrate their GPS co-ordinates as there had been a few degrees of shift of the magnetic North. He continued to surf the internet and learned that new islands were emerging from the seas, some were small and might be temporary but some were larger and scientists think these would remain visible for some time. These islands that rose up were usually seen after an earthquake near the region. Some psychic also mentioned that part of what was Atlantis might even rise up again, thus proving its existence and no longer remaining a legend as it had been for almost more than ten thousand years.

While Dr. Looi was doing his internet surfing, so was his friend Albert, who was doing his research on his favourite subject of UFOs, since he too could not venture out due to the rains and some flooding around his neighbourhood. Like his doctor friend, Albert had always made sure there was enough of stocked food items and water to last around a week should any natural disaster occur or state of emergency due to citizens unrest. They had discussed this before and made a list of things to stock up ever since Dr Looi brought up the subject of the Mayan's Prophecy about 21st December, 2012 as well as the Hopi's Prophecies. That is why both of them were not too unduly worried about the flood situation as they were well stocked up.

Lately Albert had noticed that the TV, Newspaper and Internet were abuzz with stories about Aliens and UFOs. There were numerous reports of UFOs in the skies of many countries and old stories of reported UFO crashes like that of Roswell in USA were again being discussed, while latest reports about a huge vehicle that was spotted on the Moon and strange occurrences on Mars set the internet abuzz with discussions and updates.

Albert then chanced upon a write up about the detailed structure of some UFOs. It seems that a Mothership is the usual name for the biggest craft that is accompanied by smaller ones. A typical Mother ship can be fifty miles across in diameter and it can change its shape or decloak to be visible to human view. Otherwise sometimes it may look like a huge cloud in our skies as one of its ways to be camouflaged. These huge Motherships are actually a bio-mechanical form with consciousness. It will be divided into at least twelve levels or horizontal compartments.

At the bottom level 1, is the UFO Hangar where the much smaller UFO craft are kept. At Level 2 is the Supply Deck, Level 3 is the Zoo containing animals saved or for research collected from many planets. Level 4 is their Agricultural farm, orchards and gardens.

Level 5 is where they house the technical staff. For Recreation, they have extensive parks with various landscapes at Level 6. Their Medical Complex is at the next Level. Higher level staff will be housed at Level 8. A University and Academic Level is maintained at Level 9 complete with Libraries, Laboratory, Concert Halls and other facilities. Level 10 will be Accommodation for visiting dignitaries from other Dimensions. At Level 11 will be the Headquarters and Command Centre. At the highest Level 12 is where the Pilot and Observation Centre is located.

When Portals or Gateways are opened, these Ships will use them to travel to the different Dimensions. Usually there will be Guardians at these Portals and the way the Dark Aliens like the Reptilians, and some of the Greys gain entry to our world is when some aberration in the matrix allows unguarded portals to open briefly. Reptilians are the bipedal types that came from the Draco Constellation some three hundred light years away from Earth. Other hostile ETs are the Zeta Reticuli and Alpha Centauri. Albert then discovered the benevolent ETs comprise those from Vega, Sirius B, Pvila, Pleides, Orion, Maldeck, Arcturus, Apollonia and Andromeda. However there are those from Orion that could be hostile. This is not a complete list as it seems there are more than three thousand ETs in the cosmos, so we are really not alone in the Universe.

Then Albert strayed to a particular website by accident and he was shocked to learn of some civilizations in underground cities of Earth. It seemed there are two advanced civilizations established in Inner Earth. One is that of the Agarthans and the other of survivors of the Atlantis and Lemurian Wars more than twelve thousand years ago. The Lemurians were originally of very high vibration and thus their bodies were not physical like ours. After the Fall of Atlantis, only 25,000 out of the original 150,000 managed to escape to deep underground caverns and some Atlanteans made their escape to S. America and some others to the Far East. These stayed on as surface dwellers but the group that went underground remain more isolated and pure. However in the subsequent years, their vibration lowered and they became more dense in their body composition. Albert suddenly thought about his friend Dr Looi, because he was sure the doctor would be as excited as he was about this bit of information he chanced upon. He reached for the telephone.

"Hi, Doc. I have some very exciting news for you!" said Albert.

"Yeah? Me too!" said Dr. Looi, not to be outdone. 'But are you alright there?"

"Yes, quite safe, thank you. I suppose you are fine too, right?"

"Yes. So what is it that you have discovered?" asked the doctor.

"I stumbled on things more exciting than UFOs!" exclaimed Albert.

"Really? What is it?" asked Dr Looi, now really eager to know.

"You won't believe it. There is a thriving civilization beneath Earth!"

"What? Sure?"

"Yes, I didn't believe it myself at first. But I have found enough information to think it is true."

"OK, this means I will need to check up myself to see if I can get some other confirmation." replied the Doctor.

"Great idea, in this way we can cover more ground," but before Albert could finish his sentence, he felt the ground shake for a few seconds.

"Whoa! What was that? Did you feel it or was it my imagination?" he asked Dr. Looi.

"Yeah, I felt a tremor!' exclaimed Dr. Looi. "Hey, it is a tremor! My cup of coffee even spilled!"

"Doc, what is going on?"

"Albert, I am going back to my Notebook to check it out. Talk later."

"OK, me too!"

Both of them raced to their computers. As is his habit, Dr Looi always had available the website that tracks all earthquakes happening in the world and he fixed his eyes on the screen now. There was nothing reported yet, He could feel the after shocks now. Four minutes went by and then on his screen, came the report. He could not believe what he read and saw on the world map depicting all earthquakes occurring. The epicentre of a powerful 8.2 earthquake happened in Bukit Leuser National Park in North Sumatra, Indonesia. He rushed to the phone and called his friend.

"Albert! The quake is in Bukit Leuser, near Medan in North Sumatra!"

"What? Must be a big one for us to feel it so strong here.' replied the equally excited Albert.

"Yes, it's a 8.2 on the Richter Scale!"

"Oh, no! I hope there are no casualties, Doc."

"I hope so too, but being in the National Park area of Bukit Leuser wouldn't result in much damage...I hope." said Dr. Looi. 'Hey, listen, let's go get more information and report back, OK?"

"Good idea, Doc. Bye."

They both switched on the radio for news as well as looking at news websites for any details about this strong quake. But these news portals could not beat individuals who phoned each other and among the first few was Heng, the tow truck driver. He was informed by a fellow clansman via his mobile phone of a great devastation that had occurred in the small town of Taiping, about 130km south of Penang island. It seemed an earthquake had struck the town and many buildings had collapsed and absolute chaos resulted. His fellow clansman, called Ah Kow, had called for Heng to get help for the people of Taiping. According to Ah Kow, almost half of the town buildings had collapsed and that was all he said, not knowing any more details.

Heng swung into action. The people of Penang, though experiencing floods, were better off than those in Taiping, as many must be trapped in the collapsed buildings. He used his walkie talkie to summon all his tow- truck friends, even those from rival companies, and they in turn called for crane drivers and other heavy machinery. His own boys, Mokhtar, Ramu and Ah Boey were ready to be picked up by him. They had, on their own accord, bought some emergency supplies like bottled water, packets of easy to cook noodles and even some bandages and plasters with whatever money they had on them while waiting for Heng.

Danny had by this time got wind of the disaster in Taiping too as he had some close friends there. He then talked to some men around him and these total strangers decided to assemble a volunteer team to get to Taiping. He did not have to abandon the girls under his care as their parents, siblings and boyfriends had picked them up by then. They were not the only team heading towards the stricken town, he saw many others forming a loose posse and were all heading there.

Having no friends or relatives in Taiping, both Dr. Looi and Albert depended on news channels but even after half an hour of surfing for news, they had no idea of the quake in Taiping town. Albert got wind of the disaster in Taiping almost at the same time as Dr. Looi from a news broadcast of a local dialect radio station that interrupted it's regular programme. There were no details given apart from the description of buildings collapsed but no casualty reports yet. They contacted each other and Dr Looi mobilised his nurse to get medical supplies from his clinic while Albert did his part by getting another friend, Ah Beng, to use his 4WD vehicle to carry some supplies and to ferry them there. The rains in Penang had somewhat slowed down and the flood waters were draining faster now. It seemed that the worst was over for Penang folks.

CHAPTER 26

Back in the jungle, the five minutes of rest turned out to be more than forty- five minutes, they were all that tired. However Keat used that time to meditate when he saw every one had fallen asleep from exhaustion. He was brought out of meditation when Ranger Michael woke everyone up.

"You were meditating?" Mike asked Keat.

"Yes," replied Keat, looking rather disappointed.

"Any messages?" asked Robert.

"Nothing, just saw the image of an old man, who keeps appearing but said nothing."

"Do you know or recognise him?" asked Joseph.

"I don't know him but it seemed that he is known as, as bird something."

"How does he look like?" interjected Sobri.

"Grey long hair, quite tanned for a Chinese man, thin and wearing ragged clothes. Let us get going. How is Inspector Hassan?" He was quite concerned about Hassan's condition.

"He's still sleeping." said Mustafa.

Keat went over to Hassan and felt his forehead for any signs of fever and this woke Hassan up.

"Sorry I woke you up Inspector, but I was checking to see if you are having a fever," said Keat.

'Well?" replied Hassan, now fully awake.

"There is a slight fever still," said a concerned- looking Keat. "Let me check the wounds," and he proceeded to remove the bandages. "It looks quite bad, there is pus and the edges are still red and swollen. I will need to change the bandages and get some more herbs."

Keat proceeded to tear up his already tattered shirt into strips and joined it to form a sort of bandage and proceeded to do some cleaning of the wound first before bandaging it again.

The jungle now seems more like normal, for the birds were again flying about and calling one another and even butterflies were fluttering about as though nothing had happened. It seemed that the earlier danger was gone, they could feel it as the jungle was once more alive with the activities of its inhabitants. The men were waiting for Keat to give the order to get going, that much they trusted and depended on him now.

"OK, let us get ready to move." said Keat. The men got their things and were ready to march when suddenly a voice said, "Wait! Don't go anywhere yet!" It came from behind some foliage. This jolted everyone, especially Keat because there were no giveaway signs like birds flying away suddenly or silence. Usually when an intruder is around, like a big cat, birds will fly away and so stop chirping suddenly. They all turned to the direction of the voice and the Rangers had their rifles up ready to shoot. Every one was on edge.

A man appeared into the open from the dense foliage, carrying a big dirty bundle slung over his shoulder. Now with a target in sight, the Rangers and the two policemen all had their firearms trained at the visible target, fingers at the triggers, ready to shoot.

"Don't shoot!" said the old man as he approached the startled group.

Then Keat shouted out loudly, "You, you appeared in my meditation!! Who are you and how did you find us in this jungle?" As Keat had described to everyone how this mysterious old man kept appearing in his meditation, now everyone was even more surprised and a chill ran down their spines.

"Sorry for the surprise. I will explain everything." said the old man, now putting his bundle down when he had reached the group, with rifles and pistols still pointing at him.

"Who are you and how do you know that we are here?" demanded Mustafa, pointing his pistol a few centimetres away from the old man's head.

"I am just an old man and mean no harm. Look, I have brought some food and water for all of you...including some medicine for your injured friend," said the old man calmly.

'Answer me and don't try to evade my questions," continued a stern- looking Mustafa.

"Very well, I am the old man of this forest and my name is Cheow Chek. I am a Wanderer and Watcher and if you want to get out of here in one piece you better listen to me. By the way, I am also unarmed, so please put your weapons away."

Rangers and Policemen looked at each other and Hassan gave the nod to put their weapons down. Slowly all weapons were put away.

"You have a lot to explain then, old man," hissed Mokhtar.

"Yes, I agree. But first you hungry people must eat something." Cheow Chek opened his cloth bag to let them help themselves. The men hesitated at first but soon they gave in to his invitation and one by one they picked up an assortment of edible jungle fruits, cooked tapioca roots and smoked deer meat.

"Eat slowly, we are all safe here. In fact I recommend that we make camp here today first. I shall now tell you what you all need to know," the old man said.

The hungry men distributed the food among themselves and tucked in for the much needed calories. Cheow Chek then attended to Hassan's wounds while encouraging him to continue eating.

"Please continue eating while I brief you people," said the old man after dressing up Hassan's wounds and giving him some herbal paste to swallow, saying it would hasten up the healing. They now sat down in a circle facing Cheow Chek, still munching their food.

"OK, while you eat and gain back your strength, I shall introduce myself to you. I am called Cheow Chek and I travel all over to help those in need of assistance. I use my sixth sense and my training of the Tao to perform my duties. I am indeed very old according to your standards but we of the Tao consider ourselves ageless and Time has no meaning to us. That is all you need to know about me for now."

"My friends, the world is changing very fast. Mother Earth is actually a living Being and she has decided to change from the Third Dimension to the Fifth Dimension and even beyond. The process has started, that is why you have the climatic changes all over the world with some parts having floods, other parts experiencing severe drought, still others having severe winters. Volcanic activities too are getting numerous and greater eruptions are still to come all over the volcanic belts of the world. Then earthquakes are also happening at the same time and the great quake is yet to come." The men were listening in great silence and awe.

"The reason is that Mother Earth is getting rid of all the negative energies that had been stored for ages, that had resulted from the wars, atrocities, hatred, pollution of her air, water and ground. These negative energies will need to be transmuted, released and re-cycled. She is doing it as gently as she could and that is why several earthquakes have been comparatively moderate. But very soon, they will hit the top end of the scale with devastating effects. In fact as we speak, one just hit North Sumatra measuring at least 8.2 and a small town in the state of Perak shook badly because a new fault line had emerged that extended to this town."

"Which town in Perak?" asked Hassan.

"Taiping. That is why I need to give you some information now as I need to go there to render some help."

"How did you know?" queried Keat.

"Actually you, among this group, know the answer. Same way as I know where you people are exactly. Anyway this is not the issue now, I must give you the information before I leave for Taiping as there is very little time left before it happens."

"What is going to happen, old man?" asked Joseph, after swallowing another mouthful of tapioca. Cheow Chek realised he made an error. Actually he was telling them many hours before the Taiping quake is to occur! He quickly deflected it by saying something else.

"I am coming to that. For decades, the leading governments of the world had interacted with Extraterrestials or what you call ETs." Everyone's attention is now doubled, all except Keat were in disbelief.

"One US President, Eisenhower, even signed a Treaty with some rogue ETs in exchange for technological secrets. As you will have noticed, there are now so many convincing reports of UFOs all over the world that many governments are unable to suppress them. In short, the ETs now are more benevolent, as the rogue ETs with dark intentions were either chased off the planet or are in quarantine in another world, watched over by several Light Forces.

In other words, Humanity will encounter and acknowledge these ETs. And there is one other thing that humans must be told, even more unbelievable to you than the Extraterrestrials."

"And what is this?" a very curious crowd said in unison and now very excited too.

"You will also meet your Family from Inner Earth. These people are of three groups: the Agarthans, Catharians and the Lemurians."

"You really mean there are people living deep underground?" asked Mike.

"Yes indeed, my friend. And they are beings that are very highly evolved spiritually. Their underground cities are also huge, with all amenities, for example gardens, parks, recreational areas, farms and so on. They had gone into hiding and also to escape the great disaster when Atlantis civilization was totally destroyed by their wars, which had resulted in a huge calamity. Of the 500,000 that were to escape to these underground dwellings, only about 250,000 made it. But since then, their population had grown. Others fled to mountains of South America and Tibet."

"Who are the Lemu..what is called?" asked Joseph.

'Lemurians. They are the original souls of Lemuria, from the Continent of Mu. These souls were originally peaceful souls but were cheated by a clever scheme hatched out by the Dark side of the Atlantean people. They were attacked by the Atlanteans, hence the great war started. Their leader is Adamos, who is still alive, and he led many to safety into the underground chambers. Ever since living in these underground cities, their vibration had somewhat faded and thus now they have a much more solid, material body. Previously they were more like pure Light- bodies. They have life-spans of thousands of years, Adamos is about 25,000 years old."

"I find it hard to believe that there are people living inside the Earth!" said Mike. "What sort of life is that?"

"A life far better than ours on the surface," replied the old man.

"How is it?" quipped in Hassan.

"OK, let me tell you more. They are more intelligent than we are and as I had said, highly evolved souls. They move in huge transportation vehicles that levitate and use the earth's magnetic energy with no need for petrol. These vehicles travel at the speed of sound. And everything they require is free. There is no money being used. Everyone works on the farms to produce the food they require, which is mostly fruits, vegetables, nuts and grains. No chemicals are ever used and they eat freshly harvested produce. Meat is never eaten. The quality of their food is of such a high standard that the Life Force contained is tremendous. That is one of the reasons why they live for hundreds of years in the same body, have no illnesses and are very tall, growing to their full physical potential."

"How tall?" asked Mustafa.

"The Lemurians can reach 15 feet tall while the Atlanteans are above 7 feet tall. The Catharians are even taller than these two types. They live in huge caverns because of their size and their lightings are from crystal energy, which is free and lasts as long as the crystals are there. They can communicate with their animals and plants and even their sea, rivers and lakes can talk and sing to them, because everything has a consciousness an ability which humans on the surface of the earth have lost. They live a peaceful, serene life. There is no pollution of their air, water or food and this contributes to their longevity as well."

"How deep into the earth is their place?" asked Mike.

"Their cities are from 200 miles deep into the earth's crust but most are about 800 miles from the surface. There is a sun and is called the Central Sun, but is less bright than what we see in our skies of our own sun. Yes indeed, it is another Earth there, but so beautiful and peaceful unlike what we have on the surface."

"Why are the ETs showing themselves up and those of Inner Earth as well?" asked Keat.

"I am about to come to this, and I am not surprised at all that you are able to ask this question. In fact, you know the answer deep within your heart. Later I shall tell you your life's mission. But first let's answer your question."

"Mother Earth is unable to wait for all her inhabitants to be upgraded to bodies with a higher vibration which is crystalline-based rather than carbon-based; besides karmic Law dictates that those souls who are heavily in karmic debt will not be able to change in time and these will continue to live on in another very similar holographic 3D earth to let karma takes its course. In order for Mother Earth to shift into the higher Dimension, old energies must be released and be transmuted into Light and this results in a Magnetic Polar Shift which causes massive changes. This can result in tsunamis with waves more than 30m high slamming into the land, and great earthquakes along with volcanic eruptions. The Agarthans and Lemurians are coming to the surface to disseminate some Truths about the history of Earth and Humankind as a preparation to the arrival of Extraterrestrials in their spacecrafts, what you people call as UFOs."

"This is too much for me! Who are you?" shouted Mustafa while raising his gun and pointed it at Cheow Chek's head. Everyone was taken aback. After a few seconds, Hassan intervened.

"Take it easy, Mustafa! And put your weapon down, now!" ordered Mustafa's superior. If anyone who is able to control the policeman, it is Inspector Hassan. Slowly but quite reluctantly he lowered his weapon.

"I think we can at least listen to this man. As a matter of fact, my fever is broken and my wounds do not hurt that much anymore. His medicine really works," said Hassan. The whole group turned to have a close look at Hassan. Keat was the first to check on Hassan and as he opened the dirty bandage to see the wounds, he was taken aback – there was no more inflammation nor pus but a clean and healing wound. Every one gave a clap. Mokhtar now felt very embarrassed, his face turning red.

"This is simply magical!" said Keat.

"No, you have treated him very well yourselves under the circumstances, I only happen to have the correct herbs that you didn't manage to find. You could have done the same had the herbs you were looking been found." said Cheow Chek. Keat knew that the old man was just trying to be humble as Keat had found the herbs he was looking for. This old man is something else, Keat thought to himself.

"OK, we better make camp here for the night and then let me brief all of you with more information," the old man said, mainly to distract them from asking too many private questions, but it is also true they had to settle in for the night there.

The Rangers needed not be told, they went off to look materials to make their camp, followed by the two policemen, who by now are happy that their superior, Inspector Hassan is out of danger. Keat stayed behind to have some quiet moments to himself. He was in deep thoughts.

Within an hour and a half, the men had their makeshift camp set up and they ought to be comfortable for the night.

"OK, men, gather around and listen. I still have more to tell you all," Cheow Chek said. All of them stopped what they were doing and sat down in a circle around the old man.

"The situation will get worse and tomorrow all of you will need to get up early and leave this place and you (pointing to Keat) will lead the group." Everyone then looked at Keat.

"Me?" said Keat in a sort of protesting way.

"Yes, but don't worry as I will give you a plan of how to get out later. Let me continue. As I said, things will get far worse all over the world. The sea level will rise, affecting the UK, Europe and even the California coast and elsewhere. Coastal cities will then be flooded out, affecting millions of people."

"Then you will have fireballs raining down from the sky. First they will fall into the sea, and soon after falling onto land, causing minimal damage and casualties but followed up by falling into heavy populated cities thus causing severe damage and many deaths. On top of this, undersea volcanoes will erupt, causing tsunamis of greater than that which occurred in the Bandar Acheh Quake in Indonesia. You can imagine the destruction and death it will cause as it will travel about 25km inland."

"How true can all these things that you tell us be? Impossible!" said Hassan, shaking his head.

"If what I tell you, and I have revealed a lot, starts to happen, then you will know it is true but by that time, the knowledge will be useless." replied Cheow Chek.

"And I need to add one more point- the Great California Quake will happen. California will get a series of huge earthquakes, each one bigger than the previous one, the final one will be of magnitude 9."

'Why are you telling us about a place like California which is so far away from us?" asked Mustafa.

"First because it will cause untold destruction, death and suffering. Second because this will open up fault lines and sink holes all over the world and our country can be affected. Already you have escaped from several sink holes not too long ago."

The men were shocked, how did this stranger know when no one had spoken about it? They looked at one another in amazement.

"What to do then, old man?" finally Michael spoke.

"This is what I am coming to." Then he turned to Keat. "This man will first lead you out of here. You are to then gather your families and head as far inland as possible and better still, to higher grounds. Those of you who are from Sabah and Sarawak, you are to inform your families to do so without delay. There is a chance that the destruction may be rather limited as the Agarthans and Lemurians have great technology to try mitigate it. That is why they will have to come to the surface to help as they themselves will be affected in their underground world too. However if it goes full scale, especially when all the nuclear plants are being destroyed, then and only then will help come from your brothers and sisters from the Stars."

"So that is why you started off by talking about these Inner Earth Dwellers and the ETs?" asked Richard.

"Yes."

"And how would the ETs help us if the Inner Earth Dwellers can't?" queried Hassan.

"Planetary Mass Evacuation will be done by them," said Cheow Chek.

"What? They can put everyone in their flying saucers?" said Mustafa in disbelief.

"Well, they have millions of such crafts in readiness in the skies all over the world, only thing is that they are all cloaked and so no radar can detect them nor are they visible. Some are disguised as clouds."

"And how will they get us into their flying machines?" Keat finally asked. He was silent because lots of things were going on in his mind.

"They have only about fifteen minutes to evacuate everyone before they too are affected by the adverse earth conditions. They will shoot beams of transportation light to sort of pull you up into their ships. First the adults will be beamed up, then the children. Families will be reunited again should they be separated in the confusion." replied Cheow Chek. Every one looked in amazement. No one had any questions as all were dumb struck.

"But there is an issue I need to inform about being rescued in this way. You must have no feelings of fear in you or otherwise you will not be able to be beamed up. Next, keep your vibration high, which also means that you must have feelings of joy, humility, gratitude and keep away dark thoughts like anger, jealousy, revenge and such. People with low vibration will in fact disintegrate in this powerful beam of light. Thus keep away these dark thoughts from now on to practice being in high vibration." Cheow Chek stopped talking for a while to let them assimilate what has been told. He could only hear murmurs among them.

"Here, have some more food as soon the sun will be down and you need all the rest tonight for tomorrow you will have to get out of the jungle." Cheow Chek rummaged his hand into his cloth bag and took out more food.

Every one ate what they could and then the Rangers began to collect branches and twigs to build a fire. Hassan got up and found now he could even walk almost normally. Every one was amazed but carried on with their individual tasks for settling into the night.

It was then that Cheow Chek took the opportunity to contact Keat via his Mind. He had to try a few times before Keat was able to receive the telepathic thought.

[Do you know who you are?] projected Cheow Chek, the third time to Keat..

Keat looked around, thinking he heard someone talking to him. However he sort of knew it to be a mind to mind communication and he then looked at the old man.

[Are you the one talking to me, old man?] answered Keat.

[Yes, who else?] projected the old man.

[Why are we communicating in this way?]

[I need to test your telepathic ability.]

[Why? And how do you know I may hear you in this way?]

[I just know. Do you know who you really are?]

[I am Keat]

[I know. But you are more than just "Keat". Do you know that?]

[Votek?]

[Yes! Good, you are remembering who you actually are. Very good.]

[This is all I remember.[

[Be patient, soon you will remember more. But now I wish to state your mission. Votek, you are first to lead this group to safety, and back to the city, then you are to go back to your adopted tribe and await for more instructions. But suffice to say, you and your tribe will play a very important role for Mankind and Mother Earth.]

[How can I lead them to safety when I don't even know which direction to go? Besides I am now a prisoner.]

[Not to worry, Heaven has ways to help you fulfil your mission. That is all for now.]

The men are now preparing to settle down for the night and gathered around the small fire that the Rangers built. They were all exhausted.

"Gentlemen, I will take the first watch so that all of you will be able to get as much rest as possible for tomorrow you have a long journey and I will leave very early as I need to get to Taiping." The old man said.

No one said anything and all of them started to get into the shelter they built as they were extremely tired, including Keat.

CHAPTER 27

Ranger Joseph was the first to wake up. It was early dawn. All the rest were still sleeping. The sun had not yet risen and the fire was flickering away and still had quite a lot of branches and twigs yet to be burned. He looked around but could not see the old man anywhere. Well, the old man did mention that he would leave them quite early and so he must have gone then, thought Joseph. He got up to tend to the fire and also noticed there was some food left behind by the old man. Joseph thought it was strange, how could the old man gather the food in the night? Indeed this old feller is very strange.

Soon it was Keat who woke up fully refreshed after a good night's sleep. He was never disturbed by the jungle mosquitoes, unlike the rest of the group. Within half an hour, all the rest of the men were up and ready for the day. Joseph told them of the food that old man left behind and they helped themselves to cooked jungle tapioca, bananas, guava and jackfruit. They ate in silence, everyone in deep thoughts. Uppermost in everyone's thoughts is when will they be safely home.

No one noticed Keat, who actually was trying telepathically to contact Cheow Chek. Finally when he had almost given up, he received the old man's reply. He was supplied with some directions to take and warned to be in a hurry as the place they were in now is very unstable with the possibilities of more sinkholes appearing. The old man also advised that the Rangers should try to contact their

Base and then suddenly there was no more telepathic transmission. Keat has to act fast now.

"Everyone, please let us proceed, this place will not be safe anymore," announced Keat to the rest of them.

"Who are you to give us orders?" barked Sobri.

"Yeah, you better watch your mouth!" chipped in Mustafa.

"OK, stop it!" Interjected Hassan, who by now is back to his normal self. "Keat, do you have any idea of how to get us out of here?"

"Yes, certainly. We shall need to go in this direction for another five kilometres and then, looking for signs, I will know where to go next."

"What signs?" asked Mustafa.

"Signs from Nature," replied Keat, not wanting to let them know he will need to contact Cheow Chek via telepathy.

"You see, he is lying and just making this up so that he can escape!" shouted Mustafa.

"We are the best Rangers from Sarawak and we can find our way out of here without your help. We trust this!" said Joseph, holding out his compass.

Keat just kept quiet because he knows he is facing a hostile group that is panicking now.

"Then we shall let the Rangers take us out of trouble," said Hassan.

The men started to take their belongings and Joseph was studying his compass, looking rather puzzled. He was joined by his fellow Rangers and they huddled in a small circle, mumbling among themselves in low voices.

'Well?" asked Hassan.

After some silence, that seemed very long to all of them, Joseph answered, "I don't know what is wrong with our compass, the needle is unstable and turning circles!"

Every one, including Keat, tried to look at the compass held out by Joseph. Indeed the needle was turning in circles, first clockwise, then anti-clockwise, then stopping at random and going unstable again. They gave a gasp and then fell into silence, all looking at each other perplexed.

"We will use the sun then to find our bearings," said Joseph, to break the silence. He then looked up into the sky, located the direction he intended to take and pointed it out to the rest of them. All of them then started the journey with the Rangers leading.

They had not started more than ten minutes when Keat received a telepathic message from Chew Chek.

[They are going in the wrong direction, Votek. Stop them.]

[How? They had refused to listen to me.]

There were no more forthcoming messages and Keat had to think of something. He stopped and then said to the group, "Stop, we are going in the wrong direction!"

Everyone turned around to look at him. Joseph then took wide strides to get to Keat in a menacing way and caught hold of Keat's shirt in a firm grip, cursing Keat and hit him with the butt of his rifle. Keat was knocked to the ground, bleeding from a wound on his forehead. Hassan then reacted, "Stop it!" and pulled Joseph away. No one helped Keat up, who slowly got up holding his forehead. There was a dead silence.

"What are you up to, Keat?" shouted Hassan, who felt sorry for this prisoner.

"Nothing, I just want to warn that we are going in the wrong direction, it is where the danger is," said Keat, wiping the blood trickling over his eyebrow.

"What danger?" asked Hassan.

"I think there will be more sinkholes there."

"How do you know?"

Keat kept quiet for he dare not reveal how he got his information.

"See? He is just trying to scare us so that he will lead again," said Joseph, trying to justify his attack on Keat, who just looked down.

"We follow the Rangers." Hassan barked out the order and they all started their trek again. Keat tore a strip of cloth from his shirt to bandage his forehead, which now hurt a great deal They trekked on for another twenty minutes when all of a sudden they heard a loud rushing sound. All of them stopped at once.

"What was that?" Sobri whispered. No one answered for all of them had no clue. Joseph signalled for all of them to continue slowly with their weapons in readiness. They now were moving stealthily. Keat's heart was beating fast, they had walked into a sinkhole area, he thought. He tried to make contact with the old man, but the knock on his head still hurt and the bleeding had not stopped either, which distracted his concentration. He got no response from the old man.

As the men were proceeding gingerly, they heard another loud sound like a massive rush of wind and this time the ground shuddered under their feet. This panicked the men who then ran helter skelter in all directions. Keat in fact was left standing alone, that was how fast all of the rest ran for their lives. It took another few seconds before Keat took off, rather slowly because he wanted to be sure that he did not run into danger. This actually saved his life for Sobri ran right into the ground that swallowed him up. The rest had disappeared into the forest, only Hassan and Keat witnessed the tragedy and heard Sobri's chilling yell for help. Keat stopped dead on his tracks and tried to get to Sobri. When Hassan saw this, he too changed his direction towards where the ground had swallowed up Sobri. They only saw a huge hole in the ground now covered with fallen jungle vegetation and churned- up earth. They had to back up when the still unstable edge of the hole started to give way under their weight. The men stepped back into safety just in time. There was nothing they could do for Sobri and as the ground started to tremble again, both of them turned to run, with Keat signalling Hassan to follow him.

Keat led Hassan and himself to safer grounds in the direction the old man had told him. It was only after more than half an hour of running that they stopped to assess the situation. They were panting hard by then. The jungle seemed quiet now.

"We need to look for the others." said Keat. "They ran in the wrong direction, I hope they are safe."

"Yes, but do you think the ground will break up again?" asked a worried Hassan.

"Don't know, just be careful. Whatever happens, we must stick together." Hassan nodded in agreement. He should have trusted this Chinese man, he thought, then none of this could have happened. He had made a wrong decision that had caused the life of Sobri. Hassan was full of regret. Sobri was always a good policeman.

However to find the dispersed men, they had to go into the dangerous areas. Both men started to shout for the missing men as they went gingerly along. After about an hour, they found a backpack that belonged to Joseph. It was a bad sign. Where is Joseph? Further on, they found the radio transmitter that Mike always carried. They also picked it up. The men could not be found. They could still feel minor tremors off and on so this made their search very dangerous.

"Inspector, I find it very hard to track them because of the chaotic tracks made, they must have been running in every direction."

"Do you have any suggestions what we can do to find them?"

"I will build a fire with plenty of smoke to get their attention so that they can locate us. It is far more efficient this way," explained Keat.

They thus went to collect materials for the fire and Keat got a fire started easily. Making it smoky was the easiest with the green leaves of live branches. All they had to do was wait and hope that the men would see the smoke and come looking for them. They could still feel a bit of earth movement but no new sinkholes appeared.

It was an agonizing wait for the two. All the while they made no conversation, each man in deep thought. Keat was trying to establish telepathic contact with Cheow Chek, but the headache from the blow to the head was still there, though the bleeding had stopped.

Mustafa had hurt himself when he tripped over an exposed root, he had sprained his right ankle and was hopping around, trying to find his friends. He had a glimpse of Joseph while running for his life and he went looking for him in the direction he last saw Joseph. Shouting Joseph's name as loud as he could, Mustafa tried his best to locate Joseph. It was then that he noticed the thick smoke and he decided that it must be one of them pinpointing his position to the others so he continued towards it.

Within the hour, Mustafa was the first to appear and it was a great relief for both Hassan and Keat to see him, although he was covered with cuts and bruises. Now Keat hoped that the others will be there soon. They started to exchange news of what happened to them, catching up as much as they could.

Within another hour, the three Rangers Mike, Robert and Joseph appeared together and the anxiously waiting men cheered and welcomed them back literally with open arms. They were all catching up when Keat interrupted their conversation.

"Men, I have something to say. We need to get out of here. I suggest we proceed in the direction I originally pointed out for I am sure it is the safest."

"We agree with you wholeheartedly this time." said Mike.

"Thanks, I also would like to suggest that one of you keeps trying to get a signal from the transmitter as we need to get help out of here. We need to try get Sobri's body and I will lead us to the spot where he was swallowed up by the earth. We leave now."

Keat led the men back to where Sobri met his death and when they arrived at the spot, the deep sinkhole had slightly stabilised at the sides as they tested the ground and it felt safe and solid around the edges. It was about six metres deep. The men then set to work immediately. The Rangers secured their ropes to a strong tree. Mike and Robert started to lower themselves down. Although they spent a good forty minutes down in the sinkhole probing for Sobri's body, they failed to locate it. It was then decided too dangerous to carry on and they reluctantly abandoned the search. Before they left, Robert tied his handkerchief to a tree nearby to help in re-locating the area for when they will come back with better equipment.

The men rested for a while and Keat again tried to make contact with Cheow Chek but with no success. Then he changed tactics, he started to send telepathic messages to the old man regardless of whether they would be successful or not, hoping that the old man would receive the messages. He decided to state in which direction he was leading the men and any other relevant information.

The men trekked for several hours, with Keat leading. He noticed that when he was going in a certain direction, he would get a severe headache which was only relieved if he changed course. In this way Keat was sure he was still being guided by the old man to safety. Joseph noticed that the transmitter was getting very weak signals on occasion. He also noticed that whenever Keat was changing direction, the signals would get stronger and he told this to the others. Their spirits were lifted since it is clear now that Keat knew where he was going. After another hour and a half they saw a natural clearing in the jungle.

"We shall take a break here." Keat told the men. They were exhausted and all welcomed the suggestion.

After a few minutes, Joseph yelled, "I've got a signal! It is a strong one!"

The men now gathered around the transmitter and they heard a crackle. Joseph wasted no time to make a call to their Headquarters, and to their surprise, they managed to make contact. Information was quickly shared, especially their present position. They were told by Headquarters to stay put as a helicopter would be dispatched immediately as it was still daylight. Everyone cheered. They would be rescued within a few hours.

Hassan spoke. "I wish to make a suggestion. Let us have a minute of silence in respect for our fellow colleague, Sobri. May his soul rest in peace."

Everyone then stood up with bowed heads and observed a full minute of silence. Now all they have to do is wait for the helicopter. The men then started to clear the area, removing small rocks and stones, a few dead branches and anything else that would be a danger to the landing helicopter. They also prepared a small fire to create a smoke signal for the approaching helicopter.

It took the Air Force about three hours to arrive. They could hear the familiar roar of the helicopter approaching them. Everyone was excited. Then Inspector Hassan spoke, "Mr. Lim Ah Keat, I am sorry to say that I will have to arrest you and put you in handcuffs." The Rangers actually had forgotten that they have a prisoner in the excitement of being rescued. Keat had no emotions showing on his face but turned around slowly and put his hands behind his back for Hassan to put the handcuffs on. He gave no resistance.

CHAPTER 28

Heng and his team were among the first volunteers to arrive in Taiping. They drove at break neck speed, thus reaching the town south of Penang, in thirty- five minutes instead of the fifty minutes that most would take. As they entered the town, they were caught in a huge traffic snarl on both sides of the road. It was chaotic. What seemed strange was that the cars ahead were giving way to any tow truck, tractor or jeep. It thus seemed that many had already known of the disaster in Taiping and knew these were volunteers going to render assistance. When they got into town, they saw civilian volunteers directing traffic. These young men were all holding their mobile phones to their ear talking and directing traffic at the same time. There were no traffic policemen in sight. As they got to the volunteer who was directing traffic, the man told Heng, "Brother, you are needed in Jalan Kota area! Go straight, just follow the truck in front of you!"

Heng nodded and gave the thumbs up sign. So, the residents were out in force to help in anyway they can, thought Heng. He drove on, following the truck closely. As they approached the town area, it was only then did they know of the great destruction the earthquake had caused. Many buildings were either completely destroyed or parts of them were left standing. Piles of rubble were everywhere and the roads were covered in debris There were many men looking for survivors in the ruins. A man came running to Heng and told him where his toll truck was much needed to remove stalled cars or those involved in accidents due to the mayhem so that bulldozers and other heavy machinery like cranes could come and clear the building debris to look for survivors. Heng thought that the way the locals could organize such a team of volunteers who know what to do in such a short time was really amazing.

As Heng and his buddies drove into Jalan Kota, they were shocked to see the devastation that had occurred. Almost seventy-five percent of the buildings had toppled. Many cars were also buried under the bricks and mortar. Among the landmarks that Heng knew, Restaurant Kum Loong and the Old Clock Tower, were reduced to rubble. Heng and his gang swung into action. They started to pull the wrecked cars out of the way with their tow-truck as well as distributing bottled water to survivors. It was plain chaos there. Because of their efforts, along with the bulldozers and other tow-truck operators, they did a splendid job of clearing the roads so that ambulances and the Fire Brigade could come in. Members of the public were also seen helping in whatever way they could. They were seen dousing small fires that had broken out, helping the injured into private cars to be ferried to the hospital, distributing bottles of water to anyone who needed it, directing traffic, keeping the crowds under control and so on.

Dr. Looi and his small team were already in the thick of the action. They too were directed by local townsfolk to a makeshift First Aid tent to render immediate treatment for those injured or rescued from the rubble. He found out that these volunteers were members of the Tzu Chih Organization and they are well known to be amongst the first responders in any disaster that occurs in any part of Asia. Dr Looi also heard that the Taiping Hospital had suffered partial destruction from the earthquake and those with serious injuries were being transported by relatives, friends or just strangers to private hospitals nearby, which had suffered minor damages only. Taxi drivers made their valuable contribution by ferrying those injured at no charge.

It was several hours before the Police, Army and Rela Corps showed up. Despite their presence, the locals and volunteers from nearby villages and towns continued their valuable help. As the people went about to help, all of them were wondering how was it possible that there could be an earthquake in Malaysia as she is not in the Ring of Fire where volcanoes and earthquakes are mostly found. At most when a huge earthquake occurs with its epicentre in Indonesia, some parts of Malaysia may feel a slight tremor for a few seconds only. This is the reason why so many buildings collapsed in Taiping, because local buildings are not built to withstand any earthquake. Moreover Taiping has many old buildings built in the 1900s when it was an old town engaged in tin mining.

There must have been scores if not hundreds of deaths as lorry loads of dead bodies were seen being transported out, most likely to the hospital morgue. News of the devastation had reached the whole country and more help was being organized to be sent to Taiping. Schools that were not damaged had been turned into relief centres to house those made homeless, and one of these schools was King Edward VII, a very well known school founded in 1883. It was a suitable location because it was near the town centre and it has a sprawling perimeter. Other schools being turned into relief centres were Hua Lian and Treacher Methodist Schools. Heng and his friends and Dr Looi's small team worked their hearts out to help.

Taiping is the second largest town in the state of Perak and is very scenic with it's large and sprawling Lake Gardens which are a major tourist attraction. The quaint town is well known for its rain and for being the wettest town in the country, with almost twice the national rainfall average. The townsfolk are well known to play a betting game on predicting the time of rainfall and they have worked out a system of betting that is rather ingenious. However, in recent times, this wettest town in the country experienced prolonged dry weather and water rationing had to be implemented, while the driest region in the country, Jelebu in the southern state of Negeri

Sembilan, now is supplying water to its surrounding areas. The weather had changed so much, and now this unheard of earthquake in Malaysia. Although Taiping town has grown in size with respect to the many new housing areas and shop houses, it still has managed to retain its charm and this is the beauty of the town. It is unthinkable that this beautiful small town at the foothills, full of local history, is now reduced to rubble, bricks and mortar leaving its residents to death and destruction and total chaos. Taiping means 'Peace" and the town got its name when peace finally was attained when the rival gangs of Ghee Hin and Hai Sun laid down their weapons for good in late 1874 with the signing of the Pangkor Treaty. The two triads had fought a bloody war from 1861, totalling four wars altogether.

News of this disaster spread fast and more aid and help were being organised by people of neighbouring towns that were not affected by any floods or landslides, which were still occurring in most parts of the country.

Keat was being brought to Kuala Lumpur by the police after being evacuated from the jungles of Pahang. Despite the natural disasters happening around the country, his capture managed to be aired over prime time news of most TV and Radio stations. He felt very sad not because of his arrest but that he could not fulfil his mission to get back to his jungle family and lead them to safety. It will be a long ride to Kuala Lumpur from Rompin in an uncomfortable old Police van. Two Policemen were assigned to escort him. When he was handed over to the Rompin Police by Inspector Hassan, everyone had forgotten to give him food or water. No one thought of his needs, since he was just a prisoner and convict. The hunger and thirst he felt was made worse by the little ventilation he gets in the back of the old van. Keat felt that he was like an animal now.

Almost three hours into the journey, Keat was startled by a telepathic voice. It was the old man again.

[Wake up!]

[Huh? Old Man? I mean Cheow Check?]

[Yes, it is I. Pay attention now. There are many changes all over the world. The energies of today do not support the Negative anymore. The DNA of many who are Truth themselves are changing into the original 12 stranded. Your every cell is also changing to be crystalline based rather than carbon- based. This is to accommodate the higher frequencies that you will vibrate to so that you will be aligned with the Higher Fifth Dimension.]

[What has it got to do with me now that I am a prisoner?]

[Just remember your mission, and that is to go back to your friends in the jungle. Gather them at a spot which will be revealed to you later.]

[I thought I told you I am a prisoner!]

[I heard you. Your mission will be fulfilled. This is enough for now.]

And with that, Cheow Chek's telepathic transmission ended. Keat was then left with more questions and worry now- how is he to complete his mission in his present situation? After much contemplation, he decided to just let it be. He slipped into deep sleep and waking up off and on during the long journey. Unknown to him, he was receiving energy from the Sun when the sun flares occurred. Keat actually fell asleep not because he was sleepy but in actuality his body was being recuperated rejuvenated and repaired and indeed, as Cheow Chek mentioned, his DNA in every cell was being activated and the Three Fold Flame within the secret space in his heart burned brighter and expanded. The changes his physical body was undergoing were now accelerating.

They reached Kuala Lumpur late in the evening and the police escorts were relieved to arrive without any incidents. Keat was then woken up and brought into the station lockup for the night. He finally had some water and stale food and and he gobbled it up. The next morning he was rudely awoken by the Police Officer to be transported to Penang where he would face his charges filed by Inspector Hassan. He was given only slightly more than thirty minutes to get washed and supplied with some plain buns with water for breakfast. By now the Press had got wind of his arrest and they tried to interview Keat as he was led to the black police van to be taken to Penang. He had grown to be quite a celebrity because of his exploits as a robber but with a kind heart and living in the jungle to escape the authorities. Keat's hair had grown rather long and with his tanned, sinewy and fit body, he was quite handsome too. But hard luck for the Press, both foreign and local, he was whisked away via the back entrance in another similar police vehicle and so the Press could not get to him.

It will be a journey of about six hours to Penang by the Highway and a less bumpy ride compared to the previous journey. This time around, the police escorts were a bit kinder in that they removed his handcuffs when they put him safely into the black van as his wrists were swollen and bruised from the previous trip. Including the driver, there were another two policemen. Keat felt very tired and this puzzled him and his tiredness led him to fall into a deep sleep now and then. They made a stop at the Rest and Recreation station just before Tapah. The police put on his handcuffs again before escorting him to the toilet and after some refreshments, they were on their journey again.

Torrential rain fell as they left the R&R with thunder and lightning in the darkened skies. The careful driver switched on the headlights and reduced speed. Visibility was poor due to the heavy downpour. The driver, Suleiman, could not recall a heavier downpour and neither could the other two police escorts, Daud and Sharifuddin. Keat looked out through the small barred window of the back of the van and he was worried about the bad weather. He could sense that something might happen, but he hadn't a clue as to what it might be.

They were approaching Ipoh city and this part of the journey is very hilly and the highway winds round the hills. They could hear the winds howling fiercely and blowing the rain into waves of water. Suleiman slowed the vehicle even more and none of them talked as all eyes were on the road and witnessing the wrath of Nature. There were very few vehicles on the road as many had even stopped at the nearest rest areas to avoid the atrocious conditions. For the Police Van, they had to continue according to Standard Operations Procedure.

Keat too was restless as he felt very uneasy. He literally could not keep still. Be calm, he told himself.

[Do not worry] came the telepathic thought.

[What's happening to the weather, Old Man?]

[Forget about the weather. Listen to me. This is part of the change that has been predicted by many wise ones.]

[Wise ones? Who are these Wise Ones?]

[The Hopis, the Mayans, and others from every Indigenous groups from the Amazons to the Aborigines of Australia.]

[Funny, my Tribe in the jungles never said anything about this crazy weather.] Keat was more comfortable now with this conversation as he was bored and lonely.

[Your Tribe knew but very little. They don't understand too much and so they never mentioned it. Here is where you come in.]

[There you go again, my Mission!]

[Indeed. I want you to remember that you are now even more powerful than you ever were.]

[Don't kid me.]

[In actual fact, every human. They just forgot who they really are.]

[What do you mean, Old Man?]

[Look at the tigers and lions in the circus. They obey what the ring master signals them to do. These powerful animals forgot their power and strength. In the wilds the lions can take down a huge African buffalo. What more of a mere human? If these animals remembered their courage and strength, one bite to the human's neck will crush the neck bones and sever the jugular of the human. If only the lions and tigers remembered their ferocity and might, there would be no more circus shows.]

[So what exactly has that got to do with me?]

[It means you are a very powerful Being and that you have forgotten who you really are. Just remember that the spark of God is within you and each and every Human. Reclaim your Power. You must remember this and everything else will fall into place. Do not hold onto the Past. Everything is in the Now, for it is in the Now that we create the Future. You are not the same person as before for you have received downloads of energetic codes to awaken your DNA and your carbon- based body has indeed changed to crystalline type. Besides Earth herself had her grids all up graded and infused with plasmic photon energy from Alcyone via the Sun.]

[Is that the reason I feel so tired, out of sorts?]

[Indeed. And also your karma that needed to be cleared are all happening. Oh, I need to do something urgent, remember what I told you about getting your power back and believing in your gifts and new abilities. You will soon need them]

[Wait! Old Man?]

With that, Keat was again left alone at the back of the Police Van. He looked out through the back window and saw the heavy rain still going on unabated. In fact it seemed to be even more ferocious. Suleiman kept his eyes wide open while driving gingerly across the hilly area, and now they are going up an incline. The winds were also very strong and howling across the Highway. His companions were just as alert. They kept shaking their heads as they were so bewildered at the ferocity of the storm. Thunder and lightning were more frequent now and this really put the men on tenterhooks. Sharifuddin then pointed out to his colleagues to look at their left because he spotted a swift river of water along the lower ground as they climbed the small hilly area. The river was never there before and Sharifuddin was very sure of that as he is from

Ipoh city and he travelled very frequently to Kuala Lumpur using this Highway. This showed how heavy the rain was. Sheets of rain water were gushing down the hill slope on their right and flowing across the Highway to the slopes on to their left. This only made everyone worry even more and also had everyone's eyes peeled for danger signs.

It was proving difficult for Suleiman to steer the vehicle in the torrential rains with poor visibility and the very strong winds that blew down from the hills. At times they get the feeling that the winds could blow their vehicle off the Highway. Even Keat who only had a small window view at the back of the Van could see the big picture that the weather and road condition was getting dangerous. They did not have to wait long for a disaster to strike. In fact it was barely half an hour later that both Daud and Sharifuddin shouted out in unison, "Look out!" at the top of their voice. They had spotted some loosened rocks and pebbles falling on the road in front, along with the gush of rain water. Seconds later, all three of them saw some trees about to topple down on the slope of a hill about two hundred metres ahead. This could only mean that there must be a land and mud slide ahead of them. Suleiman knew that they could be swept away and be either buried in the massive landslide or be knocked into the newly formed river below and he hit the brakes on as hard as he could.

The road was slippery in the heavy rain and on top of that, the tyres were not exactly new, thus the van continued its forward momentum and every second they were getting nearer to the edge of the landslide. The loose stones and sand on the road was another factor ensuring that the van continued its momentum as they prevented any sort of firm grip on the road. Suleiman shouted to his colleagues to jump out of the van as he knew they would soon be in the path of the landslide that seemed to get even bigger as it rushed down the slopes. The other two policemen need not a second shout from Suleiman, Daud opened the door as the Van slowed down and was the first to jump off, closely followed by Sharifuddin and Suleiman was the last to do so from the driver's side. As the men rolled on the ground, they saw a large boulder came crushing on to the side of the van and pushed it down the slope and into the raging newly formed river about five metres below. The van was last seen floating and bobbing about the fast flowing waters and then it went under with the prisoner in it.

policemen, having gathered themselves up, stood rooted for a few seconds before running away from the area as more landslides were occurring nearer to where they had jumped out. None of them had been hurt badly from jumping out of the moving van, except for several small cuts here and there. They stopped when they were at a safe distance from the landslide and looked at the river again but all they could see was the raging murky waters that swallowed up the whole van and the prisoner inside.

Daud then started to make a phone call from his mobile phone to Bukit Aman Headquarters in Kuala Lumpur (KL) to report what had happened. When the call was over, he looked very worried.

"Hey, Daud what happened?' asked Suleiman.

"I spoke to Boss in Bukit Aman about what happened to us. Then he said that they will not be able to send any rescue party here because many parts of KL are flooded. In fact they think some disaster had just occurred in Taiping and most parts of the country!"

"What happened in Taiping?" asked Suleiman.

"I don't know if I heard correctly, something like an earthquake!"

"Earthquake? How can it be, in our country?" chipped in Sharifuddin.

"That was what I thought I heard. The line is not so clear, you know. Perhaps it was something else."

"Anyway, if help is not coming what are we to do? What about the prisoner?" asked Suleiman.

"I think the poor guy must be drowned by now. No one can survive that accident," replied Daud.

"Then let me try to phone the Plus Highway Patrol to pick us up." said Sharifuddin.

Keat was thrown about inside the back of the Prison van when the small boulder knocked the van off the road and into the raging, newly formed river of flood water. When the van was sinking under the water, it was then that Keat realised the danger he was in. The first thing he knew he had to do was to get out of the van fast, so he kicked the door as hard as he could but it didn't open. Water was gushing into the van from the broken glass panel of the back window but the bars remained intact. The rolling van made it difficult for Keat to position himself for a good hard kick at the door. Soon, the van was submerged in the flowing water and Keat managed to gulp in a full breath of air before he too was completely trapped under water in the rolling van. This can't be the end, thought Keat. The water was full of sediments and made visibility very poor and the rolling van further disorientated Keat as to where is up and where is down, not to mention where the back door was.

Keat tried his best to find a way out of this death trap that he is in. The seconds ticked by and he was just flipped around as in a giant washing machine as the van was tossed around like a toy. His body hit the sides of the van several times but the impact was somewhat cushioned by being completely submerged in water. This disorientated Keat even more and his lungs could hold out no longer. The build up of carbon dioxide levels in his blood would trigger a reflex action of taking a deep breath but when underwater, this is the most dangerous part when water fills the lungs rather than vital air. He tried his best to buy some seconds by still holding his breath, refusing to succumb to the strong reflex action. However the over powering reflex won and Keat took in a deep breath and water rushed down into both lungs. He kept struggling, trying to find a way out of the van but he was getting weaker and weaker as well as falling in and out of consciousness.

The feelings of panic, fear and desperation suddenly disappeared and were replaced with great calmness and peace. Even the roaring sound of the water was gone. Keat felt totally numb, no pain or even the coldness of the water that surrounded him. Although his eyes had been open before when he was trying his best to escape, yet the very poor visibility was only a few centimetres in the murky waters, so now he closed his eyes and yet he could make out a strong, bright light shining ahead. Keat felt very drawn to the Light source. He then found himself in a sort of tunnel with a bright loving source of Light at the end of the tunnel and he was hurtling towards it. Then he saw before his eyes, a flashback on his life. He was about eight years old and he got a severe beating from his father for throwing a tantrum. But now he saw that his father regretted hitting him so hard. This made him forgive his father instantly. Then he was shown his first theft that he committed at age fifteen where he stole the purse of a school mate and that the poor boy was beaten by his father for being careless in losing the purse with some money. That boy came from a poor family and losing the money really angered his labourer father. Keat felt so remorseful and was so ashamed of what he had done and which propelled him into a life of crime, hurting more innocent people. He had no idea his crimes hurt the victims so much, leaving all of them traumatised. He had thought they were richer than him and thus would not mind "losing" some money or personal possessions.

In the next instant he felt serene and peaceful and a Voice spoke to him.

"My dear Child, do not be afraid. Step forward."

"Where am I, who are you?"

"I am Prime Creator, my child. And you are in my Kingdom."

"Why am I here?"

"In fact I should ask you, why are you here!"

"Now I remember…I was drowning!"

"But you have a Choice, my child. In fact all my children are always given Free Will. You can either stay on here in my Kingdom or go back and complete your mission in life, Beloved One."

It was clear to Keat that there were other Light Beings around and he looked at each of them. One by one, they became more visible and then he could see his father, who had died when he was about twenty years old. His father gave him a big smile and waved at him. Then next he saw his cousin, Jerry Ong, who died rather young of a heart attack. As small boys, they were best of friends. Jerry was very mischievous and always played practical jokes on Keat, who was always on the receiving end. Jerry gave him his trademark mischievous smile.

"Dad! Jerry!" shouted Keat.

'Ah Keat, we are fine. You must go back and finish your job," said his father.

"Yes, Keat the people of Earth need you very much. Go back," added his cousin.

Then Keat saw his old pet dog, a black cocker spaniel he had when he was a small boy.

"Blackie!" exclaimed Keat. His faithful dog wagged its short tail and barked.

"Son, we have to go back now. God has given us this rare chance to meet you again. Go back son." And they waved good bye and Blackie turned to follow his old master and turned its head to have a last look at its young master, now a grown man. Then they vanished in a flash of light. Keat tried to follow but his legs would not move. Keat felt sad again.

"Keat, Beloved One, you heard what your father had said. You need to go back," Prime Creator said.

"My mission, everyone tells me that, but I have no idea what it is!"

"My child, let me explain. It is time for Mother Earth, Gaia, to evolve to the Fifth Dimension and above. She had waited very long for her inhabitants to be ready but She could wait no longer ever since the special alignment of the Planets created The Grand Cross on 23rd April, 2014, bracketed by first the Blood Moon Eclipse and the Eclipse of the Sun thereafter. She had first to release and cleanse the dense negative energy that had been generated by humans over the centuries of war, conflict and bloodshed. This huge cleansing will start soon. It will result in hurricanes, tropical storms, volcanic eruptions and earthquakes, to release and transmute the negativity. Many of your people all over the world will perish, especially those who had ignored the warning signs as told by the Mayans, Hopi people and even that of your forefathers in Ancient Egypt, Tibet and China. Many had refused to change their evil ways while others prefer to ascend as Spirit bodies rather than in their physical forms. Those recalcitrant ones will then be transported to a parallel holographic planet like Earth in a far away Galaxy to live out their karma."

"Those who survive and remain behind or will be evacuated by an Extraterrestrial Race from the Orion Constellation to stay temporarily in their massive Motherships until conditions return to normal. However these ETs as you call them have their own motive, which is to slowly take over your Planet for their own benefit. At first they will share with your new governments their technology to enhance your lives and rebuild the Planet. Then your people will feel very indebted for their help and that is when they will take over control of your world for their own benefit. Then it will be too late. Humans will be reduced to their slaves. It has happened before in other worlds. This is where you come in, My child. The people of Earth who survive The Great Change will be all the native people of every country because they are more attuned to Nature. They know how to survive without the modern contraptions, they can make a fire, hunt and gather jungle produce to sustain themselves. Their simple life and knowledge of survival will see them through. You will lead these people to form a Resistance Movement later to overthrow the invaders from Orion and make Earth free and a member of the Galactic Federation and be the 33rd Full fledged Member."

'What? Me? Of all people?" asked a bewildered Keat.

"There will be one person for each country to lead their indigenous people. The descendants of the Aztecs, Mayans, Native Americans and Australian Aborigines will need no outside leaders as their Shamans are well versed as to their tasks. There is very little time for you now, please make up your mind or it will be too late."

"If I can make a difference to Mankind, then the task is mine to take, to make up for the crimes I have done. But all I know is how to rob, how can I be of any use?" answered Keat.

"You are more than you know, My Child. Soon you will remember who you are and what you are capable of. I love you my beloved one."

Then the bright light began to fade and soon Keat found himself back in his physical body. He began to struggle again and when he kicked wildly, his left leg kicked the broken back door of the van and it opened. He could feel a cooler wave of water entering and he struggled with his last ounce of strength to push himself out of the still rolling van. The current caught him and pushed him out and soon he surfaced. However he could not breathe yet as his lungs were filled with water and he was just being carried by the swift current down the river. He lost consciousness soon after.

It could be coincidence, but a group of Orang Asli from a nearby settlement deeper in the forest were making their way back to their huts when one of them saw Keat's lifeless body bobbing up and down in the river. He alerted his friends and two of them lost no time diving into the water to save Keat. They were the best swimmers among the small band of Orang Asli Tribe called Jahai, a sub- division of the Negrito group found mostly in the Lower Perak forests and they are still nomadic, and as such no one really knows their total population. In fact this band of Jahai is almost unknown among the state's Aboriginal Department. It was Bung and Akai that managed to pull Keat to the bank of the fast flowing river and like expert medical doctors, they resuscitated Keat. Bung, who was the bigger and stronger, held Keat upside down while Akai worked on his abdomen and forced as much water as he could out of his stomach and lungs. Keat was almost blue with lack of oxygen but they never gave up. Soon Keat coughed and vomited up more phlegm and water and took his first breath but choked again. The rains had not stopped and they moved Keat to the shade of a big tree nearby to work on him again. By this time the rest of the hunting group had arrived and wasted no time to start a fire to warm Keat up as he was also in danger of shock from the cold. No words were spoken, they just sprang into action. To start a fire in the pouring rain was indeed a challenge but these group of mysterious Jahai Negritos managed to do so.

Slowly Keat's lips turned pink and he continued to cough and gasp for air. The oldest of this small band of wandering Jahai, called Danai, laid both his hands over Keat's chest and murmured some incantations while what appeared to be giving Keat some form of Energy Healing, as do the Reiki Masters. Keat was now breathing more and coughing less and his body warmed up little by little. They continued to work to revive Keat until Keat looked more alive than dead and his breathing normalized. However he was still semi-conscious. There was just a short discussion among the Jahai and they started to make a jungle stretcher to carry Keat back to their village, a good three hour trek along jungle paths that only they knew. The Jahais knew that taking Keat to the nearest town would do no good for him as they mistrust the small Government clinic and the red tape that would ensue. Moreover they were in a hurry to get back to their village to evacuate their families to safer grounds as they sensed something big was about to occur. The other reason was that Keat looked more like an Orang Asli than a town person with his sinewy and tanned body, long hair and talisman hung around his neck that seemed like that of a southern Tribe. They set out on a trot while heading back to their village but their special way of running brought little discomfort to Keat as he was not rocked very much. It was as though they glided over rocks, tree roots and uneven grounds. These tough men of the forests did not stop for a rest, and there was a certain urgency to their running.

CHAPTER 29

One of the Jahai men broke into a faster run back to their village to inform their people of Keat's fragile condition so as to prepare herbal medicine for Keat's treatment. He left the rest of the men trailing far behind within minutes. When the rest of the party arrived, their shaman had prepared a herbal brew for Keat. They put their patient in their larger hut and he was the centre of attraction and curiosity. Many of the children gathered around the hut to see what was happening. Keat was frothing at his mouth and falling in and out of consciousness. He was certainly still in great danger. The old shaman started to pray for Keat's recovery and he performed the sacred dance and many other rituals rarely seen even by the villagers themselves. The shaman's assistants were learning valuable lessons as a result. For the next three days Keat hovered between life and death but he did show some progress albeit minimal at most. The old shaman used all his powers and skill and never left Keat's side. He fasted so as to increase his powers, he meditated to make contact with Keat's soul and he also went into several trance. He managed to feed Keat the special brew he had made and Keat's fever began to drop.

"What do you think, can this one make it?" asked Chief Jak to the shaman.

"I have done what I can for him. But I have a feeling this one is special and he can pull through," replied Tokuh, the Shaman.

"I thought so myself."

'He is strange, this one." Tokuh continued.

"Why?"

"In my meditations and trance, his soul appeared and told me he needed his body to be well as he has an important job to do. And that he has a special message for our people. His soul then told me he is using the time to travel back to his own people, the Temian who live in the interior of Pahang state to inform them of what happened to him.. That is why he is still semi- conscious. Then The Great Spirit told me that the Heavens are repairing his body in many ways to prepare him for his important job. Yes, this one will live and he will have powers more powerful than mine!"

"Well, he better wake up fast as I am worried about the weather, it seems to get worse and we may have to move." replied Chief Jak.

They had to wait for a further two days before Keat opened his eyes and stretched his body and slowly got up to sit. News of his recovery spread fast and almost the whole village came to see him, including the children. For a man who nearly died he looked rather healthy now. The first thing Keat did was to kneel before the Chief and the shaman to thank them, though his legs were still weak and wobbly and his coordination was still less than perfect. Then he looked into the crowd and spotted his rescuers and hugged and thanked each of them. It was a source of amazement to many how he could recognize his two rescuers, know who is the Chief and who the shaman was when he was never conscious in the five days he was in their village. By now the entire community had known what the shaman had told the Chief. Keat asked for some food and water and the shaman told him to eat some fruits first. Then Keat spoke to the whole community in Malay which the Jahai understood although they had their own dialect.

"My name is Keat but you can call me Suntek, my name given by the Temians with whom I had lived in their jungles for many months. I was on the run from the police because I committed some crimes. They caught me and I was being sent to Penang to face my trial but on the way the police van that took me was washed into the river. I could have died if not for your brave men who risked their own lives to save me from drowning. I am indeed indebted to your tribe as you people have nursed me back to good health."

All of them were caught by surprise about Keat's story but they were very happy that he was truthful. From then on, Keat was much respected by all. One by one, the Jahai folks, men, women and even kids came to welcome Keat into their Tribe. After all the greetings, Keat talked to the Chief softly and Chief Jak nodded. Jak asked everyone to be seated and announced that Keat has something important to say.

"My friends of the Jahai Tribe. Please listen to what I have to say. As you know the weather has been very bad lately and this is because Mother Earth is changing. Strange as it may sound, while drowning, I had what is known as a Near Death Experience and I was given special knowledge which I shall now reveal. Also, while in a semi- conscious state after your people had brought me to your village, I had further communication with Light Beings.

I was told to lead you to safety and as for my own Tribe people, the Temian, I need not worry as they will know where to go because in my sleep state, I had visited my Chief and given him specific instructions as to where to lead our people to the safety of higher grounds. This is because I was told that an old continent called Atlantis will rise from the seabed very soon and this will cause gigantic waves to hit all parts of the world as it will displace the oceans in what is known as a tsunami."

"This tsunami will have waves as high as forty- five metres that will smash into cities that are near the coastal regions and it will go inland for about twenty to thirty kilometres, destroying everything in its path. Many people will therefore die but it was their soul agreement and their choice. And not only that, it will be accompanied by great earthquakes and volcanic explosions. In fact while in my spirit *merkaba* body, as I travelled, I chanced to see an earthquake just shook a town in the north of where we are and the destruction is really very bad. But many people from many parts in the north have gone to help the people of that town called Taiping. As you know, our country never was hit by any direct earthquake activity but things have changed so much.

This will be followed by blazing balls of fire falling from the skies that will light them up. They are the debris from the Photon Belt of the skies and will cause further damage and destruction. Many who escaped death by Water and Earth activity will be killed by Fire now. There will therefore be complete chaos everywhere."

"I had also during my unconscious state, entered the dreams of many native shamans of many Tribes near and far, warning them of these events and had told them where to go and to look for signs to lead them to a safe place and many tribes will gather in such places, until they are ready for the place where I shall lead all of us. So there will be a rather big gathering there and we shall build a new community together to face the challenges. The united force that we create among ourselves will be the new nucleus to lead into the New Earth.

However, when the destruction is too great and widespread, some Star Beings in their spaceships will land to help evacuate the city people to the safety of their gigantic Motherships. When conditions are better on Earth, these rescued city people will be brought back to Earth to start the human civilization all over again, but this time with the involvement of the Star Beings using their superior technological machines to rebuild and to clean the polluted waters and air." Keat then took a sip of water. No one asked any questions. Then he continued.

"Then, slowly but surely, the Star Beings will become the Masters to rule our world, making humans the slaves. They came to take away our natural resources for their own Planet. So I ask you to stay with me, and never be tempted to board the Spaceships if they land to evacuate us. Our job is to survive the difficult times, be united with all the other Tribes and later it will be our job or that of our children and grandchildren to drive off these Star Beings from our beloved Planet." Then there were a lot of murmurs among the crowd now. They just could not believe their ears and no longer could they hold their mouths. Every one could not keep quiet after Keat's last sentence and Keat let them talk.

The Chief then asked Keat, "Suntek, when will we be moving?"

"As soon as we can get ready Chief"

"And how long will it take us to reach the safe place you talk about?"

"I think it will take about two weeks."

After some more discussions among the Elders of the Tribe, Chief Jak spoke, "It will take us one whole day to pack our belongings and so we can start moving day after tomorrow."

"Good, and do not dismantle your huts as they will be shelter for other tribes from far off on their way to the designated safe place." replied Keat.

"Tribe, let us now disperse and go pack your things and from what Suntek said, there is very little time left."

As the tribal folks were leaving the meeting hall, they all clasped both their hands around Keat's and hugged him as a sign of deep respect for the man who would save them now.

"Chief, I will need to rest as this new body of mine will take time to get used to. Also I have meditation work to do," said Keat.

"Good, we will talk more later."

Keat was left to be by himself while the whole settlement went to pack their few belongings. Since they were still leading a nomadic way of life, they had few possessions to pack. Keat was doing some exercises and getting used to his newly charged body with its DNA upgraded and activated. He was actually rather worried about the tasks that lay in front of him and missed his tribe back in Pahang. As he missed his Temian friends so much, he was in such deep thought about them that in an instant he found his consciousness was suddenly among them! He was surprised to see them but no one could see or notice him. Keat could see Jatek and his wife Som in their hut resting, then his consciousness wandered about and saw Balang the trekker cooking his meal. They had settled in a safe place. In an instant he was back with the Jahais and back into his body. He realised he had just acquired this ability but instead of shouting out for joy, he kept very quiet. Everyone here had not even noticed anything about him as they were all very busy doing their chores in anticipation of a move. Keat had visited Jatek in his dreams to let him know that he was recovering from a near- drowning accident and that he had a new message to ask them to do the longest trek, from their usual place in Pahang, cross the Main Range and to get into Perak and join him and other tribes there. The idea was to keep all the native people of the various tribes near to one another rather than to be spread out all over the country. In this way it would be easier for them to meet urgently if needed and their numbers would be far greater if indeed more natural disasters were to strike and they would be able to help one another, rather than being small, isolated Tribes living on their own, who can be so vulnerable in times of hardship and danger. The other reason Keat had in mind was should he need to raise a Resistance Force,sometime in the future, then it could be done at a greater speed and so much more easily.

There was no trouble in contacting and persuading his tribe to do so, but he was unable to reach, much less convince many other aboriginal tribes. In many such tribes, they may not have a shaman if their group is very small, in others their shaman may not have reached a high level of training and thus he will be unable to communicate with them at all. Keat had requested those tribes that shared his vision to try to convince other bands of native people by word of mouth about the coming event of Earth's cleansing. In fact Jatek had sent out small groups of his people to get in touch with other small and isolated groups of Orang Asli and explain to them about Keat's vision. Jatek's men were to then accompany those they managed to convince to an agreed location to be united and proceed onwards together from there.

Keat had proposed the same method as that of his own Chief, Jatek, to Chief Jak about sending small bands of men to locate and persuade other small tribes and Jak agreed. They gathered early on the day of departure to start their long trek higher into the mountains, led by Keat. They could travel faster as the Jahais are nomadic and so very fit and experienced jungle travellers. And thus began the great exodus. As word spread, more tribes of aborigines started their trek. It was not long before government officers of the Department of Aboriginal Affairs noticed abandoned Orang Asli villages. They were alerted when schools built for their children reported total absenteeism. The officers were greatly puzzled. It had never happened before. However the Government had low priorities for aboriginal welfare and sat on the issue, doing nothing to investigate. Moreover, it had its hands full in organizing relief operations to several towns hit by floods, landslides and the destruction of Taiping town was taking most if its attention.. At times there were even minor clashes between relief workers of different political parties, instigated by the heartless politicians out to capitalise on the occasion to promote their image.

Many sections of the affected population were left to rescue each other, being ignored by the relevant authorities altogether. When ordinary people are left to fend for themselves in times of natural disasters, complete chaos results with law and order in total disarray. Looting becomes rampant and crimes of all sorts are committed. The absence of Police, Fire and Rescue Services, Para-medics and Relief workers were obvious in several places. Floods in Kelantan, Trengganu and Pahang states where relief aid and personnel were sent, exposed the incompetence of the government bodies concerned. In comparison, the Orang Asli Tribes were in a much better position, seemed to be more well organised and were capable of taking care of themselves.

As the Jahais led by Keat continued in their long trek, much was happening around the world, to which the tribe except Keat were oblivious. He needed only to focus his mind on a locality and he would be able to see in his mind's eye what was going on there. And when he did that, what he saw confirmed what he was told by several of his spiritual sources. The climate change was world wide. Severe winter storms, blizzards and very heavy snow fall were seen in the UK, Europe, USA, China, Japan and N. Korea, along with severe flooding, sink holes that swallowed up roads, houses and oil spills. Australia suffered it's worst ever drought and soaring temperatures with wild fires destroying vegetation and homes. Its neighbour, New Zealand, had earthquakes of magnitude 6.5 and above while Fiji, Vanuatu and the Solomon Islands suffered quakes of lesser magnitudes. The Philippines and Vietnam were having severe tropical storms where houses were destroyed with flooding occurring in most areas. Keat was disturbed by these events and he tried to look calm but pushed the Jahais to cover more miles each day so as to reach the safe place he had for them the sooner the better.

Keat was not wrong in his feelings because the dreaded California Earthquake, which had been expected by scientists for years as it was long over due, finally came to life with a huge quake that registered a massive 7.2 on the Richter Scale. However this was the lull before the Big One came, measuring 8.9 which completely destroyed most of California with an immense loss of life. In the first quake, there was little damage and minimal loss of life which gave the Californians a false sense of security. Within days came the Big One and everyone was caught by surprise. This triggered the Yellowstone volcano, Caldera, to explode with all its might. It was equivalent to fifty atomic bombs. America was split right down the centre. A few years ago animals like the bison and elks had been seen migrating away from Yellowstone Park and no one seemed to take the cue. With these two catastrophic disasters, the Federal

Emergency Management Agency (FEMA) was caught off guard and badly so.

The world could not help the USA, as they had their own disasters too. War in the Middle East continued unabated, with the threat of the use of nuclear weapons of mass destruction very imminent. The possibility of the total destruction of the entire planet was a high possibility this time should nuclear weapons be unleashed, unlike the situation in WW2 where only one country had this capability. That is why Keat now is now using his ability to keep a watchful eye on the situation there and this is actually his worry number one, for no one can survive the nuclear fallout however far away one is from the explosion.

They had been on the move for four days and nights now. The progress got harder as they were climbing hill after hill for the higher grounds. Keat had instructed some of the men to mark their route for others to follow. Keat would spend time in meditation and deep contemplation at every opportunity when they stopped to rest. This was to get insight as to the best route to take them to the safety of some hill caves that had never been discovered by any aboriginal tribes before. It will be there where they will live to escape the coming Armageddon. And he also kept in touch with Jatek telepathically to find out their situation and progress. Jatek too had undergone a great transformation albeit less that that of Keat's as the former's telepathic ability was a recent development Keat's abilities seemed to grow more powerful as the days went by. It would be only a matter of time before he could bilocate in his physical form because now his ability to travel in his Consciousness has been perfected. He could go anywhere and witness in real time the events there, thus he knew what is happening around the world but just kept it to himself, there being no point to alarm the simple Jahais. However he failed to locate Old Man, Cheow Chek, try as he would. As usual, when one needs somebody urgently, he or she is usually not available.

Keat felt he could not handle this project alone and needed someone of Cheow Chek's calibre to help him. But where is this Old Man? In particular, Keat wanted his opinion about the subtle alien invasion that humans are about to undergo. Keat was actually looking far into the future.

He had stumbled upon their plans during one of his meditations when he was contacted by the Unseen Ones, comprising a group of intelligent Beings from a very far away Planetary System who had been observing Earth for a long time.. He was told of their sinister plans. There had been several Alien abductions of humans over several years since 1951 and the intention was to create Alien – Human hybrids and their program had been very successful as there are now several such hybrids among humans whose life span has been increasing with some reaching adulthood. These hybrids look exactly like humans but their intelligence is far superior and they are aligned with their Alien Forces. In time to come, they will gain positions of power in politics, commerce and religion to greatly influence our planet. This is the long term plan. However things may now be speeded up if these Aliens come to rescue humans from the great disasters that are to happen. Who would not run and board a spaceship if the ground under you is trembling, buildings collapsing and fireballs raining from the sky? Humans will be indebted to these so called friendly Aliens, who will then use their technology to solve several issues plaguing Earth as well as to rebuild Earth and before we know it, we will be enslaved by them and our planet will be ruled by Beings from afar.

Humanity is still in the infant stages as far as living in the Cosmos is concerned. Our Planet had been in quarantine mode for the last 25,000 years since the Fall of Atlantis. This quarantine as decreed by Prime Creator was to protect Earth from being otherwise conquered militarily by aggressive Alien Races that scout the Universe to take over planets for their own selfish needs. However this led to Mother Earth being unable to evolve higher. It was only recently that Mother Earth called to be released from this quarantine as she needs to ascend to a higher vibration as she can no longer wait for ever for Humans to be fully awakened. This was finally granted and as of 21st December 2012, this veil was lifted as predicted by the Mayans. However, in this new situation, no military conquest is yet allowed and no more Galactic Wars as well, there being no provision to bar them by using deceit and cunning from taking over any world. The influx of Energy from Alcyone and reflected by our Sun had done a lot to enlighten many but still the Dark Forces managed to keep people unaware of the Truth.

Keat was thinking how stupid humans can be. They can't live in peace and harmony but fight and kill each other to be dominant. Humans are still thinking along the lines of politics, race and religion. Humans pollute their own environment to the extent that Earth may no longer be able to sustain her inhabitants, whether human, animal or plant life. They do not realise that Earth is a valuable prize for those Aliens who come from planets that are barren. There are so many Aliens that are eyeing Earth at the present moment, and yet Earth's wilfully blind governments are trying very hard to cover up reported UFO sightings by many. Then again the blinkered scientists keep denying that there can be other intelligent Life in the Universe and maintaining that we are the only planetary civilization in the Solar System. How naive and stupid can these men of science be, thought Keat. He was getting depressed with all these and so he stopped thinking about these matters. He now shifted back to trying to contact Cheow Chek again but the exercise proved futile and he gave up.

The exodus of the Aborigine people was now in full swing in the entire country. Businessmen who depended on these natives for the supply of honey were among the first to feel the impact. They waited for their honey consignment day after day but no one turned up. And those natives who worked in National Parks were nowhere to be seen either. Furniture makers did not get their supply of bamboo and cane. Markets had not received their supply of *petai*, a local jungle produce. The most uncanny occurrence was that Forest Rangers had not seen any wild animals and the usual forays of wild elephants into plantations were no longer reported. Even poachers who trap endangered species for the illegal wild life trade found their traps empty.

The group led by Keat continued to make good progress and Keat estimated that he needed another full day's journey to reach his safe place where a system of huge undiscovered underground cave systems should accommodate them and the rest of the other tribes. They would settle down to make camp soon as daylight was fading. Keat told the group that tomorrow they would begin their journey at dawn and so advised all of them to get as much rest as they could that night. It will be a rather cold night as they are now at quite a high altitude and night temperatures in the jungle anyway are so much cooler than in the cities.

Keat tried to sleep but he felt restless, although he was physically exhausted. Almost all of the others were fast asleep, except those who were on guard duty. Then he tried to meditate, but his mind could not get into the deep state that is required. After a few hours of tossing and turning, Keat drifted into a deep sleep.

[Wake up! Wake up!]

"Huh?" Keat was rudely awaken and he was confused. He sat up and was now fully awake but no one was talking to him, everyone was in deep sleep, except a lone sentry far off. Was it a dream? Keat thought.

[You are not dreaming.]

[Old Man?]

[Yes. I have very little time to have a conversation with you. I know you had been trying to talk to me but I had so much to do as many people are suffering and dying. Wake every one and start going to the Caves now!]

[Old Man...wait...Old Man!]

If Keat had not been not really awake, he was now. There must be something about to happen and there is no time to argue with Old Man, he thought. Keat woke up Chief Jak first and told him what he knew. Then they sounded the alarm and the whole band of nomadic Orang Asli woke up. It must have been very early in the morning as it was still dark. There was no need to coax the whole group as everyone got ready within minutes and some of the men made torches of fire to light their way. The Tribe started their journey again, led by Keat, who used the feeling in his heart to lead the way since he could not be guided by the stars as they were hidden behind the dark clouds

Just after an hour of trekking in the dark, then all Hell broke loose. First the skies suddenly lit up. Everyone looked up and saw a huge fireball hurtling down and crashing into the forest behind them with a big boom! This was followed by yet another fireball and then another. The women and children of the Tribe screamed in fear and part of the forest hit by the fire from above started burning. In their panic, many ran helter skelter in all directions as fireball after fireball came raining down, some near them and some far off. This barrage of fireballs lasted for a full ten minutes and then as suddenly, it stopped. By then the first rays of the sun were breaking the dawn. Smoke filled the air as the fires burned. Lucky for the Jahai Tribe, they only suffered minor cuts and bruises and there were no casualties. Chief Jak and Keat then called out for them to re-group for a head count and when all thirty-eight were accounted for, Keat led the men to fight the forest fires. It was back-breaking work, using branches to douse the fires. The quick work by these tough jungle people paid off as they managed to stop the fire from spreading. It was indeed tough work, battling the flames.

The exhausted men gathered in a clearing to rest and recover from their ordeal. One of the men then commented that they were very indebted to Keat because the first and largest of the fireballs fell right on the spot where they were sleeping. Keat was shocked and all he could do was to thank Old Man for the warning. The fireballs had rained into the seas initially. Many people living in coastal areas who witnessed it did not think they would fall onto land a few hours later. When they hit the land areas of the west coast of Malaysia, thousands of homes were struck and many died in the deadly showers from the sky. Many telecommunication towers were damaged and thus all types of communications like TV, radio, telephones and internet were knocked out. As the Jahais were in deep jungle and very much inland, they had experienced only the tail end of the falling meteors.

Many others in countries like India, Sri Lanka, Indonesia and Africa were facing a different kind of disaster, that of a gigantic tsunami caused by the undersea explosion of a concealed volcano. The tsunami warnings could not save many people as it happened very fast. The huge fifteen metre waves crashed into land and swept away villages and towns as far as twenty kilometres inland. Hundreds of thousands of people perished. The world therefore was in complete chaos and disaster. Since Sumatra took the brunt of the tsunami waves, it deflected the waves away from Penang Island and the west coast of Malaysia, so these places received waves of about six metres high. Even then they caused considerable damage and loss of life.

Only Keat had the knowledge of what had happened as he received fragments of information telepathically from chatter in the Devic Realms. The Great Shift had occurred to accommodate Mother Earth's ascension to Fifth Dimension. Old energies give way to New Energy. The matrix of power grids had opened fully, causing a Vortex to form. The Pyramids in every part of Earth, in many parts of the world and not only in Egypt, concentrated the influx of energy and distributed it to the Ley lines. It was synchronised with the Electronic Mass Coronal Ejection from the sun's surface that faced the earth directly. Months before this occurred, there were mass deaths of animals, birds, whales, dolphins and insects that had puzzled scientists. In actual fact, this wild life had known of the coming ascension of Earth and they had voluntarily left their physical bodies behind so as to come back to populate in Fifth Dimensional Earth with their new DNA and crystalline based bodies. For humans, many had passed on before the event via diseases and pandemics. Another group fulfilled their karmic obligations in these new disasters.

Keat snapped out of his meditative state and urged his group to gather and continue their trek to the caves as they were not completely out of danger yet. About an hour into their final lap, the Jahais got very excited and pointed to the skies. What they saw were Flying Saucers, or UFOs, in the skies. Keat looked very disturbed, as he knew now that world evacuation had started. This is it, they must get to the caves fast before some more devastating natural disaster would befall them. He could see some hills nearby and some where near the hills are the openings to the deep system of caves. He hurried all of them up and even got them running.

Keat was right to do so, as the Extraterrestrials had less than half an hour to evacuate the humans before Earth's condition become dangerous even for them and their crafts. The ETs would use several methods at their disposal. Those from Orion would just beam them up by teleportation while those from Sirius, Pleides and Arcturius would land their space ships, open the hatch and invite the humans in by gesturing as well as by verbal communication. This is to allow for Free Will to be exercised and is the Law One of the Universe. With the millions of space ships hovering above Earth lately in anticipation of the Apocalypse, the ETs have enough to evacuate Earth's population and transport it to their massive Mother Ships that are no less than three hundred kilometres in diameter, which have de-cloaked themselves for this mission.

In the method of teleportation, there are certain constraints. If the person has low vibration, they would not be able to survive the teleportation and would just be disintegrated. Low vibration is the result of fear and fatal to those who are living a life of deceit, hatred, jealousy and self-centredness. However, it is the fastest method and puts the ETs in less physical harm from the adverse Earth conditions.

In Taiping, the aftermath of the earthquake was still devastating and it was now being hit by meteoric fireballs. This added to the confusion and mayhem. The volunteers and local Taiping folks ran for cover when the meteors rained down. Some were struck by the fireballs and died instantly. Kim Heng and his team of Mokhtar, Ramu and Ah Boey braved the meteor showers to continue with their rescue efforts as they were right in the midst of pulling out a badly hurt survivor from one of the ruins. It was not their way to abandon the poor guy and run away. Just then the fleet of UFOs appeared in the sky and this really shocked everyone. In fact those who never believed that Aliens and UFOs exist, died from sheer shock. This time, upon seeing the UFOs, Kim Heng and his friends just looked up with dropped jaws. Then a beam of white light shot down from the UFO hovering above soundlessly about thirty metres above. In seconds, all the four men along with the just rescued man, were lifted up and disappeared into the UFO. In very quick succession, the UFO kept shooting the beams on as many people as possible. Those who struggled, those in fear and whose vibrations were unable to withstand the energy beam, could be seen to just vaporise in mid-air.

The ground shook as another magnitude 7.6 quake hit Taiping and its surrounding areas. Any remaining building that survived the first quake was brought down like a house of cards. Luckily for Dr Looi and Albert, the commotion caused by the appearance of the UFOs brought them out in the open.

"Doc, look!" shouted Albert as he pointed to the sky.

"What? It's a UFO!" exclaimed Dr Looi.

They had just run out of the makeshift Medical Tent when the quake struck, bringing down the tent and collapsing on the patients inside. Then a UFO landed and opened its doors. They saw the tall

Arcturian coming out, who stood on the ground and beckoned those there to board the ship. Every one hesitated although it was very clear what the Alien wanted them to do.

"Doc, why is the ET asking everyone to go into the spaceship?"

"Albert, this must be Evacuation Team. It is the Apocalypse!" Dr Looi made a quick assessment of the situation. They had nothing to lose if really the world was becoming what the Hopi Indians predicted and Dr Looi was well versed in that. Dr Looi made his decision and walked up to the Alien.

"Doc, what are you doing? Come back!" shouted his close friend.

"Wait where you are, Albert. I am going to test them."

Dr Looi walked up close to the Alien and then he asked, "Which planet are you from?"

"Arcturius of the Bootes Constellation." replied the Arcturian, towering almost two metres tall.

"I ask you once, do you believe in God?"

"Yes."

'I ask you twice, do you believe in God?"

"Yes"

Dr Looi then repeated the same question one more time and the Alien answered in the affirmative again. This was the test Dr Looi wanted to do to confirm if the Alien was a member of the Galactic Federation, a benevolent Cosmic organization. All Aliens whether of the good or bad type, know the consequences if they lied three times in succession to the same question. This Law is Cosmic and the repercussions are meted out by the Cosmos and will be severe. It is also used by Buddha in his sermons, where he would say, "For the first time, I tell you..." and he would repeat it two more times.

As more and more fireballs rained down, Dr Looi called out to Albert and everyone else to board the UFO for safety. At first only a few followed Albert to board, then more and more people found the courage and rushed to board it. Two more UFOs landed nearby and evacuated more frantic people. The UFOs were silent and took off with tremendous speed and within seconds were thousands of metres up in the sky. One was hit by a meteor but apparently suffered no damage.

In Ukraine, where a war had been raging on for quite some time, it stopped suddenly when soldiers of both sides laid down their arms on seeing a huge UFO appearing in the sky. Before the UFO appeared, their weapons were not able to function and when the massive UFO de-cloaked itself and thus became suddenly visible, all the fighting men just threw their weapons down and started to head for home. It was not long after that, a massive earthquake shook the entire region. Within minutes more UFOs appeared and started to evacuate the populace.

The most dangerous areas were where the countries had build nuclear reactors to supply energy because the massive earthquakes and volcanic eruptions destroyed the nuclear plants which exploded, spewing out radiation. These areas had the most casualties within minutes of the explosions that were three hundred times more powerful than that of Chernobyl and Fukushima combined. No UFOs were seen to have made any attempt to rescue the people but minutes later, several UFOs were seen to be hovering over the devastated areas in an attempt to neutralize the radiation with their advanced technology.

Finally, the Agarthans surfaced from Inner Earth to make contact with those whose vibrations were higher and generally these were the groups of Native peoples in Amazon, Mexico, USA, Africa and Australia. Their main aim was to guide these natives to their safe haven in Inner Earth. Keat had been very worried that in their haste to flee, there had been no time to gather their food and essential water supplies. Actually he needed not to worry because as they settled in the Caves, they discovered a passage way leading deep into the Earth. As they went deeper, they too were met by a group of Agarthans who led them into Inner Earth through secret passageways and tunnels. These passage ways were dimensionally sealed and thus no one who happened to discover these secret cave systems was ever able to enter into Inner Earth unless they were able to unseal the Dimensional lock.

Of the seven Billion people that populated the Earth, about four billion were wiped out in the Great Change due to mega floods, wild fires, earthquakes, volcanic activities, diseases, pandemics, tsunamis, hurricanes, tornadoes, polar ice melt down and the man-made nuclear power station disasters. Cruel as it may seem, many humans were holding back the evolution of Mother Earth, Gaia. In fact, humans came very close to destroying all Life on Earth with the pollution of the air, water and land without even considering a Nuclear War. For the record, humans came dangerously close to annihilating all life on at least twelve occasions but nuclear war had been prevented by the intervention of Higher Intelligence in the background by de-activating the nuclear warheads. Then there was the corruption of governments that knew no limits. This was also destroying the very fabric of a civilised world. It seemed that the lesson of Atlantis had not been learned.

The Fourth Dimension, which holds the worlds of the Astral form and other lowly entities, were destroyed by Heaven's Decree and so Gaia entered into the Fifth Dimension with this quantum leap of Ascension from the Third Dimension of Form and Duality of Bad versus Good, or Dark versus Light. In the Fifth Dimension, Karma no longer holds and so there must be the fulfilment of Karma first. It will be the Golden Age of Gaia. The land mass will be stabilised after new continents have arisen and shaped the new topography. Today's continents will have been broken up into several new islands from which new Nations will be formed. Keat and his band of Aboriginals and the Native People elsewhere along with some survivors in the Polar regions will be the new hope of Gaia. Those successfully rescued by the Aliens will also form the nucleus of those who will take the lead in re-establishing the Golden Age of Gaia, which Cheow Chek estimated to be around 2038, Year of the Earth Horse. The Dark Forces had finally been defeated, never to return to Gaia. Yet the survivors will have much to do to face new challenges and a better equipped and more intelligent adversary in the form of Alien- Human Hybrids.. The climate will return to normalcy and will be universally cool and temperate. The Animal and Plant Kingdoms will again re-establish themselves with several new species appearing. There will be less and less carnivorous behaviour until the time when the carnivorous ones will take up vegetarian diets. Truly the lion and the lamb will be friends. The air will be fresh, waters sparkling clean and earth devoid of chemical pollution. It will be a pristine Earth, just like the days of Eden.

Thus shall end the Age of Kali Yuga and the New Dawn begin, The Golden Age of Aquarius or the Satya Yuga.